RAIN

A Dark Past Romance

EBONY OLSON

EBANDMUSE & PUBLICATIONS

EBANDMUSE
PUBLICATIONS

Published 2020 by

Eb&Muse Publications, Sydney, Australia

http://ebonyolson.com/

Content Warning

This is a dark past romance. During the healing process traumatic events are discussed.

Despite this, if you skip those parts you could still enjoy the read. Below is a list of trigger points. All of the triggers occur after the first split (umbrella) in each chapter.

- Chapter 6 - Bloody drag marks
- Chapter 7 - "How did it start?"
- Chapter 17 - "I don't know where to start."

— THE TORTURED SOUL, EBONY

Chapter One
CUM STAINS

SOMEONE WAS SNORING. POTENTIALLY IT WAS ME.

"Wake up, Cinderella," the sexy voice from my dreams whispered in my ear. Things tightened downstairs and I smiled.

The snoring kept going even after I became aware of being in bed and having woken up. Frowning, I forced my eyelids open. Nope, that wasn't working. They seemed to be glued together. Lifting my hand, I wiped the sleep from my eyes and finally managed to open them.

The bedside table wasn't mine. It held a glass of water with what I hoped was aspirin diffusing in it. Not one to look a gift horse in the mouth, I pushed up onto my elbows and started drinking. Turning my head, I froze at the body in the bed with me, still snoring. Looking down at my chest, I found my bra still in place but the dress I'd worn to the office Christmas party was absent. Oh, this was going to be awkward if naughty things happened. My eyes glanced at the clock, then I shoved my boss in the shoulder repeatedly until he stopped snoring and jolted awake.

"What?"

"You have to be on that teleconference in two minutes," I grumbled.

"Shit," Aubrey collected his phone from the bedside table and peered back at me obviously struggling to have his eyes open. "How's your head?"

"Holding its own heavy metal concert."

"Mine is in the snake pit. Think you can find me some aspirin?"

"I didn't find this one, it was waiting for me to wake up." Finishing the glass, I put it aside. "We didn't have sex, right?"

Aubrey laughed. "You have to ask?"

"Valid point. So, I'm half naked in your bed because?"

"Hold that thought," Aubrey held up his hand as the call connected.

With a huff, I stood up and looked around for my dress. Unable to find it, I grabbed one of Aubrey's shirts and put it on while I went to hunt for an aspirin. Searching his bathroom, I found more packs of condoms than the chemist stocks, and more variety, but nothing for headaches. My boss was a whore, but the committed kind. He always dated his sexual partners, just very few lasted the quarter mile.

"I'll fly into Auckland on Tuesday."

"Wednesday," I corrected as I passed back through the room, Aubrey's eyes tracking my legs.

"Sorry, Wednesday. I'll be at a conference all day, but I can meet you for dinner Wednesday evening."

Stepping out of the room, I walked towards the stairs. The smell of coffee captured me, so I followed my nose to the kitchen. Pushing through a door, I found two men standing in the kitchen drinking coffee. Both ridiculously handsome, one tall with pitch black hair, short and styled and looking all business in his tailored suit. The other was my height and blond, Chad, my boss's current beau. If he'd been straight, I still wouldn't have drooled because Chad's beauty really didn't penetrate his epidermis. Sadly, as my best friend's boyfriend, I had to be nice.

His eyes spotted me and glanced over my lack of clothes. "Rough night at the Christmas party, Rain?"

"Could have been worse," I shrugged.

"Really? How?" Chad moved forward all tease. "It gets worse than sleeping with your gay boss?"

"Hell, yes. I could have had sex with my gay boss."

The suit nearly spat coffee everywhere. His onyx eyes laughing as he looked me over. He looked familiar, but I couldn't place why.

"Are you sure you didn't?" Chad challenged, a tinge of jealousy showing through.

"If I had something that big inside me last night, I'd be walking rough this morning. I'm good." The suits mouth fell open.

Chad laughed. "You seriously have seen way more of your boss than I have of mine."

"Well, yes, but I'm so past walking in on him having sex in the office now, that I may as well take popcorn and watch the show," I announced as I went to the coffee machine and made myself and Aubrey a coffee. The suit spat coffee everywhere.

Chad blushed handing the suit a hand towel. "Again, I'm terribly sorry about that."

"Saying sorry after the fact doesn't undo you being bent

over my drafts table yesterday morning. Aubrey has his own office you know."

"He was showing me the plans for the tactile museum you were working on. We got carried away."

"On said plans. Cum stains is a term for a reason you know." The suit gave up on his coffee at this point, forcing himself to swallow what was in his mouth. "Now, I'm hungover and going to spend the day redrawing the plans you defaced."

Chad sighed putting his cup on the sink. "You were just in bed with my boyfriend. Let's call it even?"

"Not a chance. I didn't leave cum stains all over him." The suit was trying really hard not to laugh.

Chad's mouth fell open. "You are so vulgar, Rain."

"Blow me."

Chad gave up. "I'll go say good morning to my boyfriend."

"Take him some water and an aspirin, will you?"

Chad turned to the other man. "Aspirin?"

Opening a cupboard, the suit popped two aspirin in a glass, filled it with water and handed it to Chad.

"Thanks, Jet."

Turning my back to them as I made coffee, I bit my lip realizing Jet was Aubrey's older brother. His very straight, ridiculously intelligent, workaholic lawyer brother. Not that the entire family wasn't the same, but Jet hadn't gone into the family architecture business. He'd applied and been accepted to study at Oxford in England. When he returned to Australia, he started his own law firm, and he was now one of the most highly sort divorce lawyers in Sydney.

"I don't think we've formally met," the sexy voice that woke me up teased over my ear.

Turning around, I discovered Jet standing right behind me, hand out in greeting. Hesitating only a moment, I took the hand. "Rain Noir, one of your brother's architects."

"Jet Landy, provider of aspirin to the hungover."

Taking my hand back, I picked up my coffee and took a sip. "Thank you for the aspirin. I think your brother needed it more, though."

"I'm sure he did, but you deserved it more." Jet stepped back to the meals table as he checked his watch and started placing a notepad and file into his briefcase. "You made sure he got home safely, even though it put you out."

That was nothing new, so I shrugged. "He was off his face and Benny from accounting was all up in his ass trying for promotion. I was drunk enough that Sleezy Dudley from marketing was trying to cop a handful. If that doesn't tell you to call it a night, you deserve to wake up next to a hairy stranger."

Lifting a sexy eyebrow, Jet turned to look at me. "Speaking from experience?"

"Not yet. My drunken regrets tend not to include hairy strangers. I'm kind of picky. Thankfully, being here meant Aubrey didn't miss the important call he's on."

Picking up his briefcase, Jet looked me over again. "Do you remember much of last night?"

"I remember the work party. The after party at Murphey's gets really blurry about the fifth round of shots your brother ordered, and it is gone completely after I got him in the cab. Did I miss much?"

Jet slipped one hand in his pocket. "Not much. I need to get to work."

"Oh, do you know where my clothes are?" I asked as he turned to leave.

"Shoes and bag are by the front door. Your dress is in the laundry after my brother threw up over the both of you as you helped him in the door."

Getting a flashback of the moment, I cringed. "Crap, sorry. Did we wake everyone?"

"Just me. Luckily, mum and dad are overseas."

"Sorry."

"Don't worry about it. By the time I came downstairs, you had stripped you both off and cleaned the floor."

Remembering Jet coming downstairs in his boxer shorts wondering what the hell was happening, I frowned. I may have drooled on the floor admiring him. "You accused me of taking advantage of your brother."

Jet blushed. "If it's any consolation, I was extremely impressed you managed to seduce him. My brother has been gay since he got his first erection. He was actually ogling you last night. I wanted to film it for blackmail."

"Wouldn't be the first time he's perved on me," I dismissed. Then his words hit me. "Wait, you didn't take video of me half naked right?" I stepped forward concerned.

Jet smiled. "No, Rain. I'm not a perv."

"Right. You do realise you've talked to my boobs this entire time, right?"

Jet's eyes flashed up to mine, dropped, lifted, and lowered. He shrugged one shoulder. "Well, they are quite nice, and I did get to see quite a lot of them last night. I have to go."

"Nice meeting you," I gave a singular wave as he moved through the door. With a sigh, I finished my coffee and went out to the front door to find my bag and shoes. Locating my phone, I called a taxi, then took Aubrey his coffee. Not thinking to knock, I opened the door like I would at the office.

"Crap!" Closing my eyes, I turned around quickly at the compromising position my boss was in with Chad. "Okay, coffee. I'm heading home to change but need some pants for the trip. Do you have a pair of sweatpants I could borrow?"

"Wardrobe," Aubrey laughed.

Placing the coffee down, I crab walked to the wardrobe and borrowed a pair of sweatpants while Aubrey and Chad went back to working his hangover off.

"Don't forget you have a team meeting at nine o'clock to give us the specs for the new job," I called as I left.

By the time the taxi dropped me home five minutes down the road, it was already eight. By the time I showered and dressed and caught the bus to work, it was nine.

"I'm surprised you're standing straight this morning," Barbara, the receptionist groaned.

"Aspirin and coffee," I smiled, saluting her with the super large coffee I picked up at the coffee shop on the corner. Putting mine down on the counter, I lifted a normal sized cup out of the tray I carried and put it on her desk. With a wink, I headed back to my office.

"Lifesaver," Barbara moaned.

Aubrey arrived five minutes later, sticking his head into my office on his way passed. "Morning, Rain." When I handed him his coffee, Aubrey sighed. "God, I love you."

"That's not what you were saying an hour ago."

Settling into the spare seat in my office, Aubrey smirked. "What time is our meeting this morning?"

"Five minutes ago. I called and told them you were

delayed. Gave everyone else time to go get coffee. I think we are all a little hung over today."

"More than likely. After the meeting, I'm out for the day?"

"No, you will be in interviews for your new intern until five."

"Who scheduled interviews for the day following the Christmas party?"

"You did."

"Why didn't you talk me out of it?"

"Not my job, you have an assistant for that. Now, we need to get going."

"You're evil," Aubrey called after me. "You could have reminded me. A good friend would have."

"Pay back for puking on me."

"Oh, god. I didn't?"

"There was a reason my dress was missing this morning. I actually think I would have preferred you trying to have sex with me."

"You wish. Get your ass to that meeting." He started following me out.

"Have you got those specs ready?"

"Shit." Aubrey raced next door to his office.

Smiling to myself, I went ahead to the meeting room. The amount of groaning and heads on the table was hilarious and pathetic. It's not like any of them spent the night in the boss's bed with him snoring.

Flashes of last night passed through my head like a faded dream. Jesus, I told Aubrey I wanted to sleep with Jet instead of him. Closing my eyes in humiliation, I dropped my head to the table. I'd said it in front of Jet.

When I groaned, the others reciprocated.

Eight hours later, I was just finishing redrawing the plans for the tactile museum. "I'm heading off, Rain," Barbara called. "You're the last here so I'll lock the door."

"Have a good weekend," I answered and went back to work. I was showing these to the client on Monday, so they needed to be finished.

As I was grabbing my iPad to scan the plans, an expensive black suit stepped into my doorway. My heart raced as I stepped back. When I recognized the face, it didn't put me at ease. "Jet? How did you get in here?"

"Family business. I have a key. I quite often drop by to see Aubrey and Rae." Rae was their father and the owner of the firm.

"Oh," I frowned slightly unsettled and relaxed my stance. "Aubrey isn't here. He was leaving straight from his last meeting to have dinner with Chad."

"I'm not here to see him," Jet smiled slyly, his eyes staying pointedly on my eyes. "It's Friday night. Can I take you to dinner?"

My body charged with adrenaline, but I was practiced at pretending I was fine even when my flight system was activated. Moving back to my drafts table, I scanned the plan. "Thanks for the offer, but I still need to upload these plans before I can leave. Besides, after last night, I think a bath and bed are my only agenda items."

"I'm adding new business in the form of dinner with me," Jet informed me. "Besides, hair of the dog will help. I need a drink and I hate drinking alone."

"Don't you have friends for drinking with?"

"Yes, but they all have families to go home to. I got the impression you're single, like me."

"If you're looking to hook up, try your brother's assistant, that's kind of her thing, not mine."

Jet's lips twitched in humor. "Just dinner and a drink. I have an early morning, so I'm not up to spending hours servicing you."

Something about the comment put me at ease. Folding my arms under my bust, I noticed Jet's eyes going to them while I jutted my hip out. "Huh, well at least you know who it would be on their knees. Okay, dinner it is."

Going back to my desk, I airdropped the plans to the server, adding an item to Barbara's to-do list to have them printed first thing Monday morning.

Grinning, Jet moved to look at the plans. "Are these the plans Chad destroyed?"

"Yes," I grumbled. "They should have gone out for print this morning. Now, it will be a rush on Monday to have them ready for our eleven fifteen with the client."

"Strange, the plans don't do a thing for me."

"Good, I don't have to worry about you trashing them then." Grabbing the roll of parafilm, I pulled it out to cover the plan before laying it over and cutting it off. "Just in case." Winking at Jet, I turned to grab my bag.

"Waterproof I take it?" Jet ran his fingers over the protective layer on the plan.

"Yes. Now, changes are erasable without destroying the original. If the client likes this plan, the second draft onward is created digitally. These get archived and can always be referred back to."

"I've never seen my father do this."

"It's only a recent way to preserve our work."

Nodding as if that made sense, Jet turned his focus to me. "Are you ready?"

❖

Chapter Two
DRINKS

"We've been good friends since high school. He's the one who convinced me to do architecture and utilize my creativity."

"I got the impression last night that you've looked out for him a lot."

"How?"

"He kept saying how you are always looking out for him."

Jet's cheekiness made me smile, as did his honesty. "Aubrey did say that a lot. He also told me he loves me and wants me to have his babies, so let's not put too much stock in what your brother says drunk."

Jet's lips twitched in a smirk, his left dimple showing. "I don't know. You did manage to handle him puking on you pretty calmly."

"I've been puked on a lot. Not much you can do but clean up and get the sick person to bed or over a toilet bowl."

Tilting his head, Jet appraised me. "Wild university nights?"

Not a chance. Most of my degree happened via correspondence. "Two younger brothers whose mother refuses to deal with them when they are sick. I must be immune to the plague by now."

"I'm guessing she's not your mother?"

Understatement of the year. You could barely classify the woman as a mother to her biological children. "No, my father's third marriage. A rather rushed and disastrous affair that ended in rather a nasty divorce."

"No prenup?"

"Ah, well, yes, but then the clever little minx got pregnant with twins."

"And the prenup didn't allow for kids. Ouch."

"As my mother used to say. If you play the game, expect to claim the trophy." A lesson learned the hard way in our household.

The quote made Jet smirk and lift an eyebrow. "Does your mother get along with your stepmother?"

"They've never met," I answered dismissively. Tilting his head, brows low, Jet blinked a couple of times. Good to know he knew nothing about me. "So, you went to Oxford. Was that a wild party?"

Shaking his head, Jet relaxed with the change of topic. "I am an intensely focused person. By the time I grew pubic hair I knew I wanted to be a lawyer and I applied myself to be one. When I went to university, I kept my goals in sight. No wild parties during the semester, nothing to distract me for more than a night."

"Aubrey tells me the one-night policy is still in play, even ten years later." Okay, I was fishing, but it's best to know up front about a man's interest.

A brow jumped as his eyes lit up with humor. "You asked Aubrey about me?"

"Never," I shut down his ego. "He talks about you constantly. I think it's great you've been so supportive of his lifestyle."

"His sexual orientation doesn't bother me like it does our parents. His disastrous relationships do. He can't stick with any guy longer than an innings."

"Innings?"

"Like in cricket."

"I hate cricket," I scrunched my nose. "It's very boring."

"I put it on when I'm having trouble sleeping."

"Well, Cricket would cure my insomnia quickly, but I have better and less boring methods."

"Such as?" His eyes sparkled in the dim lighting of the restaurant.

Placing my napkin on the table, I sat back. "Not the same as your brother; that's for sure."

"So, it bothers you too?"

"Not for the same reason."

"Why don't you like his promiscuity?"

"If it were random one-night hookups, it wouldn't bother me. But, every time it's a 'boyfriend,' he wants me to be friends with them. Some are nice, some I can't stand. Then they break up and it's like losing a friend for me if I like them. Utter relief if I hate them."

Studying me, Jet peered through long lashes that fanned around his dark eyes to batter his cheeks. "Rain, I need to ask something, and I don't want you to take it the wrong way. Are you in love with Aubrey?"

Initially, my mouth fell open; then, I started laughing so

hard I nearly wet myself. Blushing a little, Jet hung his head until I settled down. "Oh, my god, you're funny. You do know he's gay, right? I mean, that's not a temporary thing. That's his orientation, and that's just how it is."

Clearing his throat, Jet loosened his tie enough to pop the top button. Spying the dip at the bottom of his throat made my cheeks heat a little, but not as much as Jet's were right this minute. "Ah, yes, I was just making sure you were aware."

"Look, I care for Aubrey. He's my best friend, but I'm not in love with him like that. I have no misconceptions about our relationship. Why would you even think that?"

Taking a drink of his beer, Jet waited until he swallowed to answer. "You are the only long-term relationship my brother has ever had. I've known about you for years. He's always talked about you, but last night was the first time I saw you together. That you slept together and you seeing him naked was no big deal made me wonder."

"Well, it's not the first time we've slept together. We've done it a lot. Not so much since we graduated uni. He's usually got company most nights now."

The deep chuckle that filled the space between us made my stomach warm. "Don't I know it. Our bedrooms back onto one another."

The idea of the noises Jet hears through the wall made the heat sear through my cheeks and chest. I wondered if Aubrey had to endure the same with his brother's female company. Now my body heated imagining facing up to Aubrey after a night in his brother's bed. Fanning myself a little, I decided it was time to change the subject. "Why did you need a drinking buddy tonight?"

"Tough week."

"Clients?"

"Yeah. The one I was in court for today, neither of them wants the kids, and all they want to know about is the money."

"Why did you get into divorce law? Your parents are still happily married."

"I'm in family law, not just divorce law. I do a lot of pro bono work with legal aid, but I've made my name through a few high-profile divorce cases."

"Do you love your job?"

"I do, but times like today, I don't. You can't stand up in court and tell a judge neither are worthy parents. You can't even say that about your client even if they are a psycho and aren't fit to raise little humans. Days like today, I hate my job and wish I'd gone into conveyancing."

"I'm sorry your day sucked."

"It could have been worse. I could have woken up half-naked in my gay boss's bed." The lift of his brow and sparkle in his eye was cheeky.

"Would have been more awkward for you than me, that's for sure." I could give as well as I took.

Jet shook his head with humor. We sat quietly for a few moments while we finished our drinks. There was something comfortable about Jet. Familiar, but not, yet, his cheekiness relaxed me enough that I hadn't looked at my watch or checked my phone once.

"Have your boyfriends had an issue with your friendship with my brother?"

The question made me smirk. "Boyfriends?"

"As in past relationships."

Lifting my wine to my lips, I paused with the glass hiding my mouth. "No. It's never been a factor."

"Has Aubrey ever not liked you dating someone?"

"If he has, he's never voiced it."

"So, he's never told you not to date someone?"

"I haven't exactly had him screening guys for me. Plus, with Aubrey's love life, I could get married and he wouldn't know what I was doing outside the workplace unless I told him."

"So, you don't tell him everything?"

"No, and he doesn't tell me everything either. Why so curious?"

Smirking, Jet snatched the bill as it was placed on the table. "I guess I like you."

Shaking my head as I stood, I leaned over the back of my chair to whisper. "No, you like the look of me. There is a difference."

"Where are you going?"

"Home, for a swim." Picking up my bag, I made my way outside. He hadn't lingered about the bill, and the way he took it announced his determination to pay. I wasn't going to argue about it.

Outside the restaurant the hot humid air of spring hit me. Now that night had fallen, a light southerly was blowing off the harbor, but it wasn't enough to tame the heat.

Stopping beside me, Jet watched me in my peripheral. "Can I give you a lift home?"

"You can."

"And how far away do you live?"

"I live in Bellvue Hills, literally fourteen minutes' walk from you."

Unlocking the door to his car, Jet smiled. "I could run home and get a swimsuit then come and join you."

"Or you could just swim there since you have quite a size-able pool of your own."

Starting the engine, Jet put his arm on my head rest as he reversed. "You've spent time at my place, but I've never seen you there?" Shifting into drive, we were off.

"I spent a lot of time at your place in high school. You were in Oxford. Aubrey and I used to lay out in your back yard and watch the stars move overhead."

"I have to admit. I've never really just laid around and looked up at the sky."

"How come?"

"I'm not one for laying around."

Eyeing Jet, I nodded in agreement. "Actually, I can see that about you."

"You don't approve?"

"I don't disapprove. I'm the creative type. Sitting around daydreaming inspires me, which in turn, helps my career. Your job isn't like that. It's about law and remembering rules and cases and precedence. It's an active thinking job. It's strategy, and out playing your opponent. Your job is chess, mine is Meccano and Etch-a-sketch." Jet was smirking at me again. "What?"

"Nothing," he shook his head, "nothing at all."

"Okay, well, tell me something you've always wanted to do, but never found the time to do it, or learn it?"

Jet's brows lifted then drew together in deep concentration. "I was a real Gene Kelly fan growing up. He was always classy, none of the crassness of modern day. I used to copy his dance moves around the rumpus. I guess, I would have loved to learn to dance. You know, the classics. Waltz, foxtrot, tango. Those kinds of dances." Peering at me in the dim light of his dashboard, I sat looking at him with a huge smile. "Too cheesy?"

"Is it a pickup line?"

"No." His deep vibrato filled the car with happiness.

"Then it's not cheesy."

Ten minutes after leaving the restaurant, we pulled into the small driveway for my place. I pressed the button for the gate. "Thank you for the lift home."

"Do you have flat mates?"

"Like you, I live at home still." Opening the car door, I stepped out, before turning to smile in at Jet. His eyes went straight to my breasts, which I'm sure my bending forward allowed a glimpse down my top. "Thanks for dinner."

"Your welcome. We should do it again." Eyes still on my rack, Jet looked hopeful.

He didn't even try and pretend he wasn't ogling. The honesty in his actions made me smirk. "I wouldn't say no."

"Good to know." Jet backed down the drive as I walked into the courtyard and closed the gate.

Once through the front door, I turned right down the hall to where it opened up onto the open plan kitchen and informal living areas. Kicking off my shoes, I dropped my bag to the floor. My skirt and blouse followed after. My dad was away for the weekend, so the place was all mine. Home was my safe place, where I didn't have to fight my body's anxiety all the time.

Grabbing a vodka twist from the fridge, I stepped out onto the terrace. Skipping down the stairs to the pool, I pulled open the gate and placed the bottle by the spa. With a running leap, I dived in the pool and swam laps to wear myself out. When I finished, I climbed over the divide and hit the button to turn on the spa. Sitting back, I opened my bottle and stared up at the beautiful sky. Peace filled me, the stars twinkling in my vision, creating buildings in my head, each star acting as a corner or intersection.

When I finished my drink, I climbed out and walked back inside. In the lower level of the house was a pool shower room. I dried off, then wrapped a towel around me.

Upstairs in the kitchen, I placed my empty bottle in the bin and put the kettle on. After the two glasses of wine at the restaurant, I was slightly tipsy, but nowhere near drunk yet. Just happy. As I pottered around, I was thinking about Jet. I'd seen photos of him as a teen, but he'd been tall and gangly then. He'd really filled out since going away to university and the years that followed. Remembering him in his boxer shorts last night, my cheeks heated. Jet was fit and strong, with a v-pack that made me want to peak beneath the waist band and see if he was as packed as his brother in his pants.

Moaning at the thought, heat bloomed between my legs. Needing to distract myself, I took out my sketch book from my work bag, and quickly roughed out the building I'd just imagined. Not the one in Jet's pants, but out in the stars. Despite focusing on the edges, sharp and crisp, my mind kept coming back to Jet and his almost black eyes.

No, that wasn't a good idea. Jet was Aubrey's brother. He didn't have relationships, just the occasional one-night stand. He was curious about my relationship with Aubrey, and probably wouldn't mind getting in my pants. Okay, the last was very likely. It didn't make it a good idea for me.

The intercom buzzed surprising me. Walking into the hall, I saw Jet looking back at me on the camera screen. Taking a deep breath, I hit the talk button. "Hi, again."

"I swam but wired as I am, I thought I would run down with your dress. It's been dry cleaned."

For the first time since the office, I hesitated to be around Jet. He was a relative stranger, and I was home alone. Still, he was Aubrey's brother and I'd felt safe enough to go to dinner with him. It's not like he knew I was home alone coming back here. Pressing the pedestrian gate button to unlock, I watched in the camera as Jet walked in, then shut the gate. Quickly racing across the room, I pulled my top on over my head. When Jet knocked at the front door, I was zipping my skirt up.

Opening it, I took the dress he offered me. "Thanks, you didn't have to do this."

"I couldn't sleep and could use the run."

"Do you run a lot?"

"Only when my brain won't switch off." Jet's eyes swept over me as his hand swept through his hair in frustration.

Jet had large hands. They looked strong. There was no trouble imaging them cupping my breasts, supporting the weight of them, and molding them while his thumbs played over my nipples. Jet's brow lifted a little in humor, his lips twitching.

"Um," I snapped back from my daydream realizing we'd stood there for several minutes. "Did you want to come in for a cup of tea?"

"Herbal? The last thing I need is caffeine."

Letting Jet inside, I showed him to the informal living area in the back of the house. Making us both teas, I then took us out on the terrace, overlooking the pool to sit. The silence between us was comfortable, Jet taking in the paintings on the walls and photos on the shelves. Every time I looked at him; I felt my cheeks heat thinking about his hands. Was I really that pent up that I couldn't keep my head straight? Or, was Jet exuding some sort of pheromones which made women randy?

We sat drinking for several minutes. Jet watching me now, seeming humored by my lack of conversation. That's when I realized I probably did need to talk. "Why do you need to be up early tomorrow?"

Sitting a little straighter, Jet checked his watch. "I have to be in Homebush for a tournament by eight. It's how I burn stress."

"I didn't realize you were still doing martial arts. Aubrey stopped competing years ago."

"It keeps me steady and focused. How about you?"

"I run." Shifting in my seat, I was very aware that Jet could not only overpower me in strength but also with his martial arts experience.

"You look unsettled. Did I say something to upset you?"

Honesty was the best policy. "I'm not going to have sex with you."

Jet's lips twitched up on one side, his dimple showing again. "I don't remember asking for sex."

"Jet, I didn't come down in the last rainfall. We both know one night is your thing. It's all you offer. It's not good enough for me."

Moving closer, Jet sat with his knee touching mine. "When was the last time you were involved with a guy?"

Way too long ago. "It's been a while."

Jet touched my cheek, turning my face towards him. "How long were you with the last guy?"

"Months."

"The guy before that?"

"Years."

"If I promised it wouldn't just be one night, would you still say no?" His face moved close to mine. Closing my eyes, I held my breath, eager and hesitant.

"I want to play Halo."

"Yeah, well I say Lego dimensions." Two young male voices were bickering at the front door.

Pulling back with my eyes wide, I cursed under my breath. "You need to leave." Standing up, I stepped into the lounge when two tired and obviously sick ten-year-old boys walked into the open area.

"Rain," they both greeted and ran over to give me hugs.

"What are you doing here?"

Jet walked inside carrying our teacups, looking confused and annoyed.

"We caught the bug going around the school, so Mum is ditching us again. Can we play the PlayStation?"

"Its nine thirty, you can go to bed."

Both of them groaned, but then raced back down the hall and upstairs. When I get up there, they'd be playing their PlayStation.

"Oh, good, you're here," Penelope greeted as she dropped the boy's bags on the floor and checked her nails.

"I live here. What are you doing here?"

Penelope flicked her fading red hair over her shoulder. "I'm dropping the boys' home. A friend invited me to Bali for the week, and I'm flying out in an hour, so I've got to run." She turned to leave.

"Wait. The boys aren't due here until Monday. Dad isn't here this weekend."

Turning back annoyed, Penelope spied Jet looking through my sketch book and her eyes widened in surprise. She blinked, fluttered her lashes at him, and forced a fake smile. "I didn't know you had company. My, my, Rain, aren't you a sneaky one. He's quite the dish."

"Stop changing the subject. You can't just ditch your sons here so you can run off with potential husband number three. This is your weekend."

"I expected to walk in and find your dad with some bimbo. Never thought to find you with one."

Jet's eyebrows raised.

"Typical, not getting your way, so you turn to insults. What would you have done if I wasn't home?"

"The boys are ten. They would have been fine for a few hours on their own. I really have to go. Thanks for being here for them, Rainbow." Penelope trotted down the hallway before I could say anything more.

"Argh!" I looked to Jet who was scowling at the empty hall. Grabbing up my bag, I pulled out my phone. "I'm sorry, Jet. Looks like I'm babysitting this weekend. You should go. I need to call my dad and..." Seeing the screen of my mobile, I stopped at the plethora of notifications of missed calls from Aubrey.

"Your stepmother has a key?"

"No, the boys do for when they get home from school. Shit, Jet, you need to go. Aubrey has been calling for the last fifteen minutes."

"And that is bad because?"

"He never calls if he's on a date. I dare say Chad is off the scene." Sending my dad a text message about the boys, I then sent one to Aubrey telling him I was home.

"About time you answered the phone," Aubrey called from the front door. "Were you swimming?" He slurred as he stumbled down the hall.

"How did you get inside?" I asked panicked as he stumbled over to my lounge and dropped.

"Relax! The ex-trophy wife let me in. I made sure the gate was closed after she drove off." Aubrey spotted Jet in the kitchen. "Why is he here?"

"Oh, it's going to be one of those nights," I groaned.

"I was dropping off the dress you puked on last night."

"Personally?"

"I'm not paying a courier to walk fifteen minutes down the road."

"You could have just given it to me."

"I didn't know if Rain needed it this weekend."

Aubrey looked to me, confusion showing at the statement. "You let a man in."

The night was getting better by the second. I cleared my throat. "Well, he's not just a man. He's your brother and you've always told me he's honorable."

"I've also told you he's a manwhore."

"An honorable manwhore," I corrected.

"You let him in. You served him tea. You're not drunk enough to sleep with him."

"Aubrey!" I snapped in annoyance. Aubrey lifted a brow surprised. Sighing, I sunk onto the lounge. Deflection was best. "What happened with Chad?"

❖

Chapter Three
INTRUSIONS

"Come on, heart breaker. Let's get you home. I need to sleep before the tournament tomorrow, and I think you need to sleep it off."

"Alright," Aubrey slurred leaning into his brother's side. "Thanks for listening, Rain."

"Always have, always will."

"I know. You're the best friend a guy could have, Rain. So, sweet, and kind, and hot." Aubrey drunk-smiled at Jet. "Rain is going to be my baby mama. When I find a guy I want to be with for life, we're going to take turns knocking her up."

Having heard it all before, I was shaking my head humored. Jet's brows went up. "What if her husband objects?"

"Husband?" Aubrey laughed. "See, I told you he could be funny, Rain."

"Yes, you did." Escorting them both to the front door, I turned to wait for them with my hand on the handle.

Frowning at his brother, Jet shouldered his weight with ease. "Why is Rain getting married such a ridiculous idea?"

"For the same reason you won't ever marry," Aubrey

blurted. "You both know the reality of how heartbreaking it can be, so you won't take the risk."

Rolling his eyes, Jet got his brother to the door. "It's not about risk. I haven't had time to date a woman I would want to marry."

"Pfft. Well, Rain could date, but doesn't. So, she's going to be my babymaker." Aubrey lurched away from Jet to lean on me, only I didn't hold up his weight as well as Jet and struggled to keep us upright. "Our babies are going to be so pretty."

"You know that means you have to have sex with her," Jet rolled his eyes.

Aubrey laughed. "You don't have to be in a woman to stuff her duff, just-"

"Enough! No one is knocking me up tonight, so let's save this discussion for when you find a guy you can be involved with for more than a week."

Aubrey huffed. "You're still pissed about Geoff."

Opening the door, I basically threw Aubrey out. "Yes, I am. Your jealousy ruined a good thing. I am never putting myself in that position again."

Juggling his brows at me, Aubrey smirked. "I thought you liked that position."

"Night." Shutting the door with an annoyed sigh, I turned around to find Jet still standing behind me. Heat raced up my neck to bloom in my cheeks.

Jet lifted a brow. "Geoff?"

"Long story. The moral is, I learned my lesson. Apparently, Aubrey did not."

"Well, as long as someone did. Can we maybe do drinks again sometime?"

Blinking a few times in surprise, I took a moment to find my words. "Ah, sure. I'm free most weekends."

"Weekends only?"

Pointing upstairs, I exhaled. "Someone has to take care of them. They are here every second week, Monday to Monday. My dad works late a lot, so I make sure they get fed, homework is done, and into bed at a reasonable time. The week they aren't here, I tend to stay late at the office." An hour ago, I'd left Aubrey and Jet on the terrace while I tucked the boys in and gave them paracetamol.

Pulling out his phone, Jet handed it to me for my number. "What about your life, Rain? When are you allowed to go away for weekends and date?"

"Weekends, as I said."

"Like tonight? How often does your weekend get canceled because of their parent's selfishness?"

Taking a deep breath, I understood how it looked to outsiders, but it didn't seem like a chore or inconvenience to me. "It is what it is. They are my brothers." Opening the door, I handed his phone back to him. "You've spent your twenties building your career and not bothering with relationships. Why is it such a surprise my priorities aren't so different?"

Jet looked out to where Aubrey was stumbling around the courtyard trying to get out. "Because I've met career focused women. You're not one of them."

The assessment made me laugh. "Really, what kind of woman am I then?"

Tilting his head, Jet appraised me. "I'm still trying to figure that out." Stepping out, Jet looked up at the surveillance camera then to the pin code entry. "I think your place has more security on it than a prison."

Hating the reminder that his observation caused, I bowed my head. "Goodnight, Jet. Thanks for getting your brother home."

"I think it's my turn tonight." With a final smile, Jet walked out to the gate, guiding Aubrey through.

"What are you doing at Rain's place?" Aubrey frowned at Jet.

"Saving her from another night of sharing a bed with you."

Glaring at his brother, Aubrey was suddenly more sober than he seemed five minutes ago. "You can't mess with her. She's not like the women you play with. She's my best friend."

"Just get your drunk ass home." Jet turned to look at me once more.

Pressing the button to close the gate, I waved. Closing the front door, I leaned against it to inhale a deep breath. Forehead resting on the reinforced timber door, I smiled at the recall of Jet's eyes on mine as his face moved closer. Floating on an unusual high, I proceeded to move around locking the house up for the night. After checking in on the twins, I made my way to my bedroom.

Located at the front of the house, my bedroom overlooked the street with a view straight up the road, at the end of which stood the mansion that Aubrey lived in with his family. With Jet.

Showering, I thought of Jet. Dressing for bed, I remembered the heat of his body against mine. As I lay staring up at the ceiling Jet's eyes as he sat beside me and moved his face closer to mine kept playing in my head. My phone vibrated on the nightstand. "Hi, dad."

"She did it again?"

"Yes."

"I'll head back in the morning."

"Don't. There is no point both of us having our weekend messed up. You enjoy yours, just do me a favor, don't marry and have kids with this one."

"You sound more annoyed than usual. Did something happen?"

"I was on a date. Well, I had dinner and drinks with a guy."

Dad was quiet. "Serious?"

"We only just met."

"But it ruined your night?"

"Well, it didn't matter. I got the boys to bed just in time for Aubrey to turn up drunk and freshly broken up."

My dad groaned. "Why don't I come back and you call the guy and ask for a do-over tomorrow night?"

"Dad, I really don't mind. It's done."

"Rain, sweetie, they are your brothers, not your kids. They aren't your responsibility."

"I'll make you a deal. I'll take them this weekend, but as of next weekend, I'm unavailable after work on Friday's until Monday unless booked in advance."

"Which is exactly how it will be."

"I think we need to organize an alternative option about keys too, so Penelope can't just dump and run. She was just going to leave them here unattended if no one was here, and they are both sick."

Dad was silent for a moment. "Okay. We'll organize something. You sound exhausted. Get some rest."

"Night, dad."

Hanging up, I was about to put the phone down when it rang again, this time with a number I didn't know. "Hello?"

"It's Jet," the sexy voice drifted through the receiver. "I was thinking; what do the twins do for sport?"

"Ah, soccer and whatever else the school does with them." The question a bizarre follow up to the night.

"What about martial arts?"

"Don't think dad has ever considered it. Why?"

"You could bring them to the tournament tomorrow. Let them watch."

It would do the twins good to do self-defense. "I guess we could. It will all depend on how they are feeling in the morning. What time should we be there?"

"I'll text you the details. Just message me before seven if you want me to pick you up."

"We'll find our own way out. Just in case we need to leave early."

"Well, I hope you can make it. Text me when you get there if you can, so I know to keep a look out for you."

"I will. Goodnight."

"Goodnight, Rain."

As I snuggled down to sleep, I remembered Jet coming downstairs last night in only his boxer shorts to find me in only my underwear, undressing his brother. How I had quite openly appraised and admired him. I might have possibly drooled as I offered to share the bed with him. Sobering dramatically, Aubrey told me I was too drunk, and I could share his bed to ensure I didn't wake up regretting anything the next morning.

Everything about Jet was sexy. Just like Aubrey, he was good looking, intelligent, hardworking, and cared about his family. Unlike Aubrey, he was straight. He was going to kiss me tonight before the twins came in. What would have happened if we hadn't been interrupted? Could I have found the courage to be intimate with him?

Falling asleep, I fantasized about being brave enough to take that risk, but in my head, I knew I wasn't. When I woke at sunrise, that was something I accepted. Dressing in my exercise gear, I went for my usual morning run. Every impact of my foot on the ground draining away my tensions, relaxing my body, focusing my mind. Usually, I arrived home with a clear head and tension free body. Today, dark eyes in a masculine face with pouty lips and dimples haunted me.

As I reached my endpoint, I had to accept that I was seriously attracted to Jet. Waving at the Sheriff who was standing out front of the police station drinking coffee, I huffed at myself and the likelihood I could expect anything to develop between Jet and me. Saluting me with his coffee, the Sheriff went inside. Turning the corner to circle the block, I headed home.

The boys were up and on the PlayStation by the time I came in. "Turn it off. Breakfast, then get dressed for the day. We are leaving in an hour."

"Where are we going?"

"To watch a friend compete at a tournament."

"What?"

"Fighting. We are going to watch people fight."

"Awesome!" The twins cheered and ran off to get ready for the day. Happy they were interested, I sent Jet a message to say we were coming, then went to shower.

Two hours later we had found a park and entered the arena. Nearly everyone was wearing a Gi, making us standout as we made our way to the stands. Several participants were in pairs on the floor sparring. As we walked along the upper walkway to the stands, I spied Jet standing to the side with his black belt, watching two green belts fight.

Glancing up, Jet smiled when he saw me. He gestured to the far end of the stands, then moved his hands behind his back, face focusing on those before him.

"This way," I told the boys and made my way to the area Jet had gestured to.

"Rain, what are you doing here?"

Stopping halfway down the row of seats, I found Joseph standing before me in his Gi. In his mid-thirties, Joseph was my height and a third dan black belt. He was also one of the policemen who regularly greeted me on my morning run. "Joseph, good morning."

"Hi, Detective Reed," the twins greeted. "Are you fighting today?"

"I will be, yes." His hazel eyes came to me. "I don't remember telling you about the tournament?"

"Oh, you didn't. My friend Jet did. He suggested I bring the boys to watch in case they were interested in going to the local dojo to train."

"Jet Landy?" Joseph enquired, his face showing his surprise. "I didn't know you knew each other."

"I've known the Landys since I was ten."

"Yes, but Jet?" When I just nodded confirmation, Joseph took a step closer. "So, he knows?"

Melancholy wrapped around me like a blanket of ice, my stomach hollowing into a cavernous well of emptiness. "Jet? No, he doesn't know. He was studying in Oxford when that all happened." Watching Joseph's lips thin, his hazel eyes narrowed as they assessed me didn't set me at ease.

"Rain," Jet greeted as he approached, the green belts having finished their match. He cocked his head when I was talking to Joseph. "Do you two know each other?"

"Yes. Joseph is a friend."

"I was surprised to see Rain here since she normally steers clear of violent situations. She was just explaining how you encouraged her to bring the boys to get their interest."

Jet's pupils constricted. "You sound like you don't approve, Sensei?"

"I do. It would be good for those boys to have some discipline. I'm just worried about someone getting hurt when they get carried away using it on each other. Most likely Rain."

"Perhaps, Rain should join too. It's good for a woman to learn to defend herself," Jet suggested.

Joseph and I looked at each other. He raised a brow. I shook my head. "No, I tried that once. It didn't end well." Jet tilted his head again. I swallowed. "A man grabbed me when I wasn't suspecting it. I broke his arm in two places. Sensei Joseph suggested I might prefer running. He was right."

Jet's mouth fell open, but he forced it closed again quickly. "What belt were you?"

"She wasn't any. It was her first class," Joseph answered. "The boy deserved it, mind you. It was the start of class and he put his arm around Rain's shoulders ready to put her in a headlock. He liked to initiate the newcomers and bully the white belts. He wasn't expecting Rain to have learned a few moves from Aubrey before coming to the class."

"But you kicked her out?"

"No! Poor Rain was mortified by what she had done and ran away crying. Aubrey and I eventually found her, but she refused to come back to the dojo." An announcement was made, catching Joseph's attention, before he met my eyes. "I need to go. I'll speak with you soon." Waiting until I nodded, Joseph left to supervise the sparring.

"My brother couldn't convince you to try martial arts again?"

"No. Aub thought going to the dojo would help me, but it just made me worse."

"Did you need help?"

Shame filled my chest, making it hard to breathe as I stared at my toes. "I went through some stuff in my teens. I was in a dark place and Aubrey was determined to bring me out of it."

Jet considered me. "I'm glad he found a way to help you. From what I've heard, you were there for him just as much."

That was an understatement and a half. Aubrey and I propped each other up like the slabs of granite at Stonehenge "We've been each other's rock for a long time."

Bowing his head in acknowledgment, Jet looked at the twins, totally enthralled with the sparring. "What do you think so far?"

"They're okay. We could kick their ass'."

"Storm," I sighed.

"Storm?" Jet suppressed a laugh. "Rain, Storm, let me guess, Thunder?" Jet pointed to my other brother.

"It's Zephyr, actually," I corrected.

"What? You think our names are funny?" Storm grumbled, crossing his arms across his chest.

"Not the names, no. I'm Jet, I'm the last person to make fun of someone's names. I was just considering one of your parents are obsessed with bad weather."

"My father named us so whenever Mother Nature got

lousy, it would make him think of happy thoughts, of his children."

Eyebrows lifting, Jet nodded. "Intriguing idea." He looked over his shoulder. "I've got to get back to supervising. Can we get lunch after it's finished?"

"Sure." As Jet ran back down to the auditorium floor, I took a seat next to the boys. They were really interested in the sparing and asking me to explain the scoring system, but it wasn't something I understood since I'd never come to a tournament before. By the time it was finished, Storm was ready to sign up and Zephyr was burning up.

"Ready for lunch?" Removing his belt and jacket, Jet mopped up his sweat with a towel.

"Jesus," I breathed perving on his body. "That other guy wasn't going to play nice," I covered.

"Unfortunately, you get some who feel the need to prove themselves."

Reaching out, I tentatively touched the bruise blooming across his left ribs. "Nothing was broken?" When Jet hesitated at my touch, I quickly withdrew my hand and stepped back.

"No, he barely got me. Do you know where you would like to go for lunch?" After spraying himself with deodorant, Jet pulled on a clean shirt.

"Actually, Zephyr is feverish, I should get him home," I excused steering my sick brother towards the door.

"Oh, I'll walk you out." Frowning, Jet packed up his stuff and hefted it to his shoulder. "So, what did you think, Storm? Want to join my dojo?"

"Sure. Do you go to Sensei Joseph's dojo?"

"Sure do. I'm one of the instructors there."

"Cool. Do you think dad will let us, Rain?"

"I can't see why not," I considered.

"Can you bring them down Monday night to try a class?" Jet asked keenly.

"I'll speak to our dad first. We should go before Zephyr gets worse."

"I could pick up lunch and bring it to your house? If I order from Schumachs I can shower and bring it over."

"That would be awesome," Storm answered. "I love their tropical delight burger with the mango chutney."

Jet looked at me. "Would that be okay?"

Uncomfortable all of a sudden, I was about to say no when Storm started making pleading gestures. "Come on, Rain. You had him there last night without anyone else, we'll be there today."

Not realizing the boys saw Jet last night, I bit my lip. "Bet you they were kissing before we arrived," Zephyr mock-whispered to Storm.

Cheeks heating, I gave in with a roll of my eyes. "Yes, it's okay."

"Great, what's the order?" Jet smiled, chuckling at my brothers.

Chapter Four
AN HONEST LUNCH

WHEN THE INTERCOM RANG, STORM RACED TO ANSWER IT. "IT'S Jet, can I let him in?"

"Yes, just make sure you watch until the gate shuts," I called from my bedroom. Studying my reflection in the mirror one last time, I worried the knee-length summer dress with capped sleeves I wore was too revealing, but in this weather, anything more would have made an effort to cover up obvious. Giving up, I went into the rumpus and found Zephyr curled up playing the PlayStation. "How are you feeling?" He shrugged. "Do you want more paracetamol?"

"What's the deal with you and this guy?" Zephyr asked grumpily.

"What do you mean?"

"You never have guys here."

"I have Aubrey here all the time."

"He doesn't count. It's Aub. This guy is new."

Worried my brother was picking up my anxiety, I took a breath before comforting him. "Actually, Jet is Aubrey's older brother, so he's not so new."

"I've never seen him before and all of a sudden he's here two days running."

Admitting to my ten-year-old brother who I was trying to drum safety into that I let a near stranger into our home wasn't a good idea. "Okay, but do you live here every day?" Zephyr shook his head. "So, how do you know who I have here when you're not around? You weren't meant to be here this weekend, remember. So, you still wouldn't have met Jet if you weren't sick."

His brow scrunched as he considered the information I provided. "Oh."

"Lunch is here," Storm called as the door slammed shut causing me to wince.

"Do you want to try eating?"

Rolling his eyes, Zephyr paused the game. "Sure," he answered grudgingly.

Jet was already in the kitchen serving up lunch while Storm got drinks out for everyone. Glancing up, Jet smiled, his eyes quickly scanned me, and his smile grew a little bigger before he turned back to the food in front of him.

"Right, I believe the quiet one wanted double beef," he handed Zephyr a burger.

"Thanks." Taking it half-heartedly, Zephyr went to sit at the table.

"And Storm wanted tropical delight with extra mango chutney on the side for his fries."

"Thanks, dude!" Grabbing up his meal and chips, Storm placed them on a plate and carried it over with his drink.

Jet looked at me. "Dude? Has he been watching Wayne's World?"

"Bill and Ted."

"I'm impressed you know it," Jet laughed. It was kind of deep and masculine and intoxicating to hear that laugh.

I shrugged. "I have an unhealthy obsession for Keanu."

"A girl told me I looked like him once," Jet waggled a brow at me.

"I've noticed. In the right light," I added when he kept the brow up.

"Yeah, maybe the lights out." He held a wrap out to me. "Caesar wrap," he smiled and handed me another packet. "Fried Monterey jack sticks instead of chips."

"Thanks." Grabbing a Coke, we joined the boys at the table.

"After lunch, could you show us a few moves?" Storm asked Jet as soon as he sat down. "Would be good to know something on the first day."

"Dad hasn't said yes, yet."

"He will. Anything that means less time at home gaming he's all for."

Giving Storm the stink eye, I poured my Coke into a glass. "Jet was fighting all morning."

"I don't mind," Jet shrugged.

"Really?" I checked.

"I had a younger brother who was much the same once. I've missed it."

"You and Aubrey don't spar?" Zephyr asked.

"Not anymore. I went away to university, and when I came home, he'd changed."

"Changed how?" Storm asked.

"He used to tell me everything, hang out with me more. Even when I went away, we used to Skype all the time. Then, it just stopped." Lowering his mouth to take a bite, Jet considered me, but I kept focused on eating. Forehead creasing, Jet finished his mouthful then looked back to my brothers. "So, what school do you go too?"

The meal passed with Jet chatting with the boys about school and hobbies. Then they went out in the yard, and Jet gave them their first lesson in martial arts. After cleaning up, I sat down on the back deck with my sketch pad to draw Jet and the boys wrestling. While working on the final touches, my phone rang, Aubrey's handsome face flashing at me. Picking it up, I smiled. "Hey, how are you feeling?"

"Like shit. What's that sound?"

"Boys are playing in the back yard." Standing up, I moved inside shutting the door.

"I thought it wasn't their weekend?"

"Penelope dumped them here so she could go to Bali. Zephyr is sick too. They were upstairs asleep when you arrived last night. What's up?"

"Bali sucks."

"You would know." I'd never left the country, but Aubrey's parents traveled prolifically, so before they were adults, the boys did too.

"We should go to Fiji or Tahiti for a holiday. Let's do that," Aubrey sounded excited.

"You do that."

Aubrey huffed. "You need to get away, get drunk, get laid. You are so pent up; you would have jumped my brother Friday night."

"I would not."

"Would too. You basically drooled on him."

"I'm sure he's used to it."

"True, but he's a manwhore. He'd use you, Rain, and you are too insecure for one-night stands with strangers."

"Really? And what is your solution?"

"We go on holiday, we find a bisexual guy, and we all take care of each other's needs," Aubrey cooed.

"Seriously? Back to that again?"

"It worked last time."

Crossing the arm that wasn't holding the phone, I glared at the fridge where a photo of Aubrey and I sat nestled amongst the family photos. "Four years ago, Aub. And that was a long-term thing until you turned all jealous and possessive."

"It was his jealousy. He's the one who wanted to start hooking up with you without me," Aubrey bitched.

"He was my boyfriend!"

"Oh please! Like his dick would ever have left his pants if I hadn't had initiated things." He was right, but it was still annoying that he was jealous of my boyfriend wanting to have sex with me alone. "Besides, I can't get you knocked up sitting on the sidelines," Aubrey simpered.

"Oh, would you stop with that shit! What is it with you and the baby talk of late anyway?"

"I'm clucky," Aubrey brooded. "Did you see Stephanie's baby photos on Facebook. So, adorable. And Kevin was telling me his girlfriend is two months pregnant. They've only been together a year. We've been together since we were ten. Sixteen years, Rain. It's time we talked kids."

Starting to get a headache, I shook my head. "You're gay."

"Most of the time. Like, ninety-nine-point nine percent of the time," he corrected.

"Aubrey, gay men do not have sex with women to get them pregnant. They use a turkey baster or pay a specialist a fortune to do the basting for them."

"I do my basting. Thank you."

"I can't believe we are having this discussion again." Dropping my head, I massaged the bridge of my nose.

"Me neither. You're begging for it, so let's find a guy to join us, and I'll fertilize your eggs with my great genetics. My parents will be happy; I'll be happy, you'll be glowing and-"

"My dad will kill you. Or have you forgotten what he told you when we were sixteen?"

Aubrey deflated. "No, I remember."

"Good. So, keep your pompous genes away from his daughter's ovaries," I repeated my father's words for him.

"This isn't over," Aubrey threatened.

"It's over for now."

"Can I come over and play with the boys?"

"That sounds so wrong."

"Get your mind out of the gutter. I'm bored."

Looking at the clock, I went to the fridge and pulled out the boy's next dose of paracetamol. "Later. I need to get Zephyr more medicine and have him rest for an hour or two. Why don't you come over for dinner? We'll order pizza and do board games."

"Sounds good. Text me the order, and I'll organize it for us."

The boys came running up the stairs to the terrace. "Will do." I hung up. "Hey, Aubrey is coming over for dinner and bringing pizza. What are we eating?"

The twins shouted their order, threw back the medicine, then raced for the rumpus room to get the first controller. Texting Aubrey the order, I put my phone aside as Jet came inside. "How did they go?"

"I feel sorry for everyone at the dojo," Jet laughed. "They

are a rambunctious pair. I think your father named Storm correctly."

Smiling half-heartedly, I handed him a glass of water. "Well, thank you for lunch, and I'll speak to dad about the lessons."

Lifting a brow over the rim of his glass, Jet swallowed and tilted his head, pulling off an all-too-handsome appeal. "Is that your way of telling me it's time to go?"

"No, I just-"

Jet moved closer. His hand caressed along the edge of my jaw, making my eyes flutter. "You don't have to apologize. Say your mind around me, Rain. I put up with people talking around in circles at work all day. One of the things I liked about you when we met is that you speak your mind."

"I barely know you," I whispered, meeting those onyx eyes. "You shouldn't be here."

"Do you want me to go?".

"No," I breathed as I pressed back away from him, "but I need space."

Jet backed away two steps. "Better?" Equally relieved and disappointed, I nodded. Jet tilted his head. "You okay? You're trembling."

My heart was racing, torn between kissing him or screaming and running away. "I, uh, get uncomfortable when people I don't know, touch me." Usually, but Jet's touch was gentle.

"That's all?"

"I have an adrenalin thing. I'm effectively in constant fight or flight. When I get anxious, it can get out of control."

"So, literally a flight risk," Jet teased. When he backed up another step and returned to drinking his drink, I gave him a small smile as a reward. "You don't get anxious around Aubrey?"

"We were friends before this. Did you know we dated in high school?"

Heavy brow shadowing his eyes, Jet frowned. "Wait, you were his girlfriend? The one who knew he was gay but made out with him in front of the other kids so they wouldn't suspect?" Jet looked scandalized. "Why would you do that?"

"Aubrey was the most popular boy in our year. Being his girlfriend kept everyone else away from me. Kissing him didn't set off my anxiety because I knew he didn't want anything else."

Jet considered me. "You said you were off the rails as a teen, so I was expecting promiscuity and drugs, but this contradicts that theory."

"Definitely not promiscuity. I-" I looked around unsure how to say this next part.

"You're gay," Jet blinked surprised.

"No," I laughed. "I'm not into women; I just have physical intimacy issues." I felt easy revealing this to him, which was weird but at the same time reassuring.

Jet's eyes widened. "You're frigid?"

My face dropped into a scold. "That is a harsh high school word that doesn't comprehend the many reasons females can be insecure around the male sex. I have anxiety and trust issues which prevent me from developing intimate relationships where you have to trust another person not to hurt, abuse, or exploit what you are giving them. I am not frigid. I love sex. It just has to be approached with kitten gloves with me, rather than some Neanderthal throwing me over his shoulder and taking me back to his cave."

Jet stood there amazed. Pressing my lips together, I hesitantly turned back to the fridge to grab a drink, slightly shocked myself. I'd never told a man about my insecurities, not even Geoff. Only Aubrey. When I turned back around Jet was appraising me. We met each other's eyes, he lifted a brow, my cheeks heated. Jet laughed, the sound like soft fur against your skin.

"Okay, kitten gloves for the anxious kitten," Jet assured, his eyes glimmering. "Though, you were going to kiss me last night before your brothers arrived."

My heart fluttered with his flirtation. "You were going to kiss me."

Jet stepped closer. "You were going to let me."

Tucking a strand of hair behind my ear, I looked away. "I'd been drinking."

"They say alcohol lowers one's inhibitions and reveals the true personality." He stepped closer again. I could feel his breath across the top of my head.

Lifting my eyes to his, my breath caught at the swirling depth of his eyes. "Do they?"

Grinning, Jet lowered his face towards mine. "The night we met, you were relaxed, fun, and an absolute flirt."

"Was I?" I inhaled shallowly.

"I think that's the real you."

"Do you?"

"Yeah, I do."

Any moment his lips would touch mine. My heart was erratic in my chest. To stop my hands from trembling, I clenched my fists in the skirt of my dress. Stepping back, Jet looked at the wall. "Did you paint that?" He pointed to a painting of a landscape not far from my home.

"Ah, yes."

Reaching down Jet took my shaking hand in his. When I looked up surprised, his mouth found mine. Soft, plump lips pinched mine, and his free hand caressed my hair back from my face as we kissed. My heartbeat hesitated, then calmed. My hand stopped shaking where he held it.

Slowly, Jet pulled back, his eyes glassy and dilated. His lips went to my ear. "Now we've kissed once; there's no need to fear if it happens again." With a wicked smile, Jet went to the painting. "This is beautiful."

Blood rushing through my ears, my stomach in knots, I blinked — happiness, fear, confusion. Jet turned around to smile at me. "Any other art you want to show me?" He lifted a brow, the look cheeky and inviting. He wasn't talking about paintings.

❖

Chapter Five
BUSTED

Our lips broke apart. Jet's eyes glimmered. "That's was my favorite so far."

"Really?" Every painting I'd shown him led to a kiss. We'd covered every picture on the main level and were now downstairs in the games room admiring the portrait of the boys and I that I painted.

"Undoubtedly. It has you in it." Licking his lips, Jet tucked my hair behind my ears. "Any others?"

"Ah, I think we've exhausted all the ones on public display."

"I'm open to a private tour."

Heat raced up my neck to fill my face. "Ah, not with the boys at home."

Smiling, Jet blushed a little. "Of course." He fidgeted with his empty glass a moment. "You know Aubrey is going overseas this week?"

"I do. But it's my brothers' week here, so I'll be taking care of them." I stepped away casually. "I was going to suggest a date on Friday night if you were interested?"

"Friday?" Jet raised a brow. "Why do I think you have something particular in mind?"

"Because I do, but it's a surprise."

His eyelids flying at half mast, Jet flirted his way closer. "I'm intrigued. But only if you show me one of the more private paintings you have now."

My heart raced at the idea of going into a room alone with Jet. Taking my hand in his, Jet lifted it to his lips. "You can leave the door open if that helps?"

"Jet..." Shaking my head, I stepped away, but he kept hold of my hand, massaging my fingers.

His smile softened as he kept space between us. "I understand."

"Do you?"

"Yes. I was hoping to kiss you a few more times."

"Just kiss?"

Smirking, Jet lifted a shoulder in nonchalance. "Maybe a little more to the kiss." God, it was tempting. Jet pointed to the closed-door downstairs. "Is there one in there?"

Glancing at the door to the guest room, I swallowed hard. "Yes."

Grinning, Jet took a step towards the door, causing my heart to knock against my chest and fill my ears with its beating. "We'll leave the door open." Fishing his phone out of his pocket, Jet handed it to me. "You can call emergency from the home screen if I do anything resembling a Neanderthal." It made me smile.

Opening the door, Jet turned on the light and went inside. Jet stopped when he saw the painting above the bed head. "Ah, I was not expecting that after all the landscapes on the other walls." His Adam's apple bobbed as he swallowed visibly. "Is that a self-portrait?"

"No!" Smacking his shoulder, I smiled at the illicit depiction of a man and woman entwined. "But it is based on the night I lost my virginity. It's why it's down here in this room, not out where anyone can see it."

"Does your dad know the subject matter?"

"Yes. It was part of my therapy. I used to have to paint about things that meant something to me, or impacted my life greatly, or things that affected those I care about."

"So, was that Geoff?" Jet gestured to the man in the painting.

"I didn't meet Geoff until Graduation from University. After my dad told me I either go to therapy or he'd send me to rehab, was when I painted this. The idea of being sent away to live with strangers and not even have a lock on the door nearly straightened me out on the spot."

"What was your substance?"

"Alcohol and pot."

Jet frowned. "But you still drink."

"It was the drug that was the problem. I stopped drinking until I was eighteen, but it came with its repercussions. I couldn't relax. Ever! So, I made my dad a deal. No pot, only one to two drinks a night, and the occasional splurge for special events. We haven't had any issues since."

Jet looked back to the artwork. "It's a beautiful painting. That night must have been special to you."

Keeping my emotions buried, I took a deep breath. "It was my biggest fuck up."

"First time, regret."

"No, and yes, and, this is a convoluted story. The summary is that I was high. I was with the guy from school who used to score for me, and he decided it was time that I lost my virginity. My dad found us naked and passed out in my bedroom."

"How old were you?"

"It was two days before I turned sixteen. Dad was going to charge him with carnal."

"Ouch," Jet cringed.

"Anyway, it snowballed from there and eventually led to dad's ultimatum. He sent me to therapy where my therapist made me dredge this shit up, so I painted it."

"What happened to the guy?"

"Dad let it go, eventually."

"How did Aubrey react to all of it?"

"We didn't talk for like a week, then he was my shoulder to cry on and helped me get through the worst of it."

Taking a breath, Jet lifted his eyebrows. "Well, the painting started as a good in, but that story killed my mood, so how about another soda and I'll share my virginity story?"

Chuckling, I relaxed. The non-judgmental way that Jet heard the story and let it go was a relief. "Sounds good." Leading the way upstairs, I got us both drinks before curling up on the lounge. Sitting beside me, Jet took a long sip of his soda before he started.

"I was seventeen at my year twelve formal, and my technology teacher was shitfaced. She was in her first year of teaching, so she was about twenty-four. I was sober, so I offered to drive her home."

My mouth was hanging open. "No? A teacher? Is that legal?"

"Well, I was graduating, but no, it wouldn't be legal. Still, that's not the story. So, I take the teacher home. She's unconscious when we get there, so I knock on her door and her older sister, who's a nurse, answers the door. She helps me take her sister inside, and afterward, told me I was adorable and kissed me. The kiss sort of took a life of its own. She took me to her room, and a few hours later, I went home having learned a valuable lesson about women."

"Which was?"

Smirking, Jet turned towards me. "Most guys go for the breast or clit to drive a woman wild. She taught me it was places like here," he reached up and gently caressed my pulse. My heart raced and breathing shortened. "Or here," he took my wrist and massaged across the carpal joints. My toes curled, and I bit my lip. "And here," he grazed passed my breast and placed his hand on my waist before using his thumb to stroke just below my rib. Exhaling hard, my thighs relaxed, and I felt my knickers grow wet, and my body heating.

His thumb still stroking that bottom rib, Jet smirked. "These were the places to touch a woman to turn her on." His mouth came closer and went to my ear. "See, valuable life lessons."

Pulling back, I caressed his jaw and pulled his mouth to mine. Leaning into him, Jet lay back, his hands gripping my waist to take me with him as he laid on the lounge. Moving my body over his, I kissed him deeply, loving the feel of his lips on mine. Holding my waist, Jet kissed me just as intently. His hand caressed up my arm, across the exposed skin of my back and pressed me a little firmer to the front of him. The pressure of him growing hard against my hip made me moan.

The doorbell rang. Sitting back quickly, surprising Jet with the sudden break from his mouth, I got up and went to the intercom to see Aubrey standing at the gate. He was fuming through the screen. "Shit!" Running my hands through my hair, I tried to steady my voice. "Hey."

"Let me in," Aubrey demanded, his voice not happy.

"Okay." Pressing the buzzer, I turned to look at Jet. "Um, remember the other day when I said Aubrey has never had an issue with a boyfriend?"

"Yeah."

"You might be the exception." Walking to the front door to meet Aubrey, I opened it and smiled.

Aubrey marched straight passed me. "He better be on this level, or I swear to god," Aubrey threatened.

"Excuse me?"

Jaw tensing when all I did was raise a brow at him, Aubrey stormed into the back lounge. Shutting the front door, I made sure the gate closed. Jet's car was inside the gate, so I knew how Aubrey knew he was here.

"What are you doing here? I told you last night she's off limits."

"You don't own her, Aub. Rain is allowed to have other friends."

Making my way back down the hall, I went to the kitchen to pour Aubrey a drink.

"You don't want her for a friend, you want in her pants, and I've told you she's off limits," Aubrey rumbled.

"We're dating; get over it."

"Dating? You don't date," Aubrey sounded confused.

"I do now, so expect to share your time with Rain from now on."

Aubrey's facial features cycled through shock, outrage, and horrified. Not that I was any better. I'd mentioned one date; that had formalized our relationship status. Blinking at his brother, Aubrey looked at me. "No, this can't happen. Mum and dad will flip, and you know it."

"Why would mum and dad have an issue with it? The way they talk about Rain, I think they would be quite happy for me to date her."

Gritting his teeth, Aubrey took a deep breath. "Can you just get lost, so I can talk to Rain privately."

"Sure," Jet walked up to the hall to the steps. "Hey, Storm, Zephyr, want to go another round?"

"Come up, and we'll kick your ass here."

Sticking his head back around the corner to see me, Jet raised a brow. "That okay?"

Nodding, I pushed the drink across the bench to Aubrey. With a wink, Jet went upstairs. Aubrey waited till he heard the boys reacting to the game. "This is not okay."

"Chill, it's not like he's talking marriage and babies."

"Mum and dad will flip if you start dating Jet."

"Or they might not."

"Rain, we made them a promise," Aubrey reminded.

"I was sixteen and recovering from spending two years off my face. They can't hold me to that promise. You hadn't even come out of the closet when you made that promise."

Face softening, Aubrey moved closer to cup my face in his hands. "Jet doesn't date. Does none of this seem odd to you?"

"That an extremely good looking, intelligent, and accomplished straight man might be interested in a train wreck like me?" I hissed, pulling my face out of his hands. "Why is that odd? Or is your brother too good for me? Am I tainted and not worthy?"

"You know that's not what I meant, Rain."

"It sure sounded like it." Collapsing on the chair, I crossed my arms over my chest in a huff. Aubrey dropped beside me. We sat there, staring back into the house. "I like him. I don't freak out when he gets too near. I let him kiss me while I was sober."

With a sigh, Aubrey turned to consider me. "Just don't be upset if he loses interest next week and disappears." Placing his arm behind me, Aubrey pulled me into his side.

"So, don't be so worried," I elbowed his side. "If he's the manwhore you say he is, he'll lose interest in me pretty quickly."

"And if he doesn't?"

Trying not to have any expectations, I shrugged. "Our children will be siblings with their cousins."

It made Aubrey chuckle. "You think my brother is going to lend you to me to knock up?"

"True. Guess if that's the case, you'll need to find another baby maker or be content with being an uncle."

"It would be my penance, I guess."

Sighing heavily, I leaned my head against his. "Can we talk about what's happening with you?"

"Don't know what you mean."

"You're drinking more, taking more risks, choosing real assholes to date, so you have a reason to dump them shortly after," I laid it out for him.

"Oh, that!" He thought about it for a moment. "Let's go downstairs." Placing a kiss to the point of my shoulder, Aubrey flicked his eyes up to mine.

"Our brothers are here." Why was this conversation sounding like déjà vu?

"I need it."

"After Jet leaves, but you have to promise to go talk to someone."

Aubrey kissed my shoulder again then sighed. "Fine."

❖

Chapter Six
EXERTION

FLESH RESISTED AND GAVE AS MY FIST CONNECTED. AIR RUSHED from Aubrey's lungs as he fell back and dropped to one knee. Stepping back, I waited. Jet left an hour ago, after dinner and winning Monopoly, Cluedo, and Trivial Pursuit. He at least lost UNO to the boys despite their rather blatant cheating.

Aubrey took a moment, caught his breath then swept his leg to try and take me down. Jumping his leg, I stepped in and kicked him in the ribs. Aubrey fell to his side.

Huffing, I moved back out of reach. "You aren't even trying to keep your guard up." Annoyed, I turned my back and started pulling the gloves off. We'd been at it for thirty minutes already, but what should have been a sparring session was just Aubrey getting his ass whooped.

The sparring started when I wouldn't go back to self-defense classes. It used to be me getting my ass kicked, and that was fine as long as Joseph and Aubrey prepared me for any holds or grabs. As long as I knew in advance what we were training, I could get through it.

The martial arts didn't stop me finding comfort in mind-altering substances, but it helped me walk out the door to go back to school. Then when we were eighteen, Aubrey made it full contact. My confidence improved, allowing me to catch the bus to university and leave the house alone. But it wasn't meant to be this.

"We are meant to be sparring. I'm not going to stand here and beat the shit out of you. What's up with you? It's like you want me a beat down these last few times."

"Maybe I do," Aubrey wheezed. "I deserve it."

Throwing my gloves on the lounge chair, I'd had enough. "Fuck you! Don't start this shit again. I'm too on edge to cope. Go home, or go fuck someone up the ass, but don't come here and fuck with my heart." Turning my back on him, I started for the door.

"Okay," Aubrey coughed. "We'll do it your way."

Gaining his feet, Aubrey launched at me, grabbing me in a bear hug from behind. Lifting both my arms quickly, which raised his hold to my upper chest, I dropped my hips off to the left, stepped my right leg around his legs, straightened the right leg to kick out his left knee and right ankle as I fell backward, tripping his legs and taking him with me.

We hit hard, the back of my head bouncing off the floor causing me to yelp. Throwing a right elbow into his ribs, I rolled away out of reach. Getting to all fours, my head dizzy as I started to stand, throwing off my balance. Memories of a hallway with bloody drag marks on the floor flashed in my head. Whimpering as my legs went out from under me, I had to catch myself on the floor. It wasn't real, not anymore.

"I'm safe, they can't hurt me; I'm safe, they can't hurt me," I chanted to myself trying to escape the memory before I reached the end of the hall.

"Shit, Rain," Aubrey groaned getting to his feet. "I'm sorry," he apologized as he reached for me.

"Don't touch me!" Pushing him away, I put my back to the wall. Tears rushed down my face as I met Aubrey's eyes. Scurrying along the wall, I found the corner beside the television cabinet, hiding in the recess with my knees tucked up.

Crestfallen, Aubrey scrubbed his face with his hands. "Fuck!"

"I'm safe here. I'm safe." The hallway was growing shorter; I needed something more. "Aubrey, help!"

Inhaling deeply, Aubrey winced and put a hand to his ribs. "I'll get help, Rain." Stepping back two steps, Aubrey took out his phone. "Joseph, it's Aubrey Landy. I was a dick and triggered her." With a sigh, Aubrey hung up the phone and squatted, the discomfort of it showing on his face, but his eyes stayed locked on me. "I don't deserve you; you know. The shit I've put you through." Taking a shallow breath, Aubrey schooled his features again. "Rain, you're safe. We're alone. Sensei Joseph is on his way over, and you are going to need to put in the code to let him inside to help you."

The detective's face flashed through my memory, his eyes full of kindness and sorrow as paramedics loaded me into an ambulance. My hand went to my abdomen for the memory of pain and blood. It didn't hurt, and when I lifted my hand, there was no blood.

"Rain, can you unlock the gate for Sensei Joseph? He'll make sure you are safe."

Frowning at the sound of the doorbell ringing, I struggled to pull free of the memory. "Move," I managed to gasp as the room came more sharply into focus.

Moving as far from the intercom as he could, Aubrey

squatted down to look less threatening, holding his ribs in pain. Using the wall to help me stand, I went to the intercom and saw Joseph on the screen, his partner beside him in the passenger seat.

"Joseph, he can't come inside."

"He'll stay in the car, Rain. I promise."

Hesitating a moment, I hit the code to unlock the gate, then stepped back and turned to look at Aubrey.

"I'll get the door and put the kettle on," Aubrey announced.

"I need something stronger."

Aubrey shook his head. "Your therapist said you should try other methods to recover rather than alcohol."

"My therapist wasn't expecting my best friend to trigger my memories to get what he wanted." Tears streamed down my face. "Why would you do that to me?"

Aubrey's eyes filled with tears. "I needed you to hurt me."

"Why?"

Aubrey met my eyes for several seconds, and then he turned away. "I'll get the door." Climbing the stairs, Aubrey left me alone. Lowering myself to the floor, I cried.

Feet skipped down the stairs, and then Joseph stopped to take in the sparring gear. Turning to me with his face full of compassion, Joseph took his jacket off, removed his gun, and wrapped it in his jacket as he set it on the lounge. "What happened?"

"Aubrey grabbed me from behind when I wasn't expecting it."

Joseph lifted a brow. "We desensitized you to that."

"In sparring, yes. The sparring finished in my mind, and I was leaving the room."

Brows furrowing, Joseph peered towards the stairs. Sides

of his mouth dropping, his eyes came back to me. "Can I come near?"

Taking stock of how I felt, I nodded. Cuddling myself in to make sure I was in a tight ball, I wiped my face on the material of my dress covering my knee.

Putting his back to the wall, Joseph slid down beside me, leaving a gap big enough for a child to fit. Settling himself, he sat quietly, waiting.

"This wasn't me. I've been good and controlled for so long now. It's been years since my last episode."

"You came to tournament and handled the violence. That was a big step for you."

"I'm even dating without the aid of alcohol."

"Jet Landy?" When I confirmed Joseph bowed his head. "I noticed the way you two looked at each other today. I don't think I've ever seen you look at a guy that way."

"He makes me hungry."

Joseph lifted his brows humored. "Well, as I hear it, Jet is rather decadent, so make sure you limit yourself to a few nibbles each serving. Gluttony will leave you sick and regretful."

"Take it slow?"

"Very slow. Let's see if maybe two people can change for the better from this."

"Aubrey doesn't want me dating Jet," I pouted.

"That doesn't surprise me. Did Aubrey tell you why?"

"His parents won't be happy that it's his brother with Jet's reputation and all that." I licked my lips. "I don't think that's it, though. Aubrey's been talking about babies and making the Geoff arrangement again. He's worse than normal. His relationships aren't lasting more than a month, and he's taking risks having sex at work and places anyone could catch him. He's drinking more than usual, and tonight he wasn't even trying to defend himself. It's like he wanted a beat down."

Joseph considered his feet. "You don't know why?"

"No, and others are starting to notice."

Exhaling roughly, Joseph shook his head to himself before responding. "I'll talk to him and see if I can get him to confide." Standing up, he offered me a hand. "Let's go upstairs and get you something to help you sleep tonight."

"You know I won't."

"At least try," Joseph coerced.

Taking the offered hand, Joseph pulled me up to standing. He led the way upstairs to the kitchen, where Aubrey was making tea for us all. "I made you chamomile to help you rest," Aubrey offered a mug across the kitchen bench.

"Thanks." Gripping the mug, I held it in my shaking hands.

When Aubrey went to put his hands around mine, I backed out of reach. Aubrey looked hurt. "I'm sorry, Rain. Can I stay, so you're not by yourself?"

"Where's your dad?" Joseph asked.

"Holidays with his new girlfriend. He'll be back tomorrow."

Eyeing Aubrey, Joseph huffed as his phone buzzed. "I've got to go. Let Aubrey stay in case you need someone." Nodding, I watched Joseph start for the door. "Aubrey will show me out."

"Thanks for coming, Joseph," I sighed.

Turning back to me, Joseph gave me a sad smile. "We'll talk later. Get some rest."

Lifting the mug to my lips, I drank the tea. Rinsing the cup, I left it by the sink as I started checking to make sure everything was locked. When I got to the front door, Aubrey stood at the gate, talking to Joseph. It looked like Joseph was ripping him a new one.

Waiting until Aubrey stepped back inside the yard, I closed the gate. Coming inside, Aubrey closed and locked the door, stopping to lean on the wall beside me. Reaching out slowly, he tucked a strand of hair back behind my ear. "Sleep downstairs with me?"

"Just sleep." When Aubrey bowed his head, I pushed off the wall. "I'll get my pajamas on." Upstairs, I checked both the boys were still asleep and changed into my pajamas before heading downstairs.

Aubrey was already stripped down to his boxers and in the bed. Leaving the door open, I slipped in next to him. Aubrey rolled towards me. "Can I hold you?"

Taking a steadying breath, I prepared myself for physical contact. "Okay."

Pressing his body behind mine, Aubrey cuddled me. I didn't relax. I couldn't; especially when Aubrey became aroused. "Maybe you should hold me," he murmured as he rolled over.

Exhaling in relief, I turned and wrapped my arms around him. Snuggling me in against him, Aubrey sighed content. "Gay guys shouldn't be turned on when in bed with a woman."

Aubrey chuckled. "I told you, I'm gay most of the time."

"Gay is all the time; otherwise, you're bi."

"Okay, I'm bi. Or, maybe it's nothing to do with being male or female. Maybe, I'm attracted to you as a person and not as a female."

"So, your pan?" I tried to nut out.

"Oh, look who's been researching sexuality."

"I've been trying to work things out in my head, so I'm not so confused all the time."

Sighing audibly, Aubrey rolled to face me. "How about, I'm a guy who prefers other guys most of the time, but formed a deep emotional connection with a female friend years ago which somehow turned sexual. As much as I've tried to deny that to both of us, it comes out every time we get drunk together, and I'm struggling to understand it myself. Am I gay, not gay, or am I just as messed up by that day as you are and never realized the effect it had on me because we've focused on the damage it did to you?"

Blinking, not sure what to make of what he just said, I grasped at the bit I could understand. "But I always asked you?"

Wrapping his arms around me, Aubrey pulled me against his chest. "I know. I wasn't accusing you of being selfish. It's just what's been going through my head. I'm confused as shit, and I didn't want to confuse you more than you already were about us until I figured it out."

"Is that why you've been acting out of late? You're trying to prove to yourself that you are gay?"

"It's part of it." Settling into the pillow, he closed his eyes. "Get some sleep."

BLOODY DRAG marks down the hall flashed.

"Rain," Aubrey whispered. "Rain."

Opening my eyes, or I tried to, but the left was swollen shut. Everything hurt as I lay on the floor, drooling blood.

"Rain, I've called the police. Where's your mum?"

A woman screamed, and men laughed. My body tried to curl in on itself, but everything hurt to move, so I laid there and sobbed. Aubrey trembled. It wasn't the man he was now, but the handsome teen he'd been. Shadows move behind Aubrey. "Run," I whimpered. "Aubrey, run."

Aubrey was still confused when the shadow pistol-whipped him in the head. Falling to the ground dazed, Aubrey blinked at me as the shadow kicked Aubrey in the gut.

"Are you another brother?" The shadow asked as he squatted by Aubrey, a bottle in one hand, gun in the other.

"No. Boyfriend," I lied.

The shadow laughed as he stood up again and kicked Aubrey harder. "How about I show you a thing or two while my brothers finish up with her mother."

"Run, Aubrey," I begged.

Placing his bottle down beside my head, he knelt behind me.

Dragging himself away to the wall, Aubrey slouched there, eyes watching, fearful, helpless, enthralled.

"Run!" I screamed when the pain came. Old pain, new pain, it all blended now after so many hours.

Wide-eyed, Aubrey slowly planted his feet and pushed himself up the wall supporting him. Waiting for the right moment, he rushed the shadow, then the gun fired.

At first, it was silent. Then the noise came from every-where, yelling, screaming, more gunshots, and boots were running across the floor.

"Rain," Aubrey sobbed as he appeared next to me, rolling me onto my back. The pain of moving wrenched another scream from my throat. "It's going to be alright." Eyes searching me, his tears fell faster as he placed his hands on my abdomen, blood seeping through his fingers. "Jesus, it's going to be alright."

"Shh, Rain, you're safe now."

Waking with a jolt, I looked around the room. Not my bedroom, but a bedroom I knew was safe.

"It's alright, Rain," Aubrey soothed without touching me.

Tears fell from my eyes, but I wasn't crying. Exhaling, I leaned into Aubrey's arms. "I don't want to be like this for the rest of my life."

"You won't. This episode was my fault. It won't happen again."

Chapter Seven
THERAPY

"I'm home," Dad called as he came in from the garage. "Can I smell cookies?"

"Kitchen. You're home early?"

Rounding the corner for the kitchen, Dad observed the baked goods all over the bench. "Dad! Isn't it awesome? Rain's been baking all day. Donuts, scrolls, pastries, cookies, and now she's making pineapple upside down cake." Racing across to hug our father, Storm itemized my day's work. "She hasn't done this in years."

"I'm aware. I think you boys need to go outside and burn some of that sugar off."

"Rain has made us drink water between everything," Zephyr grumbled.

"That's a relief. Now go swim it off."

Cheering, the twins raced back out to the pool. Still assessing the table, Dad moved forward and grabbed a churro. "Joseph called me." Lifting his gaze to meet mine, sympathy, and worry creasing his brow. Closing my eyes, I kept cleaning up from the day of baking. "Even if he didn't, I would have known. You started baking when you were distressed when you got yourself straightened out. I had to hire a damn personal trainer because of it. Do you want to talk about it?" I shook my head. "Have you phoned Dr. Lind?"

"She booked me in early tomorrow morning before her first session. The twins want to start martial arts. Can I take them to Joseph's dojo tomorrow night?"

"Sure. It will be good for them." Dad considered the food in front of him. "You should set the table up out the front and have a bake sale. The neighbors used to love that when you were younger."

"I'd get the twins to do it, but they'd eat all the merchandise. I'll take it to work tomorrow and let the vultures devour it at the staff meeting."

"Be careful. They may expect it regularly." Getting up, Dad came into the kitchen. "Can I give you a hug?"

Tears filling my eyes, I nodded. "I'd like that."

"How did it start?" Dr. Lind asked gently.

Fidgeting with the hem of my dress, I kept a sterile field around my memories. "Same as always; the hallway, lightning flashing outside, the bloody drag marks."

"Give it ownership, Rain."

Saliva filled my mouth, forcing me to swallow before I could answer. "My bloody drag marks."

"It's been years, why do you think it always starts there? Not the beginning. Not when Aubrey arrived. Why do you think it always starts when he took you out of the lounge room?"

Considering her question, I shook my head, the hallway flashing in my head. "I don't know, you've never asked before?"

"You were raw when you first started coming to me, and a lot younger. I want to see if you've ever analyzed why the memory plays like it does in your head."

"I don't know."

"What happened before they dragged you down the hall?"

Gritting my teeth, I stayed focused on where my fists clenched in my dress. "You know what happened."

Dr. Lind observed my hands. "Let's take the attackers out of the equation. Who was in the room with you before the hall?"

Closing my eyes, I shook my head as the tears ran free. "Don't."

"Rain, you have come in here for over ten years and talked about everything that happened in the dining room. You never talk, dream, or address the lounge room in the hours before. I think that's what is holding you back."

Gripping my dress in my fists, I sobbed. "My mother and brother. We were watching a movie."

"What movie?"

"I can't remember. I can't remember anything that came before those men did that night."

"Why do you think that is?"

The answer flowed through my brain, but I didn't want to admit it. It made me a horrible person, a terrible daughter, and sister. I shook my head again.

"Rain, you are an intelligent girl. I think you've known all along why you never go back to that room."

"It's too much. It's always too much but going back to what was before-" Mourning, I shook my head.

"Why can't you remember your mum and brother, Rain?" She asked softly this time.

"Because I don't want to remember them alive. Not like that."

Letting me cry it out, Dr. Lind waited until I calmed myself a little, then she bridged the dangerous waters. "So, you think you have blocked out the memories of the lounge room because you don't want to damage your memory of your loved ones?" I nodded my head. "Do you ever think of your mum before that, when you were ten? Or at your birthday parties?"

Tears rolled forward as my mind stayed blank.

Dr. Lind wrote something down. "I'm going to come back to this later. Let's move on to something we've talked about before." Eager to be away from that, I nodded. "Aubrey stayed over last night? Did you have sex with him?"

"No."

"I'm not just talking vaginal sex, Rain."

"No sex."

"When was the last time you let Aubrey have sex with you?"

Not entirely sure, I shrugged. "A year or more."

She wrote a note. "Vaginal or anal?"

"Same as always."

"Does it upset you that he prefers anal sex with you?"

"He's gay!" Wondering if that label worked at all, I frowned. Still, I preferred discussing this. Aubrey and our messed-up friendship were easier talking points. "Or bi, but he prefers ass, either way."

"Were you sober the last time you had sex?"

"With Aubrey?"

"With anyone?"

"No."

"Have you ever been sober having sex; vaginal or anal?"

"Somewhat."

"I meant completely sober, no alcohol or drugs in your system."

Pressing my lips together, I shook my head.

"When was the first time you engaged in intercourse with Aubrey? And by that, I mean after the event."

"I was too smashed to remember much about that night."

"You were high on drugs and alcohol? Do you remember agreeing to have sex with Aubrey?"

"Yes." We'd covered this before.

"Whose idea was it?"

Trying to remember, I shrugged. "We were talking about Aub being gay. He'd never had sex yet, and he was wondering what it was like, both the giving and receiving."

"And he asked you what it was like?" She probed carefully.

"I told him it hurt, but it was different because they'd wanted me to hurt. It wasn't like they used lube or were gentle. Aubrey asked if I wanted to know what it was like if done right. I think I shrugged and said something like it would be nice to know it wasn't always going to be painful."

"Did he ask?"

"Yes. Aubrey asked if he could make it nice for me. We kissed for a while, and then he spooned me and prepared us both. He was gentle, cautious, and he played with my clit to make it nice for me."

"Did you climax?"

We'd discussed this years ago when I finally told her about Aubrey and me. It was old ground. "No."

"Have you ever climaxed during sex?"

"Yes. When Geoff and Aubrey shared me, I came."

"Did you like it that first time with Aubrey?" She'd never asked this question before. I sat there quiet. "Rain, did you like Aubrey having sex with you?"

"He was gentle. He made it nice."

"That doesn't answer my question. Did you like it?"

Blinking, I looked away. "I..." Could I admit this to her? I'd lied to Aubrey all these years. Swallowing the automatic answer, I met her eyes. "I didn't care what he did. I was so off my face I barely felt a thing. I'd let him do anything if he kept me drunk and high, so I didn't have to feel anything."

Blinking, she wrote on her pad. No sign of disgust or judgment. Not a trace; she just took it all in while I looked away, still feeling as pathetic as I always did about this stuff. Weak and inadequate and worthless. Dr. Lind lifted her eyes to me again. "Let's come back around that circle now. How many men broke into your house that night?"

"Three," I stared at the chip in the gyprock of her office wall.

"And all of them took turns raping you before one of them took you to the dining room?"

"Yes." It was a small chip, the size of my pinkie.

"Did they penetrate your vagina?"

"No." It was a random indent. There was nothing near it to have caused it.

"Did you have to perform oral sex?"

"No." It was barely noticeable, but it stood out like anything to me.

"They beat you between rapes?"

"Yes." There was a beautiful painting of a forest just above the chip. Beautiful lush trees of green. So much green.

"Do you remember their faces?"

Shadows raced across the painting. I dropped my eyes back to the chip of gyprock. "No."

"Rain, how many men raped you in the lounge room that night?"

"Four." She went quiet. Pausing, I blinked as I recalled the last question and my answer, then I stared at her. Breathing became hard, painful.

"Okay, Rain, relax," she soothed as she moved to sit beside me. "Calm your breathing. Passing out won't help. I want you to think about the room. Tell me what's wrong with my office, what's wrong with this building?"

"The angle," I wheezed. "The view is cut off by the older building next door along this entire side. Had they turned the building a fraction anti-clockwise, you could have maximized the view and not been looking at the building next door." My breathing settled; the tears kept flowing. Removing her hand from my shoulders, Dr. Lind sat looking at me. Lifting my eyes to hers, I let the tears flow free over my cheeks. "I don't want to talk about it anymore. Please?"

Standing up, she moved back to her chair. Writing something down, Dr. Lind then put her pen down and assessed me. "Rain, you are an intelligent and capable young woman. I believe you compartmentalized and locked away part of that night for two reasons. First, you couldn't deal with what happened in the lounge room. What they did to you or what you witnessed. You locked it away and didn't deal with it because somewhere in your psyche you subconsciously determined, I can't survive 'that' plus 'this', plus 'this.' So, you divided it all up and dealt with the part you knew you could."

It made sense. It explained why my memories of that night start with being dragged down the hall.

"The second part is you don't want to remember what you lost. You have blocked your mum and brother so hard from your memory that you barely remember them being in your life. I think you did that because coping with what happened to you was enough, you couldn't cope with losing two people you loved at the same time."

The tears picked up speed again.

"I want you to know that's okay, Rain. People do remarkable things to survive; they do horrible things too. Blocking out someone's smiles, and laughter so it doesn't hurt that you can't see them that way anymore, is not a bad thing. It was a smart way to cope. What I want you to think about before I see you next week, is if it's time you dealt with what you couldn't twelve years ago?"

Wiping away my tears with the back of my hand, I blew out a breath. "With all due respect, Dr. Lind. I am never going to go back to that room." Sucking in a deep breath, I exhaled. I did it again, breathing all the negativity away. "It's not about facing what happened to me. It's about living now. That happened to me, and I can't undo it. Nothing I do now is going to make it okay. I need to learn how to go forward. So, when I come back next week. That's what I want to focus on."

Dr. Lind contemplated me. Slowly, she nodded. "If you feel that is what is going to benefit you most, that's what we'll do."

"Thank you. I appreciate you making time for me before your normal opening hours this morning." Rising from the sofa, I turned to leave.

"Rain," Dr. Lind called to me as she stood. "You went two years without an episode. You are getting better. Don't let one back step drag you down."

Pressing my lips together, I gave her a non-committal nod, then stepped out of the office. Outside the tall city office building, it was raining. There was an umbrella in my bag, but I didn't bother with it. Walking through the plaza outside the building with my face up to the sky, I let the rain wash my tears away.

There was a rainbow just over the edge of a distant building. I wanted to chase it, find it, and stand beneath it. I knew I couldn't, but it lightened my heart and made me smile.

People passed by without even noticing me. Umbrellas up, jackets or briefcases held overhead to try and protect themselves, and I stood there smiling. Suddenly the rain stopped, an umbrella covering me, and the warmth of a hot body next to me. Onyx eyes watched me with curiosity.

"Enjoying your element?" Jet queried with a raised brow. My laughter made him smile as he looked at his watch. "I've got half an hour until I need to be at the court to speak with my client. Want to get a coffee?"

Chapter Eight
DOUBLE TROUBLE

WHEN JET HIT THE FLOOR HARD, I CRINGED. THE OTHER BLACK belt who put him down laughed. "Stop looking at the pretty girl and focus, Jet."

"She's older than you, so she's a woman." Jet sprang to his feet.

Blinking at his agility, I turned my eyes to the twins to appear not so impressed. They were sparring against each other, but they were making stuff up as they went all out on one another. It made me laugh, but I pressed my lips together and dropped my eyes back to my tablet and the digital artwork I was creating.

Separating the twins, Joseph called an end to sparring. "Hajemai. Let's line it up for kata. Black belts at the front, belts in descending order after." Everyone started taking their places. Joseph held Storm and Zephyr back. "You two can follow the white belts. Then you sit and watch the rest."

"Yes, Sensei," they lamented.

"Sensei Jet, you have the count tonight."

Winking at me, Jet started. The entire hall moved as one;

even my brothers kept up as they moved through the white belt kata. They knew it already. They had watched and mimicked Aubrey and me over the years. The twins could perform the blue belt kata, which is why Joseph forced them to sit when all the other white belts finished.

They went through every Kata, white belt to black. Joseph corrected the students as they went, and as they finished each belt, that color sat and watched the higher belts. Jet only stopped long enough to take a deep breath between ending one kata and starting the next. You could pick those new to the higher belts because they were struggling to keep up.

When it was just the four black belts left, Joseph jumped in line with them and moved through the kata. I was no less impressed than the first time I watched him do it when I was fourteen.

Joseph made a rule when I became his private student; no drugs or alcohol the days we trained. Initially, that'd been hard because I usually got high before going to school, but I'd held out after school and waited till after training to get high again so I could sleep.

Everything had been in the papers; not all the details, but it mentioned the rapes and that my family was murdered. Not wanting to go back to school a celebrity victim, I'd begged my dad to let me drop out. Joseph forced dad to keep me in school; he said if I didn't go back then, I never would, and the chances of suicide would be higher.

High school was hell as it was but trying to deal with recovery and high school...I think it was pure luck I didn't check out in that first year. Or, maybe it was Aubrey. He could always make me laugh, even if the most I did was smile on the outside.

"Rain!" Joseph called my name firmly, but with tenderness.

Jumping from the yank back into reality, I watched in horror as my tablet went up then it hurtled towards the ground. Snatching it before it hit the floor, Jet lifted concerned eyes to me. Joseph was holding the twins back, waiting for me to be back in the present. Realizing I'd zoned out and that Joseph caught the twins before they could surprise me and possibly set me off, I cleared my throat. "Sorry, I barely slept last night."

Folding the cover over my device, Jet placed it beside my bag. "You okay?"

Putting the stylus away with the tablet in my bag while I recovered, I nodded.

"The boys want to sign up." Releasing them, Joseph moved a step closer while the twins kept their distance, having learned over the years when I was on edge.

"Oh, okay." Blinking, I was a little lost. "I'm not sure how this will work with the shared custody. I should let dad arrange this with Penelope."

"I live near your stepmother. I'd be happy to pick them up on the weeks they are with her."

"And when you come straight from work?"

"We'll work it out. It's not a hassle if it means the boys get some discipline."

Storm and Zephyr glared at Joseph, then switched back to me. "Please, Rain?"

"Fine, yes. First thing I've seen you boys enthused about outside of the media room since you discovered your wee-wees at age two."

"Seriously?!" Zephyr groaned.

Enjoying the shade of red the twins turned, I smirked. "Let's sign you up then."

Relaxing now that he was sure I was okay, Joseph started chuckling. "Jet, can I leave you to do the paperwork with Rain while I size the boys up for uniforms?"

"Sure." Walking over to Joseph's bag, Jet grabbed out a folder with the paperwork and handed me the form. "You feeling better this evening?"

"As opposed to?"

"How you were coming out of that building this morning?"

Keeping my eyes on the form, I tried not to think about my appointment this morning. "It comes and goes."

"Aubrey didn't come home again last night. When he finally did this morning, it was obvious he'd been in a fight. It's not the first time. It happened at the same time last year too. I'm wondering what's so significant about this time of year that sets him off?"

Freezing as I considered the date I'd written on the form, I recognized what it was straight away. "Damn." Clenching the pen tight, I took a deep breath and blinked the tears away.

"I'm guessing you have some insight?"

"Ah, I think I've got this all correct. I should get the boys home; they have school tomorrow." Pushing the form towards him, I grabbed my bag and readied to leave.

"Rain, please, he's my brother, and I want to help him. You'd want to do the same if it was your brother."

Gritting my teeth, knowing it was the truth, I met Jet's eyes. "You want to help him? Help me get him back into therapy."

His brows bunching, Jet considered me. "Is this about that incident when he was fourteen?"

My face fell. "You know about that?"

"I know he witnessed an assault, and that he tried to stop it but got a friend of his shot as a result."

Licking my lips, I breathed through the tightness in my chest. "No, it's not that. But there was something two years later that I didn't realize had affected Aubrey to this extreme. I should have connected the dots sooner."

"Can you tell me what happened?"

The worry in Jet's eyes made me want to tell him. "You should ask your brother or your mother; it's not like your parents didn't know about it. I need to go." Turning my back on Jet, I found Joseph and the boys standing, watching. "Let's go. You need showers and to go to bed." Without looking back, I used their shoulders to steer them out.

In the reflection of the door, I saw Joseph get in Jet's path. "Jet, if you like her, let her go. She won't betray Aubrey's confidence."

"You know them that well?"

"I know a bullheaded approach won't end well for either of you," Joseph warned. Glancing back over my shoulder, I noted the concern on Jet's face as he watched me retreat.

As soon as the twins were ready for bed, I shooed them upstairs and picked up my phone. "Hey, I'm surprised to hear from you." Aubrey sounded depressed.

"I get it. I finally get why this time of year makes you spazz out. You can't blame yourself, Aubrey. It wasn't your fault."

We sat there, silent on the phone. "I want to be with you," Aubrey whispered. "I want to be inside you."

"I'm sober." Aubrey stayed quiet. "I need a drink anyway."

"Is your dad home?"

"Yes, I'll need to come to you." I was tired and just wanted to sleep.

"I'll drive down and get you. Bring your clothes for work, and we can go straight from here in the morning."

"I'll need to make sure dad is good for getting the boys to school in the morning. I'll see you soon."

Hanging up, I grabbed a vodka twist out of the bar fridge and threw the lid in the bin. Drinking several mouthfuls to get the buzz started, I headed for my father's study.

Lifting his head from the file he was reading as I walked in and sat in the comfy lounge, my Dad sat back and observed me. "You look frustrated."

"It's been a long week already."

"You're tired and should have an early night."

"I'm going over to Aubrey's. He's been out of sorts of late and needs to talk."

Clenching his jaw, Dad dropped his pen on his notepad. "He should go back to his psychologist."

"I've been telling him that." Lifting the bottle, I took a few more mouthfuls.

"How did it go with Dr. Lind today?"

Staring out the window at the darkness, I shivered. "We covered old ground, covered some new, and will be focusing on moving forward from here on out."

"Are you feeling better?"

Trying to force a smile, I sat a bit straighter, but he saw through it, he always did. "Aubrey and I prop each other up, we always do." Finishing the bottle, I stood up again. "Will you be right to get the twins to school tomorrow?"

"I'm not due in court until ten tomorrow. I'll manage. Rain, you're not going to relapse, are you?"

"Dad, I haven't gotten high in ten years. You don't need to worry about that at least."

Waiting until Dad gave me a half smile, I went to the fridge and grabbed another drink to see me through packing my bag. There was no fooling my dad, but he'd support me, and that was enough to keep me from falling back into bad habits. When he got to the gate, Aubrey messaged my phone.

"I'll see you tomorrow night, Dad." Checking the camera to see Aubrey parked in the driveway, I opened the door. "I love you."

"Love you too. Practice safe talk."

Realizing he knew what was likely to happen tonight, I cringed. Parents shouldn't be that aware. But then, he'd insisted on the downstairs bedroom for when Aubrey stayed over, so maybe he'd always known.

Ensuring the gate closed behind me, I jumped in the car. "I was thinking about the Buffy drinking game to start." We'd been playing this game since teenagers. We watched season one of Buffy the vampire slayer and took shots every time you saw a bra strap. It only worked for season one; they got wise about it for season two.

"God, I'll be drunk by the time the first episode is over."

Aubrey laughed. "That's the idea."

❖

Chapter Nine
SHOTS

"MORE!" AUBREY DECLARED.

"No, I can't take anymore."

Aubrey chuckled. "We'll do the good stuff now."

Collapsing to the side, I was toasted. Aubrey had been pouring doubles all night. "If I drink any more, I'll be paralytic."

"You are not drunk enough if you can still use big words." Opening up the directory on his tv, Aubrey scrolled through to the later seasons. I knew which episode he was putting on before he even clicked — the one where Buffy is invisible and engaging in carnal activities with Spike. Aubrey had a real thing for James Marsters.

Shifting my glass to the side out of the way, I forced myself to sit back up. On the floor at the foot of Aubrey's bed, I hung my head back, so it rested on the end on the bed. The room was moving around me. "Why do I let you talk me into this shit on a weeknight?"

"Because you are more fucked up than me and want to escape reality constantly." Touching my bicep, Aubrey wrapped his hand around my upper arm as his lips kissed across the curve of my shoulder.

"Aubrey, I don't want to do this."

Aubrey's thumb rubbed across my arm. "You've never said no to me. I know you are horny, Rain. So, am I. We always get off on each other when I'm single."

"But I'm not this time," I argued and moved a little away so I could face him. "I'm dating someone, worse still, it is your brother."

Grimacing, Aubrey picked up the bottle of alcohol and filled our glasses again. Handing me mine, he smiled at the television. "I love this bit." Xander just walked in and found Spike pounding Buffy, but, of course, Buffy was invisible, so they only see Spike holding plank naked on the bed. "I'm doing push-ups," Aubrey laughed as Spike used that excuse and started doing energetic push-ups, to which muffled Buffy giggles and moans.

Giggling myself, I threw the drink back. Refilling my glass, Aubrey put the bottle aside. Drinking it down, I hung my head back, and the world swam.

Removing the glass from my hand, Aubrey touched his lips to my pulse. "Shit, Aubrey."

Turning me away from him so he could slide his body in slightly behind me, his lips pinched, and his hand groped my breast.

"Wait." My eyeballs were fogged up and not focusing on anything. "Stop." Trying to knock his hand away, I slapped myself instead.

"Sorry, I know you can't do it like that." Pulling away, Aubrey helped me to my feet and onto the bed. He took his shirt off, but I couldn't even lift my head to watch. Moving back over me, Aubrey pushed the skirt of my summer dress up, his hands caressing my thighs as his mouth kissed around my throat.

"Aub, I'm wasted, I can't," I breathed, struggling to stay conscious. There was the soft sound of a door opening, but I couldn't focus. "I just need to sleep."

Dropping his mouth to mine, Aubrey kissed me. When I didn't respond, he pulled away, frustrated. "Damn it! I gave you one drink too much."

"I'd say you've both had several too many," a deep sexy voice filled the room.

Smiling through the fog in my head, I moaned as that voice did things to my body I never knew possible. "Jet."

"Get out."

"Sure, but I'll be taking the drunk woman with me." Arms grabbed me up from the bed with ease.

"Put her down. She can sleep it off here."

"I think Rain will be safer in the guest room."

"She's slept in my bed hundreds of times."

Teeth gnashed above my head. "And how many times have you taken advantage of her there? You told me you were gay!"

"I am!"

"So, you like to rape women? Or is it just this woman in particular?"

"You don't know what you are talking about," Aubrey snarled.

"I was walking past your door when she told you no, Aub. Rain said no, and you gave her a few more drinks until she was too off her face to resist."

"I've never raped her! She's always said yes. She said yes,

until she met you. She was mine. I told you she was off limits and you've continued going after her. Why?"

"You're gay," Jet tried to soothe. "You've been out about it for years. Why are you sleeping with her if you are gay?"

"Because I love her. Don't look at me like that. I know it's insane. I am into guys, but I love Rain, and I was never happier than when we were together with Geoff."

"Geoff? Her ex?" Jet's arms lost their tension, and I relaxed into the feel and smell of him. God, he smelt so delicious.

"I hooked them up knowing Geoff was bisexual..."

There was silence for a very long time. Taking a deep breath, I enjoyed the way my stomach reacted to Jet's scent.

Opening my eyes, I wore a beautiful dress as Jet carried me through a dimly lit room. Placing my feet on the ground, Jet helped me stand up. As Jet started dancing us around the ballroom, I smiled into his wickedly dark eyes. A thrill ran through me as his breath blew across my ear lobe. "I'm glad you insisted on these ballroom dancing lessons."

"It was something we both wanted to learn. I thought it was a good way to get to know each other."

Jet's smile grew. "Can I kiss you?" Blushing, I nodded permission. Jet's lips pinched mine; gentle at first, then with more eagerness. Starving for his affection, I kissed him back eagerly.

The room blurred into a beautiful gothic bedroom, complete with candelabras with red candles burning. Lifting me onto the bed, Jet pulled frantically at my knickers. "Jet," I moaned, eager for his exploration of my body.

"I love the way you moan my name."

Opening my eyes, both of us were naked. Peering down to ogle Jet's junk and see if he measured up to his brother, my head swam, not allowing me to view his gift to women. Dropping my head back on the bed, I wasn't worried, I'd be feeling it soon enough.

Moving over me, Jet eager in his dominance of my mouth, slotted his body to mine and shoved in. Biting my lip on a curse, I prayed to God. Yep, it was a genetic trait. Lifting my arms overhead, I pressed against the bed head to anchor us while Jet pumped his body hard and fast. Faster than ever before, I was climbing to orgasm.

"Rain, are you okay?"

Impressed that Jet was nowhere near as breathless as he should be with how hard he was working me, I nodded, biting my lip harder as I reached the edge. "Oh, Jet, make me come!"

"What?" Jet laughed.

Opening my eyes, I snapped awake and sat up in a bed in a strange room. The bedside light was on; Jet sat beside me, an eat shit grin covering his face. Panting, sweating, and blinking, I looked around Jet's bedroom. My eyes went wide open now as I gripped the blankets as panic bubbled up inside my chest. "Why am I in your bed?"

Jet's smile dropped. "You don't remember?"

Shaking my head, I fretted about what I'd done as tears filled my eyes. All humor cleared from Jet's face. "No, we didn't have sex. Well, at least I didn't." His eyes glimmered, which only confused me more. Jet cleared his throat. "You were drunk, and my brother tried to take advantage, so I removed you from his room. I was going to let you sleep in the guest room, but I worried Aub would sneak down there."

"So, you took me to bed with you?"

Folding back the sheet, Jet flashed his boxers. "I kept my pants on. You kept your underwear on."

Sidetracked momentarily by the gorgeous male specimen before me, I blinked at the rather obvious erection peeking through the opening. Yeah, Jet sized up to his brother.

Glancing down, Jet quickly covered himself. "Shit, sorry. You woke me with your dream. I thought you were having a nightmare when you called my name, then I realized it was a different sort of dream, and I, ah..." Blushing beautifully, Jet combed his fingers through his hair. "Jesus, if you were any other woman, I would comply with your request right now just to stop this being awkward."

"My request?"

Jet cleared his throat. "You asked me to make you, ah, climax."

Heat filled my cheeks, neck, chest. Oh, God, I'd been sleep talking. Covering my face in my hands, I hid as best I could. "God!"

"Relax, Rain. I'm not going to judge a woman for demanding she is satisfied. If we were having sex, I would do my best to see you were."

"You nearly did, anyway."

"So, I heard."

Peeking over my fingertips, I found Jet smirking, his eyes twinkling. Loving this way too much, Jet was gorgeous, and he made me react to him in a way no other guy ever had before. Slowly lowering my hands, I moved my face towards his ready to try kissing him. I was still tipsy, which meant I could do this.

Pulling back, Jet frowned. "Rain, Aubrey told me about you two. I think it's best, considering your relationship with my brother, that you and I are only friends."

It burned. "Friends?" When Jet confirmed I'd heard him

right, I withdrew. Taking a moment to brace against the rejection, I then pushed the sheet away. "Okay." Locating my dress across the room, I pulled it on quickly.

"Rain, are you okay?"

"I'm going to head home."

"It's three in the morning, sleep it off here. I don't mind sharing a bed with you."

"Thanks, but I'd rather my bed." Stepping out the door, I waited until it shut behind me to wipe the tears from my face. Taking a deep breath, I went to find my shoes and bag which were in the foyer. By the time I collected them, Jet was skipping down the stairs in a t-shirt and tracksuit pants.

Grabbing his keys from the tray, Jet grabbed a pair of shoes out of the coat closet. "I'll drive you home."

"It's only a short walk. I'll be fine."

Jet met my eyes. "You're not fine, and I won't get back to sleep if I'm worrying you're dead in a ditch somewhere." Opening the door for me, Jet waited. Not up to arguing, I let him drive me home."

Once we were out of the driveway and gates, Jet turned to observe me. "You weren't upset waking up, so those tears weren't related to my brother's entitled attitude last night."

"Aubrey has been having sex with me for years. I worked out a long time ago that he prefers the interactive experience. If I'm too out of it, or if I pass out on him, he stops."

"So, you just pass out and hope he's honorable like that?"

"He's never crossed that line. Trust me; I always know when he's had sex with me. There would be no missing it if he did."

Jet gripped the steering wheel. "I was sure he was gay. I didn't even consider you two might be intimate."

"He is gay. I'm a special case. He's never looked at another girl like he looks at me. I'm his best friend. He decided we would marry and have kids when we were ten, and he already knew then he preferred men. Truthfully, if I didn't let him in the back end, he probably wouldn't have sex with me either."

Slamming on the brakes, Jet gripped the wheel as we stopped in the middle of the street. "He sodomizes you?" When I chuckled over the term, Jet cracked his jaw. "Does he do both, or just-?"

"There are three holes; be specific."

Jet's eyes widened. "Jesus, I don't even want to imagine you giving him head."

"That's fine. I've never done that with Aubrey. Yes, your brother has had hetero sex with me once or twice. Every other time, it's a colonoscopy. Though, he does like to cum inside me. He gets off on the idea of getting me pregnant."

"You don't use protection?" Jet's brows were in his hair. I couldn't tell if it was shock or disgust.

"We always use condoms, I'm on the pill, and Aubrey gets tested regularly. But your brother likes to pull out, pull the condom off and shoot his cum all over my-"

"If you say that word, I swear I will lose my shit," Jet warned. His reaction made me smirk. "Chad's right. You can be quite crass when you are drunk."

"Chad was a dick!" I rolled my eyes.

"What about Geoff?"

"He was nice. I liked him, but, like your brother, I needed to be tipsy before I could be with him. It's really rare for me to be interested in a man. Extremely rare. Even more so for me to let one kiss me sober."

Brow creasing, Jet turned back to the road ahead, put the

car in drive, and finished the length of road to pull into my driveway. Taking hold of the door handle, I didn't open it.

Instead, I took a deep breath. "I didn't say no to Aubrey tonight because I didn't want to have sex. Your brother has always made it nice for me. I said no because since I've met you, it seems wrong to let him."

Jet moved his jaw to the side momentarily. "When did it happen, Rain?"

Unsure what he meant, I frowned. "The first time with Aub?"

"When were you raped?"

Tears filled my eyes as I swallowed the pain of that question. "How?"

"It was obvious with the way you are around men, and that the only guy you relaxed around, trusted, was gay. I've been trying to figure out if it was a bad experience or a horrific one. I've decided on the latter."

"Why?" Choking, I barely held my emotions in check.

Gripping the steering wheel, Jet inhaled through his nose with purpose. "You don't talk about sex as a shared experience or a joint venture. During this drive, not once did you say *'you'* have sex with my brother. Not once did you say you make love, or *'we'* have sex, or even that you fuck my brother. Instead, you talked about how he has sex *'with you.'*"

Not realizing how I phrased it before, I blinked speechlessly.

"That's class-A separation from what is happening to you." Jet lifted his eyes. "Is that what happened ten years ago, Rain? Did my brother get drunk and rape you?"

Swiping at the tears on my cheeks, I shook my head. "No. Aubrey didn't, and he's never, he's always asked."

"But I'm right that whatever happened to set my brother off involves what happened to you, right?"

Squeezing my eyes shut, I turned away from him. "Yes." Opening the car door, I stepped out and hurried to the gate.

"Rain," Jet called from just behind me. Feet halting, I turned back to face him. "I'm sorry for upsetting you, for what happened to you, and for dredging it up. I just wanted to be honest with you that I know. Maybe, you might find it in yourself to tell me how that affects my brother."

Pressing the code into the keypad, I pushed through the gate, shut it behind me, and walked the path to the front door. The tears dried up quickly inside. Standing in the kitchen drinking water, I looked out over the pool for a long time. My emotions were all over the place, and I wasn't sure what to do with them. I'd always shoved them in a bottle and tried to drown them, but if I kept doing that, I'd never let anyone in.

Yesterday, I'd wanted to let Jet in. Aubrey ruined any chance of that. How was I meant to feel about that?

Chapter Ten
A QUIET WEEK

"Thought you were staying at Aubrey's last night?" Dad frowned, coming into the kitchen.

"I came home."

Watching me stare off into the backyard as I drank my coffee, Dad poured himself a cup. "Are you going to make me ask?"

"It involves sex."

Bristling, Dad shifted uncomfortably. "Maybe you could call Doctor Lind."

"Sex didn't happen. Aubrey's brother walked in, and sort of got a slap in the face about his brother's sexuality."

Dad lifted his brows above his coffee, which seemed to have become glued to his lips.

"I don't get how he can only like guys but claim he's in love with me. I don't understand how it works, and now he gets all jealous if I have another man in my life, but it's okay for him to bang every Tom, Dick, and Harry he trips over."

Finally removing the mug from his lips, Dad looked me over. "Do you love Aubrey?"

"Of course, he's my best friend."

"No, Rain. I mean, are you in love with Aubrey? Are you thinking about marriage and kids and a happy ever after with Aubrey? Forget about the promise you made the Landys'. Do you want to marry Aubrey?"

"I thought so, especially when Geoff came along and the three of us found something that worked for us." My dad grimaced. When he realized Geoff, and I took turns playing piggy in the middle, he'd made a call to Doctor Lind requesting she see me. "Now, I don't think so. If we don't find someone like Geoff again, he's going to be constantly having other men in our lives, and that's not the kind of marriage I want."

Dad put his coffee down. "Then be his friend and nothing more."

"Is that possible? After all that we've been through?"

"I want you to ask yourself a question, and maybe it's a question you need to ask Aubrey." When Dad cringed, I could tell whatever it was he'd been thinking for a long time, but never wanted to be the one to say it to me. "When do you think Aubrey first thought about you in a sexual manner? He was certain he was gay, so were you. When did that change, for him?"

"I don't know."

Dad stood straight. "Think about it, Rain. You've avoided admitting it to yourself for a long time."

Thunder roared across the floor upstairs and down the stairs. Dad's eyes stayed on me even after the twins barreled into the room and started making themselves breakfast. Forcing myself to move because his question touched a nerve that I thought I'd long since healed. "I might get an early start in the office today. You need to speak to Penelope about martial arts."

"She's still not back from overseas. We'll have a few things to discuss when she does."

"You know what her answer will be."

"Which is why I've been keeping a diary of all the times she's dropped them off because it doesn't suit her lifestyle. We need to talk about a few things ourselves. Family dinner tonight?"

"Sounds good. Bring some Thai home with you." My smile disappeared as soon as I was outside. Last night, I hadn't gone back to sleep. Instead, I'd changed, done my morning run, then came home and got ready for work. I was beyond tired, hungover, and emotionally fraying.

Staring out the window on the bus trip to work, I was throwing dad's question around in my head, replaying Jet's rejection. Closing my eyes, I rested my head against the window, remembering how Jet just wanted to be friends now. With a sigh, I let it go. I should have known it wouldn't have worked.

My morning passed, as usual, getting stuck into my work and forgetting about life outside the walls of the office. Just after nine, there was a knock on my office door before it cracked open. Aubrey entered carrying two large coffees, of which he put one on the desk for me and took the seat opposite. He looked like a scolded child, refusing to make eye contact. "I'm sorry about last night. When you said you didn't want to, I thought you meant you weren't ready." Aubrey considered his coffee. "You've never said no before."

"It never felt wrong before." We sat there, letting my words sink in. "Jet doesn't want to date me now. He said he only wants to be friends."

Exhaling in relief, Aubrey sat back in the chair, lifting his eyes to me. "You're better off."

"Fuck you, Aubrey! This was Geoff all over again. You got jealous and ruined my relationship. What are you scared of, Aubrey? Are you worried you won't be the only guy in my life who could make me happy? Are you scared of me losing my dependency on you?"

"I'm scared of losing you, full stop," Aubrey yelled.

"I'm allowed to have a relationship that doesn't include you. You have boyfriends all the time, but a guy is interested in me, and you go out of your way to prevent it from happening. That's unfair, Aubrey. Unfair and wrong."

Gritting his teeth, Aubrey stood up. "I can't help that I want you, Rain. Always have, always will."

"Not always, Aubrey. When did it change?"

"I don't know, and it doesn't matter. You agreed to marry me and to give my parents grandchildren. We agreed if we found a guy that we both liked, he could play piggy in the middle. You promised, and my brother isn't going to agree to share, so forget him and get over it." He stormed towards the door. "I'm off to New Zealand tonight. We can talk when I get home on Sunday."

"Fine, but I want an answer when you get back."

"An answer to what?"

Tears were flooding my vision as I met his eyes. "When did your interest become sexual towards me? Think about it. Pinpoint the first time I turned you on and tell me this hasn't been wrong all along." Aubrey swallowed hard. "Then I need you to tell me if we can still be friends, and only friends."

While I tried to say it calmly, my voice broke as the first tear escaped.

Striding across the room to me, Aubrey pulled me into his arms. "Jesus, Rain. No matter what happens, whether we abide by the promise we made my parents or not, you are my best friend. I loved you before we ever had sex, and I'll love you without it." Aubrey hugged me tight while I sobbed on his shoulder. "God, it's not like we were at it like rabbits or anything and I'm suddenly going to be hard up."

When I chuckled against his chest, Aubrey released the tension from his arms. "I'm sorry I got us in this mess."

"I'm sorry you did too."

"Hey," Aubrey tickled me, making me squirm trying to break from his hold. "I wasn't all to blame."

"Yeah, you were." Blocking Aubrey's arms, I twisted out of his hold, creating distance. Taking a few stabilizing breaths, I dropped into my chair. "I can never stay angry at you."

"I know. Even when we both know you should."

"So, you agree I have the right to be pissed off with you?"

"I agree that ten years ago, I made a mistake which led to a series of mistakes that I can't forgive myself for, and you shouldn't either. I'm not agreeing that Jet losing interest in you is one of them."

"What if he was the one?".

Aubrey huffed. "I doubt it, Rain. You're not his type."

There was no need to ask why, I knew the answer. I was frigid, a recluse, and had been in an intimate relationship with his brother, who was gay. Jet was the guy every female lawyer in town wanted to catch and every other female who knew of his existence. I didn't stand a chance.

After a moment of watching me, Aubrey sighed and went to the door. "I'll see you on Monday."

"Travel safe." The door closed, leaving me alone. Closing my eyes, I hung my head back and growled at God. If Karma was real, I must have been Hitler in a former life for all that had happened in this life.

Taking a deep breath, I lifted my head, focused on my work, and buried myself in it. And, that's where I stayed for the rest of the week. With my head absorbed with my work and taking care of my brothers. Joseph picked them up for training on Wednesday night and brought them home afterward. Dad didn't bring up the subject of Aubrey again, and Jet didn't contact me. By the time Friday afternoon rolled around, I was over it.

"I'm about to head off, Rain," Barbara announced as she came to my door. "You coming tonight?"

"I am."

"Are you still bringing a guy?"

Opening my mouth, ready to say no, I was cut off by Jet's deep voice answering instead. "She is."

Closing my mouth to stop from gaping, I held my tongue while Barbara turned to consider Jet. "Jet? Well, this should be a good evening. See you there."

Waiting until Barbara left to find my tongue, I considered the tall, gorgeous man at my door. "I thought you weren't interested in dating me?" Still dressed for work, Jet was a wet dream leaning against my door jam and boy did he rock a navy-blue suit, black shirt, and sapphire tie.

"That doesn't mean we can't go out as friends." Placing his briefcase to the side, Jet slipped both hands into his pockets. "Friday nights can be quite lonely, and I found your company enjoyable last week, so, I thought, perhaps we could hang out on Fridays. Get drinks, chat, be friends."

"Shouldn't a manwhore be picking up?"

"I think my brother gives me far too much credit. My casual liaisons are few and far between. Truthfully, I'm usually too busy to bother with the effort during the week, and I like time to myself on weekends." Jet waited, watching me. "Come on, Rain. You had a shit start to your week. Let's make sure it ends on a better note."

"I'll need a few minutes to finish up here."

Smiling, Jet took the seat opposite my desk. "I'm on your clock tonight." Taking out his phone, he started browsing.

Looking him over, I admired the angles of his jaw, cheekbones, and the slight bump in his nose - the one flaw to his perfect symmetry. His eyes lifted and caught me perving. When he raised a brow, I turned my attention back to my computer. Out of the corner of my eye, Jet smirked and watched me in much the same way I just watched him.

"You're staring."

"I'm admiring. The sunset over your shoulder makes you look like something angelic."

Glancing over my shoulder, I noticed the sun was still well above the horizon, but the light had started to change. Jet smiled at the phone in his hands. "I thought you were a realist?"

"I like art, and I adore beauty."

"Art can be chaotic."

Jet turned those abyss eyes to mine. "There is beauty in chaos. Even in the darkest night, stars shine, Rain. The clouds may hide them from our view, but we know they are there."

For a moment, his passion confused me. "You're a romantic?"

Jet put his finger to his lips. "Shh. I have a reputation to keep." Winking at me, he returned his attention to his phone. My heart somersaulted in my chest, and things tightened down below. Damn, Jet was suddenly even sexier. Sitting there staring at my computer, I made it my goal to have Jet kiss me tonight. Kiss me so thoroughly I'd still be feeling him in the morning.

Closing out of the program, I started the shutdown to turn off my computer. "Okay, let's go."

Chapter Eleven
A FRIENDLY DATE

"Remind me next time to ask what I'm volunteering for before I say I'm coming." Appearing beside me at the refreshment table, Jet grimaced.

Turning to give him my full attention, I frowned. "But you wanted to learn?"

"I did, but I would have preferred you be my partner. You didn't seem to be standing on too many toes." Rotating his ankle, Jet stretched his foot back and forth while we took a break away from the others.

"I'm in the wedding party, so I have to dance with my designated partner. Trust me; I would have preferred the exchange. You have grace. Duncan dances like a pole is stuck up his ass." He was also handsy, making me nauseous every lesson just letting him touch me.

Brows pinching, Jet glanced over to the groomsman in question. "Yes, well, I think that has always been the case with Duncan."

"You know each other?"

Picking up a bottle of water, Jet nodded. "We went to

school together. My biggest competition, academically. What does he do now?"

"Law. I guess he kept trying to compete. He graduated with distinction from Sydney."

"Please, I went to Oxford, he doesn't even come close," Jet scoffed in jest, not the ego I would have expected. It made me chuckle. "I haven't seen him around."

"He's in criminal law, as is Barbara's fiancé. They both work for the same law firm."

"And how did Barbara meet Kennedy O'Harr?" Taking a mouthful of water, Jet continued to survey the wedding party.

"Ah, well, Kennedy was an associate of my father's. He met me a few years back when I dropped in to see my dad at work. He dropped by the office a few times to try and ask me out. I'd send Barbara out to respectfully decline on my behalf, and a few weeks later they were dating."

"So, no hard feelings?"

"One would think that, but Barbara has warned me that the guys here are betting on who can score with me at the wedding. It's quite a sizeable pot. Hence, why I jumped at the chance to bring a sexy stud like you to practice with me."

Raising a brow, Jet snickered over my description of him. "Well, that explains the stink eye I've been getting from the groomsmen all night."

"And your toes." Cringing in apology, I watched him through my lashes. "Melanie is Kennedy's sister, and is gay."

It started at the side of his mouth, a little twitch of his lips, and then Jet burst out laughing. Masculine pleasure radiated around me; my skin tingled, and toes curled. Everyone turned around to observe us, and I couldn't blame them. He had the sexiest laugh, all baritone, and cymatics. Turning his back to them, Jet put his mouth to my ear seductively, causing my hormones to switch gear immediately. "Is there anyone here who doesn't want to sleep with you?"

Turning my head so I could meet his eyes, I licked my lips. "Barbara, the dance instructors, and you."

Eyes twinkling, Jet took my hand in his. "You think so?"

"As I said last week. People like the look of me. If they got to know me, they would change their minds quickly." Dropping my eyes aside, I swallowed past the sudden constriction in my throat. "You did."

"People love the idea of snow, they think it's beautiful and romantic, but if they had to shovel their cars out of it every day for a month to go to work, their opinions would change quickly."

"And I'm snow?"

Warm fingers caressed my cheek, lifting my gaze to meet his. "I thought you were rain?"

"Snow is just frozen rain."

Bowing his head, Jet put his lips to my ear again. "And yet people pray for rain in its absence. It brings life to the land, and washes everything clean again." He started leading me back to the dance floor. "People dance in the rain, and the earth is renewed by it."

"You talk a lot of shit; did you know that?" I teased, but my cheeks heated at his words.

Smirking, Jet set our frame. "Let's show them how it's done."

Jet was a natural. Both in the way he took me in his arms, and how he moved us around the floor. He'd only needed a few pointers, his natural grace and practice mimicking Gene Kelly and Fred Astaire as a child took it from there.

He glided us around the floor while our dance partners watched and scowled. When I smiled up at Jet, he smiled down at me. He was so light on his feet, I wondered if he'd be as graceful in bed.

"You need to get your mind out of the gutter. I can see your thoughts in your eyes."

"Really? What am I thinking?"

"Nothing my mother would approve of."

Smile dropping, I missed the step. Catching me, Jet studied me, his brows bunching as he watched me back away. "Sorry. I think I'm done for tonight." Turning my back on him, I walked over to my bag. Glancing at Barbara, I waved. She waved back and returned to laughing as the instructor manhandled her fiancé into wiggling his hips.

Onyx eyes assessing me, Jet grabbed his jacket and bag. "You okay?"

"Yeah, just reached my limit." Heading for the door, I led the way down the stairs to the street level. Once I was outside, I took a deep breath before turning to face Jet.

Tilting his head, Jet did a stock take of me, and our surrounds then checked his watch. "Do you want to get a drink?"

"Just one?"

"Maybe two, with food." When Jet offered me his hand, I hesitated then focused on slipping into my cardigan to cover. When Jet took a step closer, I held my breath. Placing a kiss to the tip of my nose, Jet's hand wrapped around mine beside my hip. "Just so you know, I love the rain; not so keen on snow, but I've survived it before."

When he stepped away, my hand in his, I followed. I was mesmerized. Spellbound. Absolutely bewitched.

"God, I'll fall on the floor if I eat anymore, but I so want the baileys cheesecake," I moaned.

Chuckling at my drama, Jet lifted his eyes to the waiter. "Can we get two cappuccinos, and pack up a cheesecake and an apple crumble to go, please?"

"Ice cream?"

"No, I've got some at home," Jet dismissed.

"I don't have ice cream at home."

"Guess you'll have to come to my place for dessert." Picking up the bottle of wine, Jet poured the remainder into my glass. "I'm driving, so bottoms up."

Lifting a brow at the term, I raised my glass and glared. "Whatever you do, don't ever say that to me without a drink around or I'll smack you in the mouth."

"I'm not my brother, and I've never had anal sex. One-night stands don't usually go for that."

"Are you thinking I might change that?" After all, last Sunday I told him I regularly took it up the ass from his brother for years, maybe that was his game.

Folding his arms across his chest, Jet leveled me with his gaze. "If I were planning to take you home for sex, I would make that abundantly clear." Jet dropped his head a little to give serious eye contact. He gave damn good eye contact. I was just about ready to spill my sins under that gaze. "I am always up front with women. If all I want them for is sex, I'll tell them I want to take them out for a night of fun, and I always take them to a hotel, not my house."

"Why?" A little disappointed that he didn't want to jump my bones, I sipped the wine.

"You've seen our home. Women become clingy when they get inside that mansion. It stinks of old money, and that's like the best perfume to some."

"No offense, but I've never been impressed with a guy for his money. I'd take a younger version of Joseph any day over some rich, arrogant bastard who thinks they can buy me."

Jet lifted a brow. "Yet, you let my brother seduce you?"

"I met your brother because he was following my older brother around like a lost puppy. He was infatuated, and he started hanging out with me so he could come over and swoon at Harry. We just gelled from there. I didn't know he had money, where he lived, or anything about him until weeks after he started hanging around me."

With his arms still crossed in a brooding manner, Jet sat assessing me. The waiter brought our coffees and placed the bag containing our desserts beside Jet. "Anything else?"

"Just the bill, please." Waiting until the waiter walked away, Jet released his arms to lean on the table between us. "So, dessert and a movie at my place?"

"If I politely decline?"

"Then I get two lots of dessert to help me cope with having to spend another Friday night by myself." Face serious, Jet picked up his coffee and took a sip. Foam stuck to his upper lip, and my sex convulsed when he licked it clean.

Shaking the sexy image from my head, I scooped up my foam with a teaspoon and sucked it clean; Jet's pupils were dilating when I pulled the spoon free with a pop. "So, my company in exchange for cheesecake? It better be damn good cheesecake."

Finishing his coffee, Jet smirked as he stood up and buttoned his suit jacket. "It's the best you are ever going to get." With a wink, he walked off to pay the bill, our desserts captive in his hand. Finishing my coffee, I followed him. Jet took my hand as we made our way back to his car, and he drove us to his place.

As we approached the gate, I pressed my hands between my knees to hide the slight tremor in them as my nerves picked up. "Are your parents still away?"

"For a few more days. Are you worried about being here alone with me?"

"Yes," I decided to be honest.

Side-eyeing where my knees were pressing on my hands, Jet pressed the button for the automatic gates. "Anything I can do to put you at ease?" Glancing over at him, I shook my head. Waiting until we reached the top of the driveway and the house was in view, Jet put the car in park and focused those beautiful eyes on me. "Anything I shouldn't do? You know, in case it triggers your anxiety?"

Swallowing hard, I laid out my boundaries. "Never step in behind me or grab me from behind."

With a simple nod, Jet led the way inside. We stopped in the kitchen, and he added a scoop of Connoisseur ice cream to our desserts and grabbed two Smirnoff twists from the alcohol fridge in the butler's pantry. "I'm guessing my brother stocks these for you."

Taking them from him so he could carry dessert, I assessed the bottles. "I hope one of those is for you."

"You. I prefer port with dessert."

"I think one will be enough." When I put one back in the fridge, Jet's eyes smiled, but he kept his face neutral.

Following him upstairs, Jet led the way to the boy's media room. Yes, they had one just for the two of them. It had been their playroom as kids and graduated to the media room when movies and game consoles became their thing.

Setting the desserts on the coffee table, Jet handed me the remote. "Pick something. I've got a surprise." He walked towards his room.

Considering the possibility this could be his move, my mind imagined Jet coming back wrapped in a red bow and a hard on and yelling surprise.

Trying to determine how I would deal with that, I fantasized starting to pull the bow, but then I shook my head cursing my imagination. "You know you wouldn't." Turning on the television, I opened Jet's profile and hit the movie icon. Recommendations came up on the screen, and I bit my lip laughing at Fifty shades darker as a top pick.

Walking back in and seeing the look on my face, Jet glanced at the screen. "Seriously, I put number one on for background while working on a case file and now it thinks I'm down for everything with debauchery."

"Are you?"

Imitating my smile, Jet sat beside me on the lounge. "We all have to learn sometime. Here, trade." Taking the remote, Jet handed me shaved Belgium chocolate flakes.

"Jesus, I love this stuff." Opening the pack, I sprinkled it over my dessert, then did his for him.

"Yeah, you might have left some here last year. I only got one try before Aub devoured it all, so now I keep some hidden in my room for when I'm a good boy and deserve a treat."

"Have you been a good boy?"

"I haven't kissed you yet, and I got my feet trampled for you."

"Good point. Did you want to kiss me?"

Cocking his head to consider me, Jet pressed play on the remote and collected his dessert, holding it close. "Not till I've had my treat, or it would undermine the reward."

"Doesn't being naughty post-treat undermine it anyway?"

"Nope. Post-treat starts a new line on the reward chart." When I raised a brow, Jet shrugged. "Hey, that's how it worked for my mum. Don't blame me for her dodgy parenting."

Laughing, I took a mouthful of cheesecake as I snuggled into the lounge watching the movie. The entire film I remained terribly aware of Jet, his body heat, and the fact he just admitted he wanted to be naughty. He hadn't even touched me yet, and the clouds were clearing to show me that star littered sky.

Chapter Twelve
A LITTLE NAUGHTY

"WELL, THAT WAS A LAME ENDING."

Turning off the television, Jet chuckled at my groan. "It was sweet. He respected her wishes."

"He should have kissed her. She wanted it; you could tell. She was waiting for him to kiss her and say he would stay. Instead, he shrugged and walked away. Stupid!" Gathering up my dirty dishes and his, I stood up to take them down the kitchen.

Still smirking at my disappointment with the movie, Jet lifted a brow. "Where are you going?"

Smiling over my shoulder at him, I started down the stairs. "Kitchen to clean up, then home to sleep."

"Just put the dishes in the dishwasher."

Already planning to do that, I noticed Jet heading off towards their rooms with the chocolate flakes. The fact that he still had to hide his treats from his brother made me laugh. By the time I'd finished loading the dishwasher, Jet was standing on the other side of the island counter. "Thank you again for coming dancing with me. Those practices were getting annoying."

"Thank you for spending your night with me. You could sleep here the night if you wanted?"

Lifting my eyes halfway, I considered the offer. "My place isn't that far to walk."

Leaning on the bench with a cheeky grin, Jet lifted a brow at me. "Are you worried you snore? Because if so, that boat sailed Monday night."

Heat filled my cheeks and chest thinking of last weekend. Dropping my eyes away, I drew random patterns on the counter with my finger. "Did you undress me Monday?"

"Yeah, I did. I hope that didn't cross a line. You seemed uncomfortable, and it's not like I hadn't seen you in just your underwear before that."

"True." Moving around the bench towards him, I lifted my eyes to stare into the endless depth of his. "My scars didn't bother you?"

Jet's smile dimmed a little. "Yes, but not because I saw them as a flaw or detracted from your beauty. They bothered me because I know you were hurt badly." We stood there close, breathing the same air. Jet's hand slowly reached forward and caressed my scar through the blouse I wore, making my breath catch. "What caused it?"

"I was shot."

Brow creasing, pupils dilating, Jet opened his mouth a little before he caught himself and schooled his features. "You were there? You're the friend Aubrey got shot trying to save someone."

Swallowing, I kept it clinical and detached. The memory was not mine. If it were, it would break me, and I couldn't go through life broken. "Yes. He was trying to save me." Sucking in a breath, Jet understood immediately. As his hand fell away from me, I snatched it and placed it back to touch my scar. "Don't. You've already figured most of it out, so let me give you the quick version, then I'll go home and provide you with time to deal with it.

"When I was fourteen, some men broke into my house. I was beaten and raped repeatedly for hours. Your brother was coming to see me. He used to sneak over the back fence and climb in my bedroom window so we could hang out talking all night. He called the police, and then he tried to help me escape. He got the shit beaten out of him for trying. Then one of the men raped me in front of your brother."

Hand falling limp, Jet stepped away from me, shock covering his features.

"While the guy was preoccupied, Aubrey rushed him. The man had a gun. It fired, but I was already in so much pain, I didn't feel it. The police arrived a moment later and shot my attackers."

White as a sheet, Jet swallowed hard, his eyes glassy with unshed tears, and fierce with rage. "Tell me the bastards are dead."

Voice cracking with the constriction in my throat, I kept it separate. "The police shot them." As Jet crumpled into one of the chairs at the kitchen table, I resisted trying to comfort him.

Years ago, I'd realized that people wanted you to comfort them, to tell them it wasn't as bad as it sounded, to believe that because I was functioning, I was okay. It was bullshit. I'd never been okay again, and it was far worse than people could perceive it to be with a retelling. Unless they felt the pain, suffered the years of nightmares, and nearly screamed every time they saw an open window or unlocked door in their house, they would never understand just how not okay I was thanks to that experience. There was no way I was comforting anyone about my past. "Thank you for tonight. I enjoyed the time with you."

Grabbing my bag, I made my way out to the foyer and let myself out. I didn't cry. Retelling my story was done clinically and with distance. As long as I didn't mention before Aubrey's arrival, I could cope.

Feet running on the pavement behind me made me turn, always acutely aware of my surroundings when I was outside. Running after me, Jet still wore his shirt and suit pants. He stopped a few meters back, breathing reasonably evenly for the run he just did. "Thank you for telling me."

Confused by his relief, I frowned. "It's not what sets your brother off."

"I know, but it explains you and him, and frankly, that's what has been stopping me doing this all week." Taking two steps forward, Jet took my hand in his, squeezed in gently, and then he kissed me. His lips pinched gently. He didn't try for open mouth, just a church friendly but passionate kiss. Closing my eyes, I went with it, moving in to be closer to him. When he pulled back, Jet looked down on me. "Is that okay?"

"Kissing is good. I like kissing."

This time his kiss was a little bit more, a little bit deeper, a perfect kiss on the walk home from a good night. Jet's free hand moved to my waist. His thumb traced the scar through my blouse, then lifted and traced my twelfth rib along its base.

Moaning, I pressed against him, my tongue flicking

against his lip. Pulling back, Jet smiled, his eyes were shining orbs in the night. "The offer to stay the night is still open."

Rubbing my lips together, I savored the feel of him. "I'm already halfway home. Maybe another night."

"Then I'll walk you home." Keeping my hand in his, we walked together, talking more about the movie before agreeing the cheesecake was worth the exchange of my company.

When we reached the front gate of my place, Jet frowned. "Did you want to walk around the block?"

Peering down at my heels, I laughed. "I'm going to pass tonight. It's getting late, and I haven't slept well this week."

Obviously disappointed, Jet took in the heels and nodded. "What are your plans tomorrow night?"

Kind of surprised, I blinked. "Ah, I didn't have any."

"Would you consider dinner and a show? I've got tickets already, a gift from a client."

"I'll make you a deal. I'll be your date tomorrow night if you be my lunch date on Sunday. A client of mine is holding an event, and with both your dad and brother out of town, I have to fill in."

"Deal. I'll pick you up tomorrow at six."

"I look forward to it." My cheeks heated as I considered kissing him again. As if reading my mind, Jet lowered his mouth to mine. His lips were perfect, not too thin, not too big. He'd perfected his kiss, not opening his mouth too wide that you feared being swallowed, not keeping his lips glued shut. He knew how to pinch, and how to tilt his head before pinching again.

When we pulled apart breathless, we met each other's eyes and stood awkwardly — both of us, shy and unsure of what to say like a couple of teenagers. Stepping to the gate, I punched in the code. "Good night, again."

"Good night." Waiting until the gate closed, Jet turned away and strolled back down the street. Wandering up the path to the front door, I let myself inside.

"I'm home." My dad's study light was still on telling me he was awake. Making my way to the kitchen, I heated some milk and added a dash of honey.

Dad made his way into the kitchen. "You're later than usual. I was getting worried."

"I went out on that date that got interrupted last week."

Lifting a brow, Dad assessed me. "I take it that it went well?"

"We're going out again to a show tomorrow. I might be home late again."

"Should I meet this guy?"

"Not yet. Let's see how we go this weekend. If he's still interested next week, then you can meet him."

Tilting his head, Dad raised a brow. "You really like him?" I nodded. "Enough to cause an issue with the Landys'?"

Biting my lip as I considered the question, I stared at my toes for a second, then lifted my eyes to meet my father. "Yeah. I think if this guy and I get serious, it's going to be an issue."

"Does Aubrey know?"

"Yes. He wasn't happy, but I've told him we should only be friends, another guy or not."

Dad blew out a breath. "When the shit hits the fan, I'll be here if you need me."

"Thanks, Dad." Kissing him on the cheek, I headed up to bed.

After showering, I pulled on my singlet and knickers to

sleep before climbing into bed. Just as I laid down my phone buzzed.

Jet: I'm still thinking about you, and I want to kiss you again.

My girly bits tingled.

Rain: Just kiss?

Jet: Maybe a little more.

Feeling naughty, I bit my lip.

Rain: I'm going to call in a few minutes, but I don't want to talk.

Jet: Are you suggesting what I think you're suggesting?

Rain: You'll find out in a minute.

Setting the phone aside, I grabbed my hands-free headphones, and then I collected my vibrator from my drawer. Placing a drop of warming lubricant on the tip, I pulled aside my knickers and bit my lip on a moan when the cold gel impacted my hot lips, easily spreading them and mixing with my desire to allow the toy to slip along my path. I imagined Jet above me, watching my reaction as he niched himself at my opening. Collecting the phone with my other hand, I called Jet. He answered on the first ring. "Rain?"

"Ready?"

He chuckled. "I've never done this."

"Me neither, so let's not make it more awkward."

"Okay. Do you want me to talk dirty?"

"No talking." Pressing the toy inside me, I moaned. Not all the way, my body always took a few goes to open up.

"Jesus!" Cursing, Jet released a heavy breath.

Closing my eyes, I listened to him pant, matching the rhythm of movement to his sounds, moaning for him softly. My body opened, and I hit the setting I liked, cursing as that first spike of pleasure hit.

"Good?" Jet checked.

"Yes." On the other end of the line, Jet was gaining speed. "Slow it down. Be gentle."

Complying, Jet exhaled hard, his groans growing longer, slower, more intense. My body reacted to the sound of him, the long slow stroke of him inside me, the way he panted in my ear. "Oh, god!"

"Wait for me."

"Don't worry; I'm a repeater." Cursing as the first spasm of orgasm seized me, I threw my head back. "Don't stop."

Swearing in my ear, Jet moaned beautifully. "God, that sounded good. Let's do it again."

Switching to the next setting, I smiled. When Jet's breathing picked up again, I matched his pants with my own. "Not too fast." Jet slowed it down but kept the tempo a little higher than before. His grunts and the slapping sound of him slamming his fist down for that hard pound came down the line.

The rising wave of orgasm swelled suddenly, growing bigger and bigger. Listening to Jet wank was a turn-on. "Jet?"

"I'm ready."

As I imagined him pulsing inside of me, shooting his cum into me over and over again, Jet cursed and groaned as he exploded. Quickly, I covered my mouth to smother my cry as the wave crashed on me, stealing my breath, my body seizing, every muscle tightening before it snapped, and I fell limp to the bed.

We lay there, both of us catching our breaths, then Jet chuckled. "Okay, that I did not expect."

"I told you. I love sex. I just struggle to be intimate with others."

"Believe it or not, I'm much the same, Rain. That's why I've never dated. Being intimate isn't my strong suit, either."

"Well, we aren't dating. Just friends that hang out with each other."

Jet was quiet for a second. "What if I wanted the other?"

"Less pressure being friends. But, let's be flexible about our friendship."

"Like you are with my brother?" There was caution in his question that forced me to heave a sigh as I rolled to my side, looking at the window.

"We should talk about that before this becomes something other."

"Yeah, we should, but not tonight. I'd rather go to sleep enjoying the night we had, so let's not burst our bubble right now."

Wondering if his recovery was anything like his brother, I smiled. "I could go another round?"

Masculine laughter vibrated down the line, through my body, and tightened everything inside me. "I'm up for it. Literally."

Chapter Thirteen
THE WRONG DATE

STARING AT THE STAGE WITH MY MOUTH HANGING OPEN, I wasn't sure what to think. This was not the sort of show I was expecting when I got dressed up to go out tonight.

"Um..." Jet also stared at the stage agape. "This is not what I thought it was."

"What did you think it was?"

A shudder swept through the audience: not the wrong sort, but that good one. I wasn't feeling it.

"A musical romance about a golf player."

Glancing at Jet to see he was serious, I burst out laughing, annoying the voyeurs caught up in the first act around us. "What is it called?"

"The three-hole carousel." Cringing, Jet shrugged a shoulder. "In fairness, it was an easy mistake." When I snickered, Jet smiled and shook his head. "Do you want to go?"

Nodding my head, I grabbed my bag in readiness. Taking my hand, Jet stood up, keeping low not to block anyone's view as we left. "Jeez, checking out at the first hole. No stamina," an audience member muttered. My eyes went wide, and Jet flushed bright red. By the time we got outside of the dark theatre, we were both red like tomatoes.

"I should have known it was something not mainstream by its unorthodox location," Jet apologized.

Stepping over to the poster advertisement on the wall, I smiled. "As a lawyer, I would expect you to read the fine print." Pointing to the poster, I lifted a brow in a tease. "Three-hole carousel: a live porn show. Your client must think you a deviant?"

Face getting redder, Jet cleared his throat, his brows going up. "Actually, she was the star of the show. Not that I would have known if she hadn't told me."

"Ah, you never asked her occupation?"

"She said, actress. I didn't question what sort. My job was to sort out her finances and custody of her kids."

"Is she a good mum at least?"

"Yes. So, let's not judge how she earns her keep."

With a shrug, I blinked trying to get the image of what I just saw on stage to fit with being a mum. It probably required better compartmentalization of her life than I needed to get through every day. "Doesn't bother me. I'm just surprised her husband didn't try and use that to make her name mud."

Eyes glinting, Jet smirked. "He used to be her costar, so I'm guessing that wouldn't have done him any good."

"Well, that would make an interesting 'how I met your mother' story."

"More interesting than getting naked in the foyer with your gay brother?" Jet laughed at whatever he saw on my face. I loved his laugh. It made me feel all light inside. "Should we go to dinner early?"

"That all depends on what you're serving up."

"Not a sausage." Suddenly, Jet frowned. "Have you been drinking today?"

"No, why?"

"You're relaxed and making dick jokes."

Grinning broadly, I looked up at the sky, knowing that smile reached my eyes. "I had mind-blowing sex last night. The endorphins are better than alcohol."

"Remind me to give you mind-blowing sex regularly, to see if we can curb your dependency on alcohol." When I looked away, heat filling my cheeks, Jet tugged at my hand. "Let's go eat before we get distracted and you overheat."

We were over an hour early for the restaurant Jet booked, so the host asked us to sit at the bar until our table was ready. "What would you like?" The bartender requested. Jet deferred to me, handing me the drinks list.

"I might have a pineapple mojito sangria tonight."

Frowning, Jet took the list to look. "Aren't they two different drinks?"

"Normally, yes, but it's a mint and lime tropical sangria. I'm a sucker for anything with mint and lime in it."

"So, if I drank mint and lime?" When my cheeks cooked at the idea of kissing him while his mouth was bursting with flavor, Jet laughed. "I'll try a traditional sangria." The smirking bartender went to make our orders. "So, despite wanting to enjoy this date, I feel, considering the slight curve away from the friendship we've taken, that we should discuss your arrangement with my brother."

My stomach collapsed at the prospect. "Maybe we wait for somewhere more private?" Gazing around me at all the people who could witness my embarrassment should Jet lose his temper.

"That bad?" The bartender slid our drinks in front of us. Jet took a mouthful of his. My hands were trembling when I reached out to take a sip of mine. "Your anxiety has kicked in. You think I'm going to react badly?"

"Yes." Taking two large mouthfuls of my cocktail, I avoided Jet's eyes.

"Okay, well, let me tell you what I think, and you can just say wrong or right." Placing his drink on the bar, Jet angled his body towards mine. "The painting on the wall in the downstairs bedroom; that's Aub in it, right?" Jet waited for me to take another drink and nod. "So, you lost your willing virginity to him."

"Willing virginity?"

"Most rape victims don't consider that their first time. Their first time is when they willingly have sex."

"No, it was my first time having vaginal sex."

"But that was two years after-" Jet cut off, his bunched brows straightened, raised, and tears filled his eyes. "Oh!" Taking several large mouthfuls, Jet set his empty glass down before indicating the bartender he needed another. Taking a minute to get his words sorted, I watched Jet's jaw clench tight. "And my brother watched it?"

Nursing my drink, I stared into the colorful potion. "When my dad caught Aubrey in my bed, and it was evident that I was very high and very drunk, but Aubrey not so much, he threatened to have Aubrey charged with rape of a minor. That got your parents involved. They talked my dad down by persisting Aubrey was in love with me and intended to marry me. They made me and Aubrey sign agreements to our intentions."

"Wait. What?!"

"Your parents have a contract signed by your brother and I that we will marry and have kids once both the age of consenting and both ready. If Aubrey fails to uphold the agreement, they'll disown him. He loses his inheritance and his job in the family company."

Jet's jaw was on the floor. "So, you agreed to marry your best friend to protect his future?"

"Who else was I going to marry? At the time, Aub was the only male I could stand touching me. He definitely was the only one I'd been intimate with, and considering what it took to handle that, I couldn't see the potential of me ever meeting another man who I could let close to me."

"So, you signed your future away to protect my gay brother?"

"There was more to it than just that, but that's why I signed the contract."

"So, we can only ever be friends? Because I love my brother, and I can't ruin his future any more than you can."

My eyes prickled as I picked up the glass and drank the rest. Finishing his second cocktail, Jet took a deep breath. "What about divorce? You could marry him, have a baby, divorce him, and still have abided by the agreement."

The planning Jet was putting into this made me laugh. "Your brother would hire you as his divorce attorney. That would be a severe conflict of interest."

"I'll be drawing up the prenup. You won't even need a day in court because you will stay living in our house after the divorce, therefore custody of the child won't be an issue."

Blinking over his decision, I lifted a brow. "You expect your parents to be okay with me just swapping from your brother's bedroom to yours?" I shook my head. "Your mother can't accept her son is gay. The marriage, the child, is all for her self-deception. A divorce won't be an option."

Taking my hand, Jet turned my chin to look into my eyes. "It has to be because I don't believe you were meant for Aubrey."

Falling into the depth of Jet's eyes, there was a passion in them I'd never seen before. My throat constricted. "Well, it's not like your brother is going to be faithful."

Shaking his head, Jet took his hand back. "You deserve better than that. I deserve better than being secondary, and I won't accept you going back to his bed when he wants you and watching you get drunk to be with him."

"So, just friends?"

"Friends for now. I want to see this contract you signed before I stand aside for my brother. He's never going to make you happy, and you shouldn't be stuck with that."

"Jet, you've never had a committed relationship, but you're talking as if that's what you want."

Bowing his head, refusing to meet my eyes, Jet licked his lips.

"Mr. Landy, your table is ready. If you'll follow me." The hostess walked off, not waiting.

Pressing his lips together in a line, Jet stood and followed. With a sigh, I played follow the leader. After taking our seats, Jet ordered water to drink, so I followed suit. The conversation was light and superficial after the depth of our pre-dinner drinks. We ate mains, and when the waiter brought the dessert menu, Jet finally smiled at me again. "Shall we take dessert home to eat while watching a movie?"

"Is that what you really want to do?"

Tilting his head, Jet considered me. "Yes, Rain. It's the start of what I want to do. Then I will walk you home, return to my house, and call you to have sex with you again."

Blinking at his plan, I frowned a little. "You don't want to do the real thing?"

"Of course, I do. But, until you can have sex with me sober, we won't do the real thing."

"That might never happen."

"You've kissed me sober. I think there is a chance we can do more."

"Can we do more tonight? More than just kissing at least?" The potent cocktail I drank pre-dinner may still be in effect.

The sides of Jet's mouth twitched. "We'll see."

Three hours later. Kissing. Lots and lots of kissing. On the media room lounge with Jet's body lying above mine. His hands were caressing my hips and thighs, and his engorgement painful where it pressed against my hip, straining against its imprisonment. My knickers were well beyond damp.

We broke apart breathless. "I should take you home. But, god, I want you to stay with me."

"Okay." Not wanting to stop this dream, I sucked his bottom lip.

Groaning with need, Jet moved his hand up my leg, pushing my dress up until he held under my bum. His long fingers rubbed the gusset of my knickers, and the sound in his chest was as close to a human purr as you could get. "Can I taste you?"

"Okay."

Kissing down my neck, Jet dropped pecks over my body above the clothing as he pressed back to kneeling, then his head disappeared between my thighs. Covering my eyes with my hands as Jet pulled my knickers aside, I bit my lip as he licked through my center. With a growl, Jet latched on hungrily, sucking and licking me until I was walking the fine edge of climax and insanity.

"God, I want you, Rain."

Squirming in his grasp, I couldn't stay still. My body was out of control, and for once, I wanted to go with it. "Okay."

"Not good enough, Rain." His finger teased around my opening. "You need to be very clear about what you want here."

Biting my lip, I was barely holding my senses together. I was sober, not having had anything else to drink all night, and yet, I was eager for this. That meant something, right? It had to mean I could do this. That Jet was the right guy for me to be with this way. "Yes, I want to have sex with you, Jet."

Kissing me passionately, Jet slipped his finger inside me. Gripping his shoulders, I gasped as he rubbed my live wire. Seconds later, my body seized, clenching his finger, and flooding my body with feel-good hormones.

Grinning with the ego of a job well-done, Jet eased his hand free. "Okay, but not here." Taking my hand, Jet led me to his bedroom.

My heart was thudding in my chest, but my hands, they were steady. I was ready.

❖

Chapter Fourteen
SOBER

His bedroom wasn't as clean as I remembered. It wasn't a mess, but Jet was always so immaculately dressed and presented, I expected everything about him to be like that.

"Sorry." Letting go of my hand, Jet gathered the case files on his bed, piling them and neatly placing them on his desk. Like his brother, his room was huge. Unlike Aubrey, Jet didn't have a television. The entirety of furnishings was the bed, desk, and chair. All the other space was clean from clutter.

Turning to consider me, Jet tilted his head. "Something wrong?"

"I'm just imagining where we should put the cot?"

Smirking at my tease, Jet pointed at the door. "There is another master bedroom on this level with our old nursery next door. My parents moved to the downstairs master suite after we were old enough to be up here alone."

My eyes were wide. Jet had been way too comfortable with that conversation. "I was joking about the cot."

Noticing my hands, Jet stepped forward and quickly took my hand in his, giving it a gentle squeeze. "I wasn't making plans, just explaining when my brother or I marry, they'll give up their bedroom and move to the other side to live with their family."

"You haven't even considered moving out and getting a place just for you?"

Shaking his head, Jet walked me to his balcony door and opened it for us to step out. We looked over the sizeable estate of his family's home, the mansion one of the first in the area and passed down through the family.

"This place will be mine one day. Do you think I could find a place with this much space for kids this close to the city?" They had three acres of land here, and the house was three-story and could house a different family on each level. It was worth millions.

"You want kids?"

"Don't you? You've basically raised your brothers."

"I love my brothers, but they can be feral. I would love a little girl, but I'd be terrified of anything happening to her. The sad reality is that I'd be one of those helicopter mums." When Jet squeezed my hand, I instantly relaxed a little.

"That sort of history doesn't repeat itself in the same family, Rain." Shuffling his feet, Jet looked away. "If it helps, I would be the same about my children, daughters, or sons." He lifted his eyes to meet mine. Something horrible I'd never glimpsed before hiding within. "I certainly would never trust my children alone with a priest."

My chest expanded to draw in air, but my throat restricted. I couldn't do anything but watch that darkness and vulnerability pass through Jet's eyes. His mother was Italian and very religious. "Aubrey was an altar boy."

Jet looked away. "We both were."

"Jet..."

Moving closer, Jet squeezed my hand again. "I'm not going to discuss this further after this moment, but I wanted you to know that I understand why you don't like people behind you. I am not angry at Aubrey for being involved with you, but I despise him for doing it as they did."

I wasn't game to ask if he meant their priest or my attackers; it didn't matter. Jet had been the only family member to go to law. No one he was related to was even in the industry, but Jet was intently focused. He didn't go to criminal law, he went into family law, and family law wasn't just about divorces and custody.

Sighing, Jet stepped back. "I've ruined the mood, haven't I? It wasn't my intention to reveal things to you. I wanted you to understand your fears, aren't yours alone."

Blinking, I stepped back. "When did you pick that I was a victim? The night we met?"

"No. You were enigmatic, but not broken that night. Even when I took you out for that drink, you were different, but I didn't pick it. Not until Aub was stunned you let me into your house. The next day, when I came there, you confirmed my suspicions." Closing the distance again, one of Jet's hands rubbed my upper arm. "I was attracted to you physically when we met. I became attracted to you as a person before I realized you were damaged, but that revelation didn't alter my interest."

Determined that I heard him, Jet met my eyes. "It's important you know, that your past changed my interest from casual to something that affected the way I breathe in your presence. I understood why you and Aubrey were so close." Jet lifted a brow.

"Admittedly, not expecting you to be as close as you are, but even after I found that out, I couldn't stop thinking about you. The need to kiss you and to see you smile at me only grew." Jet shook his head. "I never expected this, and I can't explain it. It just is."

Tilting my head, I considered Jet and balanced his words against his actions so far, adding how he made me feel. Here I was standing in his room, moments ago ready to have sex with him, and I was sober. Jesus, Dr. Lind was going to have a party just with that alone, even if we didn't have sex. Hell, last night's phone call would probably make her do cartwheels.

Moving closer, I went up on my tiptoes. "Okay," I breathed against his lips.

"Okay?"

When I initiated the kiss, Jet pulled back a second, his eyes wary. "Boundaries." Taking my hand in his, Jet stroked his thumb in my palm comfortingly. "Always let me initiate the physical contact, but I will always make eye contact with you before I do, so you are ready."

"What if I want to kiss you? That was a huge step for me."

Jet used his free hand to caress my jaw, touching the joint near my ear. "Kiss here first. Then come forward to my lips."

Kissing his jaw just in front of his ear, I lingered, tasting him. Jet exhaled roughly making me smile. "Anything else? No-go zones?" Placing another kiss to his starting point, I merged a little forward.

"Just let me take the lead. I'll redirect you if you hit a fence." Sighing, Jet firmed his grip on me as my lips marked his jaw until I was in front of his lips.

"Do you trigger often?"

Shaking his head, Jet stepped us back into his bedroom.

"The women I've been with love dominant men, so it's never been an issue. I did a lot of research after I lost my virginity, figured out how sex would work for me, and not have a problem."

"I just got drunk and high. Your approach was probably healthier."

"Give yourself credit, Rain. You are here and willing to try." Letting go of me, Jet started unbuttoning his shirt. "I prefer to undress myself."

Smirking, I stepped back. "I'm not opposed to a strip show."

My cheek made Jet laugh. The sound of his deep chuckle was music. Sex music. When his shirt fell open, I pressed my lips together to prevent moaning. He must have done more than martial arts to keep fit. He had a defined waist without the bulging abs. Clear lines were separating his obliques from his rectus, dipping down to below his belt. He may not have a six or eight pack, but he had the V.

Jet's shirt fell to the ground. I licked my lips. When his hand went to his belt, I pursed my lips and moved my hands to unzip my dress. It fell to the ground at the same time his pants did, boxers as well. If I hadn't already experienced his brother, I might have freaked out about the package Jet smuggled. Thankfully, hanging around Aubrey and his boyfriends desensitized me to large cocks. Physically and personality-wise.

Unhooking my bra, I dropped the lace covering to his floor. As I hooked my fingers in the sides of my knickers, Jet took his erection in hand and stroked himself. Sliding them down, I stepped out of them. Without saying a word, I sat on the bed and scooted back, so I could sit with my legs outstretched.

Kneeling onto the bed, Jet shifted his body to lie beside me. "Lay down with me." Lying back on the bed, I turned on my side to face him. Taking my hand, Jet placed it to his chest. "Touch me anywhere but down there."

"Kiss too?"

Nodding his head, Jet took the hand of the arm I was lying on and held it. Kissing his starting point, then down his neck, I loved when Jet sighed and hung his head back. Feeling a rare surge of bravery, I licked along his collarbone.

"Jesus, Rain." Using his free hand to tilt my face up, Jet captured my mouth, kissing me deeply, making my stomach hollow, my sex weep, and thighs open to relieve the heat building between them.

Rolling us, Jet shifted himself over me, moving between my thighs. He still held my hand, pinning it beside my head, anchoring me while our other hands caressed each other, and our mouths probed deeper. His back was so strong beneath my fingers, his biceps hard, and I loved the definition of his shoulder muscles.

He didn't try and enter me, just kissed me, touched me, rubbed his hard body against my softer one. Yes, I did martial arts and ran, but I drank and ate desserts too. Sighing, I moaned and panted his name when I could.

Pulling back, Jet met my eyes. "Are you sure? We don't have to go further if you're not ready."

Meeting his eyes, I traced the shape of them with my finger. "I'm sure."

Moving to his bedside table, Jet collected protection, putting it on so I could watch, but not so I could help. Aubrey liked me to do it for him, but I suspected Jet didn't want me touching him there. It made me curious if their abuse was different.

Returning to me, Jet slowed his kisses and made them more purposeful. Reaching between us, he checked that I was ready. That single touch burst a dam for how wet I suddenly felt down there. Smiling against my mouth, Jet shifted his hips into place.

My hands started to shake where I held his shoulders. Jet paused. Taking one of my hands in his, he placed it beside my head and squeezed it gently. "Still okay? I won't be angry if it's all you can manage today. I don't want you ever to fear to say no to me."

Tears pricked my eyes at his understanding. It just made me want him more. "I..." Observing me patiently, concern flashed in Jet's eyes. "Just keep kissing me."

His mouth came to mine. His lips careful and gentle as Jet moved his hips slightly forward. Breath rushing out of me as he stretched me open, I cursed. Moving my mouth to his shoulder, I bit him.

"Rain?"

"Keep going. You're huge."

Jet chuckled. "I'm not that much bigger than you've had before."

"I'm normally drunk too."

"Good point," Jet muttered stopping. "I should have used lube to help."

"Too late, keep going."

"If I'm hurting you–"

"You're not. I'm just ready to come already."

"Seriously?"

"I've already gone once tonight. It doesn't take much for the second time."

Kissing me heatedly, Jet pumped his hips forward. Moaning as my body tightened, I wasn't quite there. Slow and gentle, Jet took his time with every stroke, caress, and the way he kissed. Moving deep and snuggling his hips in, Jet moaned. I wanted to climax. It was right there, but I wasn't going over. Still, it felt terrific, so I wasn't complaining.

Running my hand up Jet's back, I caressed those muscles, feeling them bunch and press as he moved in me. Hanging my head back as his lips kissed around my neck, his teeth marked his pleasure, hesitating at first.

"Yes. It feels good."

His teeth pressed a little deeper, then he sucked, and I drew in a sharp breath with the twinge of delight it sparked. My memories of sex were blurry at best; like navigating through a fog. This experience was crystal clear; my senses were lighting up in high definition. The feel, Jet's overpowering scent, the way his breath brushed across my neck, the sounds he made. It all added up to be better than I could ever imagine.

"Do you want to be on top?" Jet asked.

"I've never done that."

"I think you'll like it." He rolled us without waiting. "Sit up." Pulling my knees in, I sat up. My hands pressed to his chest to steady myself. "Okay?" Jet checked. I nodded.

Aiding me in moving my hips to start, once I had a steady rhythm, Jet placed his thumb to my clit and pressed. My eyes rolled back in my head. The noise that came out of me as the head of him flicked back and forth across my cervix, so very deep inside me, was primal.

Biting my lip, I whimpered as my entire body seized. Gripping my hips, Jet rocked me while I lost control of my body, encouraging me gently to enjoy it, to keep going. As I sagged, he sat up, lifting me enough to adjust our legs so mine wrapped around him and he could hold me close. "That's it, beautiful. Want to keep going?"

Delirious from the orgasm, I nibbled his ear. "God, yes."

Chuckling, Jet bent me back a little and sucked my nipple into his mouth. My sex clenched tight around him, causing me to curse. Jet's cock jerked inside me, and he groaned. Controlling my hips, Jet started rocking me over him. He was gentle still, but his hips ended every thrust with a hard shove.

"Okay?"

Moaning some form of confirmation, I kissed around his neck. Wrapping my arms around him, I added a little thrust with my hips. Murmuring my name, Jet told me how beautiful I was, that he would give me everything I wanted if I stayed with him.

Taking very little time to reach the pinnacle again, the fierce clench of my body had Jet calling my name roughly. He swelled and pulsed and cried out as he came, my body taking me over one last time.

Deflating in his arms, panting, I clung to reality and my body by holding him tightly. I'd never felt like this, at least, I couldn't remember feeling like this. Jet's arms tightened. "It's okay, Rain," he breathed and wiped my face. That's when I realized I was crying.

❖

Chapter Fifteen
AFTERSHOCKS

"Everything okay?" Coming back into the room with a tray of drinks, Jet set it down on his bedside table.

Pressing send on the message on my phone, I put it away. "Just letting my Dad know not to expect me home. He worries."

Picking up the two mugs on the tray, Jet handed me one. "Hot chocolate?"

"Thank you." Smiling as I took the mug, I took a sip; it was the good stuff. When Jet walked out onto his balcony, I hesitated. "Unless you want me to go home now?"

"No. I want you to stay."

"It's just, you don't normally bring women home and sleep with them."

Moving so we could see each other, Jet leaned back on the railing outside the door. "True. But you are not a normal woman, Rain, and the reasoning I apply to not bringing women here would be invalid for you."

"I am normal. I've just had an extreme life experience." Smirking, Jet shook his head as if he disagreed. I wasn't going

136

to argue with him. What was normal, anyway? "Are you sure you want me to stay?"

"Come here. Please?"

Holding the bedsheet to my chest, I chewed my lip. "I'm naked."

"Does that bother you?"

"It does if I'm the only naked person in the room."

Lifting a brow, Jet set his mug aside, dropped his boxers to the ground, and threw them back inside the door. Straightening, he collected his cup, the cheekiest of grins plastered across his face as he lifted it to his lips.

Snickering, I set my empty mug aside and turned on the bedside lamp. Picking up the remote, I switched off the room light, so there was only ambient lighting. Taking a deep breath, I dropped the sheet and walked to the balcony and Jet's bright smile. His eyes filled with heat watching me approach.

The night was warm, bordering on too hot to sleep. Summer was a month away, but Mother Nature didn't follow the sun calendar. When Jet offered me his hand, I took it and stepped into him, pressing myself to his chest, letting my head naturally rest on him. Jet moved our locked arms back and behind me, so he held my waist and hand simultaneously.

"I want you to stay." Kissing the top of my head, Jet inhaled the scent of my shampoo at the same time, then he lifted his mug to his lips and kept drinking.

We stood like that until he finished his drink, a smile upon my face, body relaxed. "I could sleep like this." Jet's hand squeezed mine gently. "Thank you for telling me about what happened to you and Aubrey. It helped me focus on how it was for you, and not solely on how it affected me."

Tensing a little at the topic, Jet cleared his throat. "Sex should always be considerate of all parties. It is a team sport, and there is no 'I' in a team. There isn't one in sex, either."

Taking a deep breath, Jet moved me back enough so he could see my face. "I should clarify. Pedophiles typically have an age bracket. I am significantly older than my baby brother, and therefore, my fate was not his. Whatever affects my brother now, it is not the same thing."

My breath rushed from me in relief. I didn't mean to, but I was consoled to know that all these years Aubrey wasn't carrying around some huge thing that happened to him, and I never noticed. "Are you sure?"

"Quite. Our family priest fell down a flight of steps when I was thirteen. He broke his hip and didn't survive the surgery."

"Oh!" Blinking in surprise at Jet's dry, unaffected tone, I felt my brows bunch and tried to clear my reaction.

Placing a kiss to my forehead, Jet used his thumb to iron the crease in my brow away. A poker face was not a skill I toted. "It was no great loss to our community, trust me. Though, my mother was devastated. She thought he was wonderful, and the priest who replaced him was modern. Absolutely disgraceful, apparently."

"Your parents don't know?" Jet shook his head. "You've dealt with this alone?" Jesus, I was going to cry. I felt so sorry for him, but at the same time, I admired him even more. He had his shit together. Yeah, he had issues, but no one would have picked them without him telling them. Even his physical contact could just be explained away as a dominate personality or alpha male shit.

"I have a psychologist," Jet answered as if that was all he needed.

Wrapping my free arm around him, I kissed his chest.

"Don't cry for me, Rain."

"Okay." Holding my tears back, I focused on the feel of his chest beneath my cheek. The strength of his back beneath my hand. Pressing my palm firmer against his back, I hugged him tighter, instantly feeling energized and happier. When I pulled back, I rose on my tiptoes and placed one single kiss to his jaw, then I moved back into his bedroom and beneath his sheet.

Coming inside, Jet shut the balcony doors. "You look good in my bed. I could get used to this."

Cheeks heating at the thought of always being in his bed, I averted my eyes. Too soon, I know. Especially with a man who has never even dated, but I hated the idea of never being here like this with him again.

Lifting the sheet back, Jet appraised me, his desire growing visually. "Up for more?"

My gaze dropped pointedly to his dick. "I know you are."

Opening his bedside draw, Jet retrieved a fresh condom. While I watched, he covered himself, the ultra-thin layer looking like it was going to split any second. Taking out a tube, Jet squirted some on his fingers, smothering his hardness in the slick fluid.

When I lifted my focus to his grin, Jet climbed directly between my thighs. "I don't want you walking rough in the morning. Well, no more than you already are."

How he'd noticed I was tender, I didn't know. It didn't matter. He paid enough attention to know and was ensuring he didn't make it worse or hurt me.

We kissed avidly as he used his already slick fingers to ready me, then he took very little time getting as deep in me as he could. Wrapping my thighs around his waist, I held him tight as he made me sing his praises. But I couldn't quite get there this time, and even though Jet had swelled impossibly big, he wasn't getting there either.

"Rain?"

"I can't. I want too, but I think I'm all tapped out."

Dropping his head to my shoulder, Jet breathed deeply. "You're on the pill, right?"

Wondering why that could help, I frowned. "Yes, of course."

"Let me go bare?"

Pulling back, I met his eyes, filled with lust and tenderness, and need.

"I've never asked this of any other woman, but they've not turned me on as you do, and it's hurting."

"Show me?"

Pulling out, Jet knelt back, so I could see how the protection had become a tourniquet on him. It looked agonizing, making me feel bad for him.

"You're clean, right?"

Opening the drawer, Jet produced a pathology report from only this week. "I get tested once a year. Meeting you prompted me to get it done again."

Handing him back the report, I nodded my head. My heart caught in my chest as he gritted his teeth and started to remove the condom. The curse that left his mouth when it tore the moment that he touched it made me blush.

Appraising me, Jet grabbed his naked engorgement as it pulsed and seeped. "We can stop."

Shaking my head, I offered him my trembling hand. Taking it, Jet gave it a squeeze and laid down on the bed, encouraging me to ride him again. As I sank down on him, the utter relief on his face settled my anxiety. If it all went wrong, it was worth seeing that pleasure radiate over his handsome features.

Rocking over him, I bit my lip as the euphoria grew inside me. Palming my breasts, Jet then thumbed my clit. Without warning, I was reaching the precipice. Crying out, Jet jerked hard inside me. His entire body was rigid as he spurted like a geyser. My eyes folded back in my head at the sensation, every pulse flicking against that profound pleasure point.

"Keep going," Jet encouraged as he recovered, his hands focusing on me, and on my pleasure.

It felt different now, better. As Jet crunched up and caught my nipple between his lips, I crashed over the edge and called my delight to whatever god was listening. Collapsing on Jet's chest, I panted for breath.

Lifting my gaze, I noticed Jet's eyes were blinking rapidly. "Are you okay?"

Jet turned his face to mine. "I don't think sex is ever going to be the same."

"First time bare?" Jet nodded. Happiness bloomed in my chest at the thought of being his first for something. "Okay."

"Okay?"

"You never have to use protection again with me. Just as long as you do with anyone else."

Jet's brows bunched. "Anyone else? Why would I want to be with anyone else when I can be with you like this? That makes no sense." Wrapping me in his arms, Jet kissed the top of my head. "What if the pill doesn't work?"

"You get to tell your parents." Lifting my face, so Jet could see me smiling, I found his eyes were intent and focused. "Jet?"

"I want to do it again." Rolling us, Jet showed me the true meaning of a quick recovery.

JET LOOKED peaceful in the early morning light. Hating the idea of leaving him, I watched him for a few more minutes. Sadly, I had a morning routine, and despite my progress these last forty-eight hours, I couldn't let this one go yet.

Slipping from his bed, I quickly dressed and wrote him a note, leaving it beside his bed so he couldn't miss it. Carrying my shoes, I jogged down the street. I'd never done the walk of shame, and frankly, the tightness down below was too good to be ashamed. Hell, I couldn't stop smiling long enough to even try feeling bad about last night.

Letting myself in at home, I changed and went out for my regular run. When I reached the police station, Joseph was out front drinking his coffee. He raised a brow and looked at his watch.

The smile couldn't be held back. "Late night."

One of Joseph's brows went up in surprise, and a smile tempted the side of his mouth. With a wave, I headed home.

"When are you seeing him again?" Dad asked over breakfast.

"Today. He's my date for the work event at lunch."

"I'd like to meet him."

"Okay."

Yes, having Jet meet my father might seem too soon, but for my father, my spending the night with a guy probably meant it was overdue. Truthfully, I was optimistic about the potential we could be something long term. Either way, the ease of my agreement made my Dad happy.

Except, by the time I was ready to go, and Jet was ringing the doorbell, Dad was on the phone fighting with Penelope about being late to pick up the boys.

"No, send it in writing or get your ass over here now," Dad demanded and hung up.

Standing at the kitchen counter, I waited. Already I'd let Jet through the gate, but I was waiting for Dad before I opened the front door. The fights with Penelope never lasted long. Dad always put the 'call my lawyer' foot down and hung up when she started.

"Ah, did you still want to meet-"

"Not now." Dad cut me off, running his hand over his face. Jolting a little at his anger, I turned to leave. "Rain, you look lovely. I hope you have a good time."

Nodding, I went out to open the door. Jet stood waiting, reading an email on his phone. "Everything okay?"

"Stepmother dramas."

Frowning, I closed the door with a huff then Jet offered me his hand. When I took it, he pulled me close, making direct eye contact as he lowered his face. "I missed you when I woke up. Next time, wake me, and I'll come for the run with you."

"I can't. That run, it's therapy for me. It took me two years to be able to do it by myself and not freak out about being alone. I'm not ready to give it up or change it yet."

Assessing my words and my eyes, Jet sighed. "Okay, but still wake me up before you leave in the future. It's disorienting to go to sleep with you near and wake up alone wondering if it was all the best dream."

"Well, I'm still feeling you too much to ever believe it was just a dream."

Eyes dilating, Jet socked me with a toe-curling kiss that left me wanting more. "How long until we can be alone?"

Licking my lips, I checked my watch and pouted. "Four hours."

Jet huffed. "I need to wind forward time."

"I couldn't agree more."

❖

Chapter Sixteen
HOMECOMING

"Is that mine or yours?" I asked sleepily.

Jet lifted his head to see his phone sitting quietly on his bedside table. "Yours. Where is it, I'll get it." Kissing my head, Jet gently removed me from his chest to find my phone. "It's Aub."

When I groaned, Jet smirked and put my phone on his bedside table. "He must be on his way home from the airport." Sliding back into bed, his hands caressing me, Jet nipped my neck.

"Jet," I gasped as he fondled my breast. "I should go. I need to talk to Aubrey."

"Stay. We'll talk to him together. I'll look at that contract you signed and find a loophole that gets you out of it without Aubrey losing everything."

"And if you can't?"

"We'll find a way." Kissing me hard and deep, Jet sank his hand into the gully of my hips.

"Jet, darling, are you home?" His mother called right before she opened his door. Jet and I pulled apart; Veronica Landy blinking at us, all of us in shock.

Making sure the sheet still covered us both, Jet held me to prevent me from jumping out of bed. "Mum, the door."

"Rain, sweetheart. I didn't know you were here. Why don't you both come downstairs for a coffee once you have clothes on." Forcing a smile, Veronica stepped back and closed the door.

"Crap!" Grabbing my phone from the bedside table, my hands were shaking so hard I couldn't even put in my pin code correctly.

"What are you doing?"

"Calling your brother to warn him."

Taking my phone out of my hands, Jet palmed my cheek. "Calm down, she's not going to eat you. Let's get dressed, then we'll go downstairs and see what she has to say about us. We can go from there." Jumping out of bed, Jet headed for his shower.

When I didn't immediately follow, Jet came back and took my hand, squeezing it gently. "I'll protect you, Rain. Come on, you shower first."

Rushing through washing and dressing, I was pacing Jet's room while he dried and pulled his clothes on. "Jet, this isn't a good idea. Aubrey should be here."

"Let's deal with my parents first, and we can talk to Aubrey after. I'm not going to hang him out to dry. He's my brother, and I love him. I'll protect you both." Kissing my forehead, calm as can be, Jet opened his door.

We were approaching the kitchen when his parent's voices traveled out to us. "Do you think that's the case?" Veronica asked, intrigued.

"It would make sense. Genetically Jet's children and Aubrey will be related, so no one would question it. My concern is if Aubrey set this up with Jet's consent or not."

"Please! Rain is frigid as snow. Aubrey and Jet would have to agree to it and plie her with alcohol for this to happen."

"She has every reason to be like she is, Ronnie, you know that," Rae scolded.

"The poor thing. After everything, she went through, and everything Aubrey has already dragged her into, to do this."

"Let's not jump to conclusions, Ronnie. Let's hear them out first."

I didn't want to go into the kitchen now. Jet saw it and squeezed my hand. "It's okay, I'm right here with you." Encouraging me forward, we entered the kitchen.

"Rain, Veronica told me you were here, how did the luncheon go today?"

Grateful to talk about work, I relaxed a touch. Rae was always the easy one to be around. "Ah, good. We secured the account for their new building in Pyrmont."

"Excellent. Well, I think you will have more than earned your Christmas bonus this year, but then, you always do. She's harder working than your brother."

"So, you've told me." Smiling, Jet pulled out a chair for me. Waiting for him to walk away before I would sit down, Jet moved to his own chair. "How was the cruise?"

Sitting down, I winced a little with tenderness. Hard kitchen chairs and freshly bruised girl bits were not really compatible. "Can I help with anything, Mrs. Landy?"

"It's all ready, Rain. Just take it easy." She served coffee and baklava. Then they sat there discussing the cruise and smiling like she hadn't just caught me in bed with her eldest son.

Not that I expected them to call me a hussy or something horrible and tell Jet I wasn't worthy. The Landy's always treated me much like they would a daughter if they had one, but I expected them to say something. I couldn't eat the lovely food or even drink the coffee my stomach was so tied up in knots. And Veronica made damn good coffee.

"I think Rain is going to pass out if you don't address the elephant in the room much longer, mum," Jet instigated the conversation.

Setting her cup down, Veronica glared at her son the way a mother did when he pushed her into something. "Okay. Has this been happening long?"

"No."

Frowning, Rae assessed his son. "Is it just a once-off like your others?"

"No."

"So, it will happen again?" Veronica checked.

"Yes." Jet could give short and sweet an entirely new meaning.

Veronica looked to her husband then back to her son. "Jet, you know she's engaged to Aub, right?"

At this, Jet laughed. "Mum, Aubrey is gay. He likes men and cock. I'm the pussy eater in the family."

"Jet!" His mother blushed, taking a second to cross herself. "That's not entirely true. Rain and Aub have been lovers since teenage years."

"I'm aware he's regularly gotten her drunk and taken advantage of her. That doesn't make her his lover. Sharing the room next door, I've heard him with his lover's regularly, and all are men, not women."

Veronica looked to Rae disgusted.

Taking the cue, Rae answered on his wife's behalf. "That may be the case, but they are engaged."

"Only because you forced a susceptible teenage girl into it." His parent's eyes widened. "Yes, I'm aware of the contract, and I'd actually like to see it because I'm pretty sure a sixteen-year-old girl under the influence of drugs and alcohol could not be held to it."

"She was sober. Your mother made sure of it. And your brother was very aware of what he was signing."

"Again, neither of them legal adults."

Veronica's mouth fell open. "Is that what this is? Aubrey traded her to get him out of the contract?"

"No!" Jet and I rejected together. Jet squeezed my hand. "I want Rain out of the contract because what you are asking of her is unfair. She can't let Aubrey touch her without being so far gone she can't tell which end is up."

"That's how she is," Rae sympathized.

"Not with me. Not once has she been drunk with me because she wants to be with me, not Aubrey. You are punishing her for him abusing her trust years ago. Worse still, you've encouraged him to keep doing it."

Rae sat back, shocked, and Veronica refused to meet her son's eyes. "She's not all innocent, Jet. Are you, Rain?" Avoiding her gaze, I looked away from everyone. Veronica shook her head. "No, I don't care if you two have it off, that is none of my business, but Aubrey is not entirely gay, and they will marry and give us grandchildren. I don't care if you and Aubrey take turns knocking her up or you end it the moment you find another woman you want. She will marry your brother."

"Mum, you're unreasonable. Everyone knows Aubrey is

gay. He hasn't hidden it. Everyone will know this is a sham marriage."

Getting up from the table, Veronica started tidying up the afternoon tea. "We've discussed this enough. I was hoping you, and your brother worked something out about getting Rain pregnant, I never expected you to try and swindle us, Rain."

"I haven't. I've never had any say in this. I agreed to protect Aubrey, and because I never planned to live long enough for this to happen."

"Well, you did! You murdered my grandchild, and you survived your attempt to end your own life. You can pay for your sins with my hell condemned son, just like you committed them."

"Ronnie!" Rae scolded as I burst into tears. "You promised never to bring it up."

"Grandchild?" Sitting back confused, Jet turned to me for an explanation.

Face fierce, Veronica slammed her chair under the table. "Well, she promised to marry Aubrey, and she's trying to get out of it. I've had enough." Turning to me, Veronica glared daggers at me. "Set a date for the wedding, Rain, and you and Jet are done." Her rage turned on her eldest. "If you try and dissolve this contract, Jet, or interfere in this arrangement, it will be you I disinherit instead."

"Ronnie, stop!"

Standing up, Jet slammed his hands on the table. "What grandchild?!"

The room went silent. Noise by the door revealed Aubrey watching the entire scene unfold. "I told you she was off-limits. I told you to leave her alone. But no, you had to chase after her."

Rage straining his voice and whitening his knuckles, Jet snarled at his brother. "What child are they talking about?"

No one bothered talking to me now, I was a blubbering mess.

"My child! I got Rain high, I had sex with her, and I got her pregnant. Then I got her high and convinced her to have an abortion."

While Jet stood there shocked, Aubrey guided me out of the chair and to the door. "Happy now, Jet? You know all my darkest secrets. Now, stay the fuck away from Rain and stop fucking up my life."

"And who's going to stop you messing up hers?"

"I already did that ten years ago."

Placing a restraining hand to his eldest son's shoulder, Rae stopped Jet from going at Aubrey. "Let them go, Jet. You can't break the bond they have."

Walking me out to his car, Aubrey cuddled me to him. "I'm sorry, Rain. Jesus, I'm so sorry."

Tucking my knees up to my chest while Aubrey drove me home, I hated myself all over again. This whole scene reminiscent of when Aubrey brought me back in a taxi after the clinic ten years ago.

Pressing the gate buzzer, Aubrey waited for my dad to answer. "Judge, Rain's falling apart."

The gate opened for Aubrey. Once the car parked, Dad was opening the passenger door and helping me out. "What happened? I thought she was on a date?"

"I don't know where she was. Where I found her was at my place trying to cancel the contract. Mum brought up the abortion, and Rain lost it after that."

Cursing under his breath, Dad, held me tight. "Go home, Aubrey."

"Judge, I didn't do this. Jet brought this shit on."

"Jet!?" Turning back to Aubrey, Dad held me to his front. I wanted to crumble and turn to dust.

"That's who she's been seeing. He was determined to seduce her even after I warned him off."

Shaking my head, I looked up at my dad, his face blurry through the cascade of tears. "It wasn't like that."

Growling, Dad glared at Aubrey. "What is it with you Landy's? Get the hell out, Aubrey. Tell your mother she can foot the bill for the next few weeks of house calls." Dad started moving me towards the door.

"No!" Shoving away from him, I walked towards Aubrey raging that his actions years ago just destroyed the first true happiness I'd experienced. He saw it coming but didn't even try to block my fist. Aubrey went down, blood gushing from his nose. Tears falling down my cheeks. "I hate you."

Cursing on the ground, Aubrey glared up at me. "Took you long enough." Watching him, my anger for those weeks raging through me, I watched his eyes fill with tears as he wiped the blood gushing from his nose. "I hate me too. I've spent a decade trying to make it up to you, but every time it matters, I just make it worse."

Turning my back, I walked to where my dad stood, his eyebrows in his hairline.

"Thank your mother for afternoon tea. I apologize in advance for declining any immediate future invites." Storming inside, I went downstairs to the room I'd always slept in with Aubrey. Lifting the painting off the wall, I traced Aubrey's body and how it fused with mine. Closing my eyes, I let the rage inside of me out. Smashing the painting against the bed head, wall, and anything that could destroy that memory.

"Shit!" Running into the room, Dad snatched the painting from my hands. Turning on the bed, I yanked the sheets from it. "Rain, honey?" As I started smashing and breaking everything in the room, Dad tried to calm me down, but he didn't attempt to grab me or hold me.

Zephyr stepped into the doorway. "What's going on?"

"Get out!" Dad warned as I hurtled the last lamp.

It smashed against the wall where Zephyr was standing. Luckily, he'd was smart enough to pull the door shut as he stepped out.

Now that I was still, Dad touched my arm, giving it a gentle squeeze. "Rain?"

Staring at the dint in the wall I'd made with the lamp, all I could think was that could have been my brother's head. "Harry."

My dad tensed up. "What about him?"

Collapsing on the floor, I wanted to vomit my heart out of my chest. "Aubrey was Harry. I let him do what he did because I wanted to forgive Harry."

Chapter Seventeen

DISASSOCIATE

IT WAS NEARLY NINE WHEN THE DOORBELL RANG. SLINKING OUT of my room to the landing, the video monitor showed Jet standing at the gate, hand messing his hair repeatedly. I didn't answer. I couldn't. What must he think of me?

Coming out of his study, Dad answered the bell. "Yes?"

"Ah, Mr. Noir, I'm Jet, Aubrey's brother." Stumbling over my Dad answering, Jet stood a bit straighter. "Rain left her things at our house earlier, and I thought she might want them for work tomorrow. Especially her phone and travel card."

Descending the stairs, I sat halfway down them, body weary and exhausted. When Dad looked up at me, I shook my head, hugging myself. It'd been hours since I tore up the room downstairs. After throwing up for an hour straight, Dad helped me to my bedroom, told me to rest and then he called Dr. Lind.

Pressing the release on the gate, Dad opened the door enough to be seen, but nothing past him. "Judge May? Rain's your daughter?"

"She goes by her mother's maiden name now, for safety."

"Jesus, your family, that was her? That's even worse than I thought."

Shoulders dropping, my father hung his head. "You have no idea. Thank you for bringing her stuff back."

"Could I speak to her?"

"Not tonight. Rain hasn't been well all afternoon. She needs her rest and time away from your family."

"Judge May, can you tell Rain that knowing the truth hasn't changed how I feel."

Covering my mouth to stop the sob creeping up my throat, I shook my head, tears running free.

"What truth do you think you know, Jet?"

"About the baby and the abortion, about why Aubrey feels guilty."

Dad's shoulders tensed. Stepping outside, Dad pulled the door across, but not all the way. "Really? You think you know the truth, do you? I bet it's your brother's truth because Rain can't even think of that day without hating herself."

"Then tell me her truth. Why did she have the abortion if she regrets it so much?"

"Because your brother got her high and convinced her to go with him for what he thought was the best way forward. Rain didn't realize what happened until afterward, and do you know what occurred when she realized? Did your brother tell you what she did after he brought her home and left her alone?"

There was a moment of pause. "No."

Lowering his voice, my father's words trembled over the ugly truth. "She killed herself, Jet. Rain overdosed on the anti-depressants her psychiatrist prescribed and walked down the park. If one of the neighbors hadn't been walking her dog and seen Rain fall off the swing unconscious, I would have lost her too. That is why your brother feels guilty, Jet. Not because he seduced her, or got her pregnant, or because he manipulated her into an abortion. He feels guilty for being the one that finally pushed her past her limit and ultimately killing her."

"I'm not defending Aub, but they were sixteen, traumatized, and showing obvious signs of barely coping after what happened. Why weren't they supervised better?"

With a loud sigh, Dad sounded dejected. "I thought she was. I married a woman I thought would care for her and help me cope with my loss. I trusted Penelope to be there when I couldn't be. Instead, she was busy stealing my used condoms and getting herself knocked up." Pushing the door open just enough to step through, my father turned back to Jet. "Do you love Rain, or was she fun?"

"She wasn't fun."

"Then winning her over isn't what you need to do. It's convincing your family. Sort them out before you mess with mine again. Goodnight, Jet." Stepping back inside, Dad shut the door, and then he turned to face me. "It's not too late if you need to say anything to him."

Shaking my head, I wiped my face dry. Standing up, I took my bag from my father, kissed him on the cheek, and went upstairs. Taking out my phone, I had a missed call and message from Jet.

Jet: *I wish you'd told me all of it. I would have told you it didn't matter.*

Leaving the message there, I opened my phone book, holding myself together until Barbara answered. "Hey. You so need to spill about you and Jet at lunch tomorrow."

"Nothing to tell. We're just friends. Look, I won't be in this week, I've caught some nasty stomach virus. Can you move any appointments on to Rae or Aubrey's books? Email me any specs I need to look at, and I'll work on them when I can."

"Sure. Let me know if you need anything."

"I will, thanks."

Hanging up, I turned my phone off and shoved it into my bedside table. Gazing at the photo of my dad, my brothers, and I at our summer beach house from years ago, I sighed and curled up in a ball in bed. We went to my mother's beach house every Christmas, which was still two months away. Usually, I dreaded leaving my secure safe place; my mother's home was my only other sanctuary. Right now, Christmas and our summer escape couldn't come fast enough.

"I DON'T KNOW where to start."

Assessing me, Doctor Lind sipped from her coffee early Monday morning. "I hear you broke Aubrey's nose."

"I lost control."

"Did it feel good?"

"Yes, but then I couldn't hold it in. I wanted to kick him over and over again, and scream, and shout at him for hurting me. I took it out on the room instead."

"You wrecked the painting. Your dad told me you nearly took one of the twins' head off, that's what brought you back?"

"I hate everything about the room, everything that we've done in there. I had to destroy it all. I would never have hurt the boys. I didn't even realize he was there until I'd let fly. I'm just glad he has quick reflexes."

"Your dad said you mentioned Harry when you calmed down. Can we talk about what you said?" Waiting for me to nod hesitantly, Dr. Lind leaned forward a little. "You said you let Aubrey do what he did because you wanted to forgive Harry."

Regretting those words, I hung my head, tears pouring down my cheeks and splashing onto the floral top I wore. "I shouldn't have said that, not to Dad. He must be so confused."

Pressing her lips together, Dr. Lind tilted her head. "Rain, do you think no one knows?"

Unsure how to answer that, I blinked through my tears at her. Moving to her desk, she collected my file from beside her computer.

"Your visits to me were court-appointed. The judge for your case set me the task of finding out what happened that night from the only witness left. I've never finalized my report because you couldn't talk about what happened in the lounge room, so the police used the physical evidence to conclude." Sitting down with my file, Dr. Lind considered me. "Your dad has seen the forensics in this file, Rain. He helped the police piece it together, and they hope they got it right."

Scared of what conclusion they came to, and curious just the same, I hesitated. "What does it say?"

Eyeing me, Dr. Lind opened it. "I'm going to refer to people as victim or attacker. This will help keep it distant for you. I don't want you to imagine faces or put names to any memories that appear. Approach those memories like a horror movie you are watching on the television. Don't give the people of the show, names or faces, okay?"

Swallowing as I imagined an old black and white version of psycho, I nodded.

"The autopsy of Victim one, female, mid-thirties. The victim's body showed evidence of repeated beatings, multiple forced entry to the anus with sizeable tears that led to hemorrhage. Multiple vaginal penetrations, some by the forced entry of a male penis, and others with a large and pointed inanimate object. Evidence of severe internal damage and hemorrhage obtained perimortem. Samples from the rape kit showed four different sperm samples. DNA testing matched those samples to the three attackers and a non-related male victim. Cause of death was multiple gunshot wounds to the chest." Stopping, Dr. Lind met my eyes.

My breathing was shallow, and my hands were clenching the armrests. Flashes of three men brutalizing a woman like a strobe light behind my eyes, all of it in black and white.

"Can you do this, Rain?"

Squeezing my eyes shut, the tears flowed as I nodded my head.

"The police believe that multiple attackers brutalized the victim at once for hours on end. Forensic testing found Gunpowder residue on her right hand."

A gun went off in the movie, making me jerk in my seat and choke on a sob. The television showed the woman's hand holding it, and the tattooed male hand holding her wrist to direct her.

"Victim two, male, eighteen. Victim showed evidence of having sexual intercourse with two females before his death. DNA found around his genitals matched victim one, non-relative, and victim three, twenty-five percent genetic match. So, cousin or half-sibling. Evidence of forced anal penetration, but relatively minor physical injury in comparison to the other victims. Rape kit determined one incomplete sperm sample that matched an attacker. Cause of death was a single gunshot wound to the head."

Sitting back, Dr. Lind assessed me. "Did you want me to keep going?"

Maybe it was the river of sorrow that was flooding my face and soaking my top or the horrible whimpering noises that sounded like a scared puppy that made her worry. From her perspective, it would be like sitting in the room next door while someone watched a snuff film. She could only judge how bad it was by my reaction. Swiping at the deluge on my cheeks, I nodded my head.

"Victim three, female, fourteen. Forensic evidence shows signs of multiple beatings, more severe external damage than that of other victims. Tears around and inside anus suggestive of multiple forced anal penetrations resulting in internal hemorrhage. No forced vaginal penetration. Rape kit revealed four different samples. DNA matched to the three attackers, and a twenty-five percent genetic match consistent with victim two. Injuries. Gunshot wound to the abdomen, multiple fractured ribs, two fractured vertebrae, fractured coccyx, fractured sacrum, fractured cheekbone and eye socket, dislocated shoulder-"

"You can stop now." Every impact or causation of those injuries showing on my black and white television.

"Your mother was your father's second wife. Harry belonged to his first and was your half-brother, right?"

"Yes."

"Did you see the movie, Rain? Can you tell me what happened?"

Covering my mouth with my hand, I bawled.

Waiting until my sobs had settled to crying, Dr. Lind picked up her pen. "Let's start with victim two, the man. Did he willingly violate victim one?"

"No, they put a gun to his head, made him watch one of them do it first, then made him."

"And the girl?"

It became harder to breathe as the movie played out in black and white. Thank god it wasn't in color with all the blood. "He refused, even when they threatened to kill him. So, they beat her, punched and kicked her until she begged him to do what they said, anything to stop the beatings. She could hear her bones breaking under their boots. She didn't want to die. Not then, but she would, every minute after, she would wish she'd let them beat her to death instead."

Writing notes, Dr. Lind kept her face neutral. "How did the male, victim two die? Did they rape him next?"

"At the same time." It was just a very horrible movie; I could talk about a film. "He wasn't doing it hard enough, so one of the men took him from behind to force him to do it properly. He pleaded forgiveness from her the entire time. Afterward, they gave the gun to the woman, pointed it at the boy, and told her to take her revenge for what he did to her daughter. She wouldn't do it, so they started beating the girl again until she pulled the trigger."

"Okay, Rain. Turn the movie off for me."

"They made the girl watch what they did to the other woman; always two with her while the third used the girl." The movie kept playing, every scene getting worse as I watched it. "One of them found a trophy with my dad's name on it-"

Face growing pale, Dr. Lind put her notes aside and leaned forward to try and touch my hand. "Turn it off, Rain. That's enough for today."

Shrugging her off, I shook my head. "No, it's not! They were tired, needing to recover, so they started talking about ways to fill in the time. One didn't like what the other two wanted to do, so he told them he was going to have some private fun with the girl. He dragged her out of the room by her feet, agony tearing her apart. She screamed for her mum, but her mum screamed for them as they started using the trophy. Then it was the hall and the trail of blood she left on the floor while the storm raged outside."

Panting for breath, I stopped. Mentally, I reached out and turned off the television. "We've seen the rest of that too many times before." Waiting to ensure the movie was off, I opened my eyes to meet Dr. Lind's. "I think I'm going to need to vomit now." Running into the bathroom, I puked until my stomach was empty, and my head felt like it was going to explode.

"Martha, can you book me a session today. I'm going to need it." Coming into the bathroom, Dr. Lind wet a washer then squatted down next to me and placed it to my forehead before flushing the toilet. "Okay, Rain. We never have to watch that movie or talk about it again, unless you want to talk about it."

Fresh tears ran free. "I begged for it, and then I hated Harry for it. He can't ever forgive me, and I can't hate him. Harry would have chosen death rather than hurt me; he loved me that much. He could have died without that on his soul, and I made it worse for him."

"Rain, you did what every human on earth would do. You

fought for your life, and you did what you needed to do to survive."

"As I said; I've wished every minute since not to."

Chapter Eighteen
LACK OF CREATIVITY

"Hey, welcome back," Aubrey stopped at the door brandishing our usual morning coffees. Across the bridge of his nose, sat a small bandage. "Is it safe?" "

"I wouldn't be here if it wasn't." Sitting back from the computer, I sighed. After a week seeing Dr. Lind daily, we'd covered my existing issues and then I told her all about Jet. Not his name, just about him, how much progress I made in that weekend with him. Dr. Lind hadn't cheered, but only because Sunday undid everything.

Shutting the door, Aubrey crossed my office in two strides, placing my coffee on the table. "I've told my parents they shouldn't expect you to uphold the agreement."

"Are they still going to disown you?"

"Probably. Jet said that would only last until mum kicks the bucket and he'd support me however I needed. I gave him a copy of the contract. He ripped it apart in seconds." Aubrey took a drink of his coffee. "I went back to my therapist last week. I've come to the understanding that we've held each other in stasis with our behavior. That neither of us have moved forward, and we won't until we let each other out of this shit."

"Strangely, Dr. Lind feels the same." Picking up the coffee, I took a sip.

Chuckling, Aubrey shook his head. "Of course, she does. I wanted you to know that I love you. I don't want to lose you as a friend, but I think, for a short time, we need to be friends here, at work, the occasional lunch or after work drink, but that's it."

"So, what we do when you have a boyfriend?"

Lifting a brow, lips thin, Aubrey met my eyes. "Speaking of boyfriends. You and Jet? I hear it was a very sober weekend?"

My smile faded around the edges. Studying Aubrey, I noticed the flare of jealousy in his eyes.

Aubrey exhaled hard. "I've spent my life looking up to my brother, trying to be as good as him. He's so focused. Anything he puts his mind too he gets. You were the one thing I always had that he didn't. Then he didn't just find his own version of you, he took my you. For the first time in my life, I hate my brother."

My eyes filled with tears. "It sucks, doesn't it?"

Aubrey frowned in confusion.

Shaking my head, I waved my response away. "Don't hate Jet; he didn't steal me, he just sat down on the other side of me. You don't lose me by his being in my life. If anything, maybe you two will become close again."

Staring at his coffee, Aubrey sighed. "He kind of hates me right now too."

"No. He understands we were both messed up. We were young and we were trying to escape the pain and we did stupid things which made it worse. The thing is, we're not young anymore and we need to start making smart decisions for ourselves. I'm sorry if that puts you in a bad place, Aub, but marrying you would be another mistake."

"Because you want Jet?"

"Because you are gay. Whatever your attraction to me, we both know what caused it, and that isn't healthy for me. You know that."

Aubrey hung his head. "I wanted to help you move forward. It was never anything sinister, Rain. I swear, I never wanted to hurt you more."

"I know. I don't blame you."

We sat there staring at our coffees. Eventually, Aubrey stood up. "I should get some work done. Try and convince my father he can't do without me here."

After I watched him leave, I looked at my phone. Jet hadn't tried to contact me since he came to the house. Whether he was giving me time or took his mother's threat seriously, I didn't know. The truth was, I needed time to orientate myself and my future.

"THANKS EVERYBODY," Rae dismissed everyone from the meeting. "Rain, can you stay behind a moment?"

Blinking, I sat back down, and Aubrey hesitated to leave.

"It's fine, Aub. This is work related."

Aubrey's brows bunched, but he left, shutting the door after him. Rae moved to sit adjacent to me and sighed. "You have always been one of my most creative staff members, Rain, but you haven't offered any new ideas or suggestions since you came back from sick leave a month ago. You've not taken any new projects on your plate, even if Aubrey assigns you one, you reassign it within a day. Is there something I should know, something I can help with?"

Pressing my lips together, I considered how to answer his question. "My head still isn't right. I'm uninspired currently and I don't want to take on anything new and not be able to deliver."

Fidgeting with his pen, Rae exhaled. "Look, I know Veronica can be inflexible. I've been married to her for thirty-two years, so trust me, I know. She always wanted a daughter, and from the moment Aubrey brought you home she's adored you as if you were her own. She cried for days when..." Rae choked, "it happened. Then we were stuck watching you and Aubrey spiral out of control and to find out he was gay at the same time." Rae licked his lips. "It was too much for her. When your dad caught you two in bed, Veronica became convinced that the gay thing was a phase, a reaction to witnessing what happened to you. Then when you realized you were pregnant, Veronica was sure that forcing you two to marry and having that baby would be the cure you both needed." Rae shook his head. "She convinced me it would work. Don't ever tell Ronnie I said this, but not having that baby was what saved you, Rain, not the contract."

Tears falling from my eyes, I frowned. "How? I committed suicide. It was the straw that broke the camel's back."

Rae's eyes filled with tears. "Exactly. But from the moment you woke up in that hospital bed, you straightened yourself out. You stopped doing drugs, you controlled your drinking, you threw yourself back into your schoolwork and went from failing to the school dux. It was like dying drove you forward. I know you've lapsed here and there, that you've never again been that happy child who stole our hearts, but you lived, and you didn't let those bastards kill your spirit." Drying his eyes, Rae took a deep breath. "Ronnie and I admire you, Rain. I didn't agree to the contract to hide our son was gay. I knew long before he told us, and I loved him anyway. I agreed because I wanted you to be our daughter. I knew you and Aubrey were having sex a year before you got busted, it's not like you were quiet about it."

Eyes wide, my cheeks flushed with heat and embarrassment.

"I figured, if you two could make it work, for whatever reason you accepted that type of relationship with my son, I would support it." Taking out a hankie, Rae handed it to me. "We were wrong."

Standing up, Rae pushed the seat under the table before leaning on the back of it. "Moving back to the work issue. It's been a month since you lapsed, I need you back in the swing of things. You are due to hand over the last project on your docket on Friday, so get Aubrey to assign you Pyrmont. The client likes you and you have a flair for the softer elegance they are asking for."

My hands shaking, and my heart falling through the floor, I removed the folded bit of paper out of my notebook. It had been there for a week, waiting for me to make a decision. "Rae." Rising out of my chair, I held the paper out to him.

Turning back to me, Rae spied the letter and his face lit up. "Is that a sketch? Have you already been thinking about it?"

"It's my resignation." Rae's face fell. "I wasn't sure. I've been thinking hard about it. When I was growing up, I wanted to be a lawyer like my dad and mum. Then, with what happened, I was so lost, and Aubrey gave me direction, encouraged me to go with him into the family business. It made sense, then. Now, I'm not sure if this is what I want anymore." Rae wouldn't take the letter, so I put it on the table in front of him. "Thank you for taking me in. Being part of your family saved me too, but I need to find my own way, figure out what I want for my future now." Kissing his cheek, I walked to the door.

"I never thanked you," Rae mourned as he picked up the letter. "When you got yourself straight, you got Aubrey straight too. You two were good for each other when it mattered. Do what you need, but if you search the world and still can't find what you want, I'll always have a job for you here. No matter what, you're still family, Rain."

Giving him my first true smile in weeks, I walked out. I needed this, some time apart from everything. Aubrey was standing outside the door, tears in his eyes. "Are you sure?" I nodded. "Where will you go?"

"Up the coast for now, stay at the beach house until new year like always. Then I'll figure the rest out."

Stepping forward, Aubrey opened his arms. Moving into them, I gave him the biggest hug. "Anything you need, Rain. I'll always be here for you."

"I'm heading off," Barbara stuck her head in the door. "You going to be okay with your stuff?"

Placing a photo of Aubrey and I in the box, I smiled. "Yeah, my dad is coming to pick me up. Thanks for the surprise farewell." I'd been tentative about quitting, but the last week of finishing up assured me, that while terrifying, it was something that needed to happen.

"So, I'll see you in the new year for your final fitting. No skipping off to explore the world until you be my bridesmaid."

"I'll honor my commitments. Is Veronica still here?" Veronica came in for my farewell. She cried and told me she was sorry and that if I really like Jet, I should give him a shot. I think she was worried neither of her son's would get married and give her grandchildren now.

"Yes, but she just went into Rae's office and shut the door, so it might be better to leave quietly," Barbara chuckled. "I hope Ken and I are still that into each other when we are that old." With a wink, Barbara walked off.

Left wondering if the boys took after their, dad and that's why Veronica was a happy wife, I cursed and covered my eyes. "Oh, god! Don't imagine that." Scolding myself, I went back to packing.

As usual, I was the last one here on a Friday night. Well, except for the boss and his wife, which is why when things started getting good in his office, it was time to get going. It happened enough times before for me to know it was only going to get worse. My phone pinged with a text from my dad telling me he was about to pull up out front.

Hearing a door shut, I looked up from my phone in time to see Jet striding towards his father's office. Rushing forward, ready to warn him, I stopped at my door when his feet stopped. His head turned, so he could listen to the noise on the other side of the door, then he stepped back shocked.

Turning, Jet saw me. "Please, tell me that my mother is in that office?"

"She is, so you might want to come back later. I'm just leaving." Going back into my office, I piled my boxes and picked up my bag.

Following me, Jet visibly cringed as the noises next door got louder. "Here, I'll help." Placing his briefcase on top of the first box, he picked it up, leaving me the bottom one. "Rae told me you resigned, and why," Jet conversed as we walked out to the elevator. "It seems to me like you are trying to distance yourself from my family."

"Your family have been my family for a very long time. That won't stop. I just need to figure out what I want."

Stepping into the elevator, we both fell quiet.

As the floor levels neared the ground, Jet sighed. "Can I call you some time?"

"If you'd like to." The doors slid open, and I stepped off the elevator.

"I'd like to."

As we walked out, my dad pulled up and popped the boot. Opening it, Jet placed his box in beside my luggage bag, ensuring he didn't damage the blank canvases and moved my art supplies case further back before taking the one from my arms and squeezing it in.

Joining us, Dad grabbed Jet's bag for him before shutting the boot. "Jet. That was a shit session today."

"Those cases always are."

"Tell me about it."

Running a hand through his hair, Jet shook his head. "Do days like today make you miss criminal law?"

"I miss my wife and son more." He'd had to give up criminal law after the attack. A smart-ass lawyer used the very publicized attack to ask for my dad to be removed as the judge on his case due to potential bias against his client. It effectively ruled my dad out from any rape or murder cases.

"Shit, I'm sorry, that was..." Scrubbing his hand through his hair, Jet shook his head. "I need a drink."

Dad patted him on the shoulder. "Then let's go get one." Handing the car keys to me, Dad met my eyes. "Drive safe. Call me when you get there, and I want at least one text a day."

"Yes, dad." Rolling my eyes, I gave him a hug and kiss. "I'll be okay."

"How are you getting home," Jet queried my father his brows drawing together.

"This is Rain's car. She wanted to head off to our beach house straight from here, so I brought in her car today. I'll get a taxi home."

"You're going away? For how long?"

"Until after new year. Maybe longer." Stepping forward, I kissed the end of his jaw just in front of his ear. "You can still call me." Stepping back, I met his eyes, but I couldn't read his expression, whether he was angry, or confused, or just resigned. Either way, he would call, or he would consider me time well spent and move on. "Bye, Jet." Hurrying to the driver's door, I slipped into the car.

"Come on, Landy. She's got a long drive, and we've both had a long day."

Adjusting the seat and mirrors for me, I locked the doors while Jet and my father walked off down the street. Putting the car in drive, I started my three-hour drive north.

❖

Chapter Nineteen
RECOVERY

SPRAYING THE SEALANT OVER THE FINISHED CANVAS TO SEAL IT, I left it to dry. My phone rang, and I smiled at Aubrey's picture. "Hey?"

"So, I was in our favorite coffee shop this morning, getting the usual, and this hunk of gorgeous in a suit came in and was giving me the eye."

"How is Jet?"

Huffing into the speaker, Aubrey grumbled. "Not that hunk. This one is blond with puppy dog eyes and thighs. Jesus, the thighs on this guy."

"Did you get his number?" I missed our conversations like this.

"Pfft! I gave him mine. He can do the chasing this time."

"Has he called you already?"

"Asked what I was doing tonight. I told him I was busy. I didn't want to come off desperate. Suggested Sunday instead."

Smiling, I moved outside to the pool. "Well, I'm glad you are getting back on the horse."

"We both know who will be getting on the horse, and it'll be Jim."

Dropping my skirt to the ground, I stepped into the heated water, walking across to the infinity edge which looked out over the beach. "Jim? That's a name to call out in the heat of the moment."

"You know I don't use names. Gets me in trouble."

"I know, but Jim? Jim, oh, Jim, give it to me, Jim, that's it, Jim, right there, oh, Jim, you're so big!"

"You know you're on speaker, right?"

"Say hi to your mother for me."

Laughing, Audrey paused. "Are you in the toilet? I can hear running water."

"Pool, by the edge. The beach is beautiful, but my pool is warmer, cleaner, and safer."

"I'm jealous. I should come up and visit you."

"Get stuffed. This is my retreat."

"What have you done to keep busy?"

"Painting, cooking, swimming, and running the beach every morning."

"So, the usual?"

"Basically."

"Are you going out at all?"

Huffing, I felt like I was talking to my dad now. "I've been down the street a few times. They have markets tomorrow, so I'll be going down for that." Aubrey hesitated. "I'm okay, Aub. I've had no triggers, and I'm relaxed."

"How about I come up for the weekend? You're going to go nuts by yourself."

"Joseph is coming up this weekend. His girls are visiting

their grandmother nearby. We're going to do some training, and he said he's bringing me a present."

"Is he staying with you?"

Yeah, that would never happen. As much as I trusted Joseph, having him in my house was bound to trigger an event. "No, just visiting on Saturday. He's staying with a friend, then will collect the girls Sunday and head home with them."

"How are they coping?"

"It's been a year since she died. They had just as long before that with her diagnosis. They miss her." Joseph's wife died from a brain tumor in October the year prior. I'd not spent much time with her or his family since I was work for him, but when he spoke of his family, it was apparent he loved them."

"Okay, well, I'll come up next weekend. We can go snorkeling around the rocks and have some fun. I miss hanging out with my best friend. It's been over two months."

"Sounds good. I'll see you then."

"I'll call you next week. Enjoy the swim."

Saying goodbye, I put my phone aside, then dove beneath the water and did as many laps as I could. The solitude was enjoyable, but it was healthy to have company on occasion. There was a park run on nearby each week. I'd gone last week and planned on it again tomorrow.

After swimming, I spent long enough in the sunlight to dry. Summer was in full swing, and that meant short spurts of the sun in the early morning and late afternoon, or I'd burn. Dressing in just my skirt over my swimmers, I moved back inside to start making dinner.

Sitting on the lounge, I was watching a movie when my

phone rang later that evening. Expecting it to be dad, my stomach fluttered when I saw Jet's smiling face. Pushing pause on the remote, my heart jumped in my throat. "Jet, hey."

"Hey. I've been trying to give you your space, but Friday nights are kind of boring without you."

Loving that he was thinking of me, I grinned and was glad he wasn't here to see how my cheeks flushed with heat. "There's a social dance on every Friday. Lots of single women looking for Gene Kelly."

Jet chuckled. "And have my toes stepped on? I'll pass. How's your week been?"

"Relaxing. You?"

"Busy. I could use a drink with a beautiful woman who happens to enjoy my company."

"Your brother is free."

"Is there static on the line? I said a beautiful woman."

"I know, but maybe you two should get the occasional drink together, hang out, and be brothers. You wanted that relationship back, but you need to do something for it to happen." The phone was quiet. "Jet?"

"I'm here. I just wish you were too. I'd like to kiss you right now."

Touching my fingers to my lips, remembering his kiss like a ghost haunting me, I closed my eyes. "That would be nice to do one day again."

"Can I call you later? Tonight, that is."

"I'm probably going to head to bed soon. Maybe tomorrow night."

Jet exhaled in frustration, the sound of it coming through the phone. "Sweet dreams, Rain."

"Night, Jet."

Hanging up, I looked at the television. With all interest in the movie lost, I turned it off and went to bed, thinking about Jet, his lips, the feel of his strong arms and back, and the way he touched me. I was smiling and relaxed by the time I fell asleep.

"Morning." Approaching the car to meet Joseph after letting him in the gate, I gave him a wave.

"Morning, I have someone for you to meet." Grinning, Joseph opened the back door, and a huge Alaskan malamute bounded out of the car. He dashed around the open space of the yard before coming over excitedly to greet me. "His name is Oscar."

Giving the friendly dog pats, I greeted him by name. Sitting beside me, Oscar leaned his head on my leg, nearly pushing me over, causing me to laugh. "He's adorable. Is he the girls?"

"Yours."

Blinking at Joseph, I felt myself gaping and wasn't quite sure I could stop myself. "Mine?"

"I should have got you a dog years ago, but you were a workaholic. Now, you have the time to spend with him."

"But why?"

"He will help you feel safe. He's fully trained, two years old, and good with kids. He will be good company for you when you are alone, and he'll happily go and play when you have company."

"You bought him for me?" Joseph was a policeman, a

widower, and a single father of two. He lived a modest life-style because he had no choice.

"No, he belonged to my friend I'm staying with this week-end. He's in the forces, and his wife has left him, so he has no one to take care of the dog. He's been trying to rehome him but hasn't found anyone he trusts to give him a good home. I mentioned I was visiting you today, and that Oscar was the sort of dog you needed. He agreed to let you meet, see if you struck a bond."

Glancing down with a grin, Joseph took out his phone. Looking down, I found Oscar lying across my feet. Joseph took a photo as I leaned down, and Oscar rolled over to show me his tummy. When I gave it a rub, Oscar lolled his tongue, and Joseph took another photo.

"My friend is here. I had him stay up the top of the drive until I spoke to you and made sure Oscar liked you. If you would like to adopt Oscar, he'll come in and train you how to command him."

Taking a backward step automatically, my attention went to Oscar, who instantly went on alert and scanned the surrounding area.

Changing his tone to soothe, Joseph made eye contact. "I'll stay with you the entire time, Rain. Plus, you could kick his ass without blinking."

"You're just saying that to make me feel better."

"True, but I train with him too. He's nowhere near as good as you. Jet could kick his ass too."

My stomach dropped at the mention of Jet. Taking a breath to center myself and focus, I took a step back and considered Oscar. "Is he house trained?"

"He is. He has a piddle pad for inside at night."

"If it doesn't work out?"

"Try tonight. If you don't feel comfortable, I'll pick him up in the morning. Otherwise, Blake will be gone for three months. You can consider it dog minding if you want?"

Liking the idea of having a dog, but also having the option of just minding him while his owner was away, I gave Joseph a nod. Taking out his phone, Joseph made the call to his friend while I opened the gate again. "Come on down."

Bounding to the gate, Oscar greeted his owner. Blake was the epitome of the military, but in boards shorts and a shirt. When he made a gesture, Oscar stopped and sat. Then Blake patted him and told him he was a good boy.

"Blake's military police. We went to high school together, but when I went police force, he went military. He did dog training with them and had a K-9 for ten years. When the dog died, he didn't get another for work. He bought Oscar to keep his wife company while he was away. She didn't take to him and preferred the company of a female tattooist she met."

Raising a brow, I bit my lip. "Oh! No kids?"

"He can't have any. Got injured at work in his first year. Lost the ability to shoot anything but blanks." Dropping his voice politely as Blake approached, Joseph met my eyes. "He's a good man. Just been dealt a few hard blows."

Nodding my head in understanding, we waited until Blake walked the rest of the way down the drive, Oscar obediently by his side. After Joseph made introductions, we went inside for coffee. Automatically, I filled a bowl of water for Oscar and found an old blanket for him to sit on by the back door where the sun was shining. Blake watched without saying anything.

Joseph was grinning while I settled Oscar, chatting to him,

before coming back to join them. "Rain has twin ten-year-old brothers. She's good with rambunctious kids."

Smiling, Blake watched Oscar lie out on the floor. "I can see that. If you put the blanket on the floor by your bed, he'll sleep there at night. I've got another dog bed in the car you can put here in the lounge and another for the yard. He likes to be outside during the day, and he has a lot of energy to burn. Luckily, you have a good size yard here."

"This isn't my permanent home. I own this place, but it's a holiday house. I rent it out throughout the year and my family, and I just come here over Christmas and new year."

Brows bunching, Blake looked to Joseph. Still smiling, Joseph shook his head. "Her place in the city still has a good-sized yard. It's half the size of this place, but there is a dog park nearby, and Rain runs over ten kilometers every day."

"What do you do for a living?"

"I'm an architect, but I just quit my job. Right now, I'm relaxing and painting. I make a small amount of money from my art, so I'll be okay for a while."

Hell, I'd been living at home all my life and working as an architect for four years. I'd saved my entire life. Add in the victims' compensation payment I'd received after the attack, and my mother's inheritance which my dad put away in trust for me, I could not work for years and still be okay. Especially with my limited expenditure. I contributed to expenses at home and took care of my own bills, but that was pretty much it.

"And you're single?"

"Yes."

"What happens if you meet a guy?"

"I don't like guys."

"A girl then?"

"Not into them either."

Brows pinching in the center, Blake titled his head. Joseph cleared his throat. "Ah, Rain has a best friend, but not a boyfriend, if that makes sense."

It didn't by the continued pinch of Blake's brows.

"I wouldn't get rid of a dog any more than I would my brothers for a guy. I can tell you exactly where any guy wanting that to happen could go."

Blake liked that answer better.

Lifting a brow, Joseph considered me. "Speaking of guys, have you heard from Jet?"

The brightness of the day seemed to dim with that question. "Yes."

"Are you two still trying to navigate the awkwardness of his family, or is it over for good?"

"I honestly don't know. I'm not ready to think too hard about it yet."

"Were you happy before his family found out?"

Meeting Joseph's eyes, I assessed his question. "He told you?"

"You talk to me during training. Why wouldn't he?"

Blinking, I guess I didn't see Jet as the chatty type. At least, not about relationship stuff. "Yes, I was happy, and I'd like to try again when the time is right if he's still interested. It's just weird and awkward since."

"You cheat on him?" Blake asked with enough accusation in his tone to let me know the hurt of his wife's betrayal was still raw.

My brows bunched at the question, but Joseph answered before I could. "No, Rain has trouble trusting men to let them close. Jet is her best friend's brother. When the rest of the family found out they were dating, they caused an issue."

"Why?"

Sighing, I stared at the tea in my hands. Conversations like this, I could use something stronger. "They expected me to marry my best friend, not his brother."

"Oh, that is awkward. Especially if the best friend thought that too."

Cringing, I took a big mouthful of tea.

"He did." Joseph stood up. "Shall we teach Rain how to talk to Oscar?"

I spent the morning learning to interact with my new best friend, and he with me. Then Blake chilled out down the beach while Joseph and I did some training. Oscar sat watching happily, but whenever Joseph got the upper hand and pinned me, setting off my anxiety, Oscar would growl in a warning and prepare to get off his outdoor dog bed. Joseph let me go quickly. It made me wish I'd had Oscar years ago.

By dinner time, I was giving Oscar commands with ease, and he was following them, so Blake felt safe leaving him there with me. "You don't think he'll get upset when you leave and miss you?"

"Sadly, while I trained him, I was rarely home after that. My wife never really connected with him. He chose you as his new owner when he cozied up to you, and you showed him affection." Smiling, Blake gave Oscar a pat goodbye. "Joseph will bring around the rest of the dog food for you tomorrow if you don't have any issues tonight. It was nice meeting you, Rain."

"You too, Blake."

"I'll see you in the morning. We can run the beach with Oscar and get some more training done."

Agreeing, I closed the gate after them. Gazing down at Oscar, I patted his head. "Do you want to run around some more out here or are you ready to come in for the night?" Rubbing my leg, Oscar wandered off.

Letting him go, I curled up on the lounge to read my book. As it got late, I went to the door and called Oscar. He came to me, stopped, waited for his pat and the signal to go inside. He trotted beside me to the lounge, then went into the kitchen to drink from his water bowl.

When Oscar came over and sniffed my toes, I giggled. Jet's face flashed on the screen as my phone started ringing. Picking it up, I answered at the same time, Oscar licked my toes. It tickled, making me laugh. "Oscar, stop. I don't like my toes being licked." Signaling he goes to his bed, I smiled as he did. "Sorry, Jet. Jet?" The line was dead.

Frowning, I tried calling him back, but it went to voice-mail. "Jet, it's Rain. I think we got cut off, sorry about that. I hope to hear from you again soon. I'll stay up a little while longer if you want to call again. Bye."

Hanging up, I wondered if his calling me was a mistake. I waited up for two hours, but he didn't call again. Not that night, or any other night over the next week. When Aubrey came to visit, he mentioned Jet in passing, that they were hanging out, and talking again. The rest of the time, we spoke about Oscar, his new guy, and work. Two more weeks passed, with no more calls from Jet.

❖

Chapter Twenty
MEET CUTE

"When can I expect you back?" I asked dad as I let Oscar out to patrol the yard for the morning.

"We'll drive up Sunday night once Penelope drops the twins off. I'm going to spend the week with Margaret at her place down the south coast." The courts closed on Friday for the Christmas break. My dad brought the boys up to stay the weekend but had to have them back to Penelope tonight.

"You don't think she will try to dump them early?"

"Of course, she will. But I'll be away, you are here, and the boys will be locked out. If she wants to drop them off before Sunday, she's going to have to drive all the way up here to do it." The war continued, albeit in a passive-aggressive way. Dad tilted his head. "You doing okay here by yourself?"

"I'm not by myself."

"True," Dad looked out as Oscar raced pass. "He's a big dog. He couldn't have gotten you a poodle?"

The look on my dad's face was funny enough, but the thought of a yappy poodle warding off intruders made me grin. "Because a poodle is going to make me feel safe."

"Does it work?"

"I'm sleeping better. I'm enjoying my runs more, and during the day, I don't feel the need to lock the back door all the time anymore."

"I take that as a yes. When I tell him to sit, he just looks at me."

"You're not his master."

"He won't hurt the boys?" Raising a brow sarcastically at the question, I watched my dad chuckle and shrug. The boys spent nearly all day yesterday outside playing with Oscar. "I'm just happy you are happy."

Thinking of Jet, my smile faltered. Dad saw it, but he didn't ask. He'd always been good at reading me, so he probably didn't need to delve into things. The boys came running out of their rooms and headed for the door.

"Stop. Breakfast before the dog!"

"Aww, Dad!" They moped their way into the kitchen area. Since I'd already made their breakfast, they cheered up, inhaled it, and bolted for the door.

Shaking his head, Dad chuckled. "I think they like the new family member."

"So, I'll see all three of you on Christmas Eve? But not in time for dinner?"

"Depends entirely on Penelope. Which is an oxymoron because she can't be relied on for anything." I couldn't argue with that.

After spending the morning hanging out, Dad headed home with the boys. Following them to the gate, Oscar looked a bit upset when they left. I don't think Blake had a hope in hell of getting him back now.

The next morning, I missed my morning run so Oscar and

I could help the ladies who ran the local shelter with a stall. I'd donated one of my paintings from the set waiting to be picked up by the gallery that sold my work. After that, we headed home, had a light lunch, and then I changed into my running gear before Oscar, and I headed off down the beach.

We were on the return when a man in suit pants and shirt was standing on the beach looking out at the water. His feet were bare in the sand, and it looked like he'd just arrived from the office, leaving what he didn't need elsewhere. As I got closer, I recognized the black hair, gorgeous looks, and those onyx eyes.

When I stopped in my tracks, Oscar stopped and sat immediately, gaining the attention of the man only a few meters in front of me. "Rain?" Jet's eyes went wide as he took me in before his face shut off all expression of emotion. "What are you doing here?"

Unsettled by his reaction to seeing me, I fidgeted with the fur on Oscar's head. "Um, I live here. You?"

Cursing beneath his breath, Jet pointed to one of the condo buildings. "I've rented a place here for the week to unwind. Is the dog yours or a friend's?"

Surprised by his cold demeanor, especially over the word 'friend,' I frowned. "Ah, mine. Joseph gave him to me after I came here." Wanting to know what I'd done to anger him, I swallowed back the sting when Jet just stood there glaring at me. "Well, enjoy your holiday. Come on, Oscar." Walking around Jet, I clicked my fingers, and Oscar followed.

"Oscar?" Brows bunching, Jet blinked at the dog and his eyebrows suddenly lifted. "The dog is Oscar?"

"Yes, why?"

Cursing again, Jet's face fell. "I'm an idiot!"

"Jet?" A woman called. "I'm ready."

We looked to where a woman in her late twenties stood at the gate where he was staying. She was blond, presentable, in a lovely blouse and skirt appropriate for the office, or a date with a hunk like Jet. My heart sank, my stomach crumpled, and I felt my heart rate nearly double.

"Just a moment, Evette. Look, Rain-"

"It was nice seeing you again, Jet." Turning for home, I broke straight back into a run to get as much distance as quickly as possible.

"Wait, Rain! I misunderstood."

I didn't stop. I couldn't. Tears were falling down my face, and I didn't want Jet to see that. I didn't care what he misunderstood. He came on holidays with another woman. There was nothing more that I needed to know.

Getting back to my place, I ran up the steps to the gate, punching in the code for it to open. "Go play, Oscar." Unclipping his harness, I made the gesture, and he ran off. Glancing back down the beach, Jet was only just walking up the sand to meet his date. Well, that was one less thing to stress over.

WHAT STARTED out as a landscape had turned dark and stormy, my emotions expressing themselves without conscious thought. The buzzer for the gate sounded. Oscar lifted his head from where he was sleeping under my easel. Frowning, I walked inside to the intercom where Jet was showed waiting at the gate.

Hesitating, I just stood there, staring at his image. He'd made himself quite clear this afternoon on the beach. I was done, fun had, and he'd already moved on to someone who probably was a lot more capable of making him happy.

Taking a breath, Jet pressed the buzzer again. Still, I didn't answer. Huffing, Jet pulled out his phone. Jumping, I clawed the phone out of my pocket to see that Jet was ringing me. Pressing my lips together to hold back the tears, I answered the phone. "Jet?"

"I owe you an apology. I jumped to conclusions. When you answered the phone giggling and saying a guy's name, I assumed you were moving on. It hurt, and I didn't want to wait around for you to tell me you weren't interested, or to string me along."

Frowning, trying to catch up with what he was saying, I blinked. "Wait, you thought Oscar was a boyfriend? Didn't Aubrey tell you I have a dog after he visited the following weekend?"

"Aubrey came and visited you?"

Rolling my eyes, I shook my head. "Jesus! I thought you two were talking?"

"We are. Just not about you?"

"Why not?"

"Because I hate what he did to you, and he hates that I'm in love with you too!"

Sucking in a breath, I tried to calm the swarm of butterflies in my stomach.

Jet exhaled hard. "My brother and I love the same woman. For the sake of our friendship, we've agreed not to discuss you until the problem can be resolved."

Standing there, speechless, I focused on keeping my breathing calm.

"Rain, can I come in?"

"What about Evette?"

Jet's brows slanted together. "What about her? She attended the same funeral as me this morning, so she caught a ride and then I drove her to the local airstrip to catch a plane back to the city after lunch."

"So, you didn't bring her on holiday with you?"

Jet laughed. "God, no. Evette is my paralegal. A colleague of ours died of a heart attack a week ago and was from Newcastle. We drove up early this morning for the funeral. Since Evette's flight home wasn't until later, she came with me while I picked up the keys and checked into my place." Some people walked past and gave Jet a strange look. "Can I come in? Discuss this in person? It sounds like we've both jumped to conclusions."

Resigning, I pressed the button for the gate. He wasn't at the street entrance, but the beach. Hanging up the phone, I walked out to greet him. Oscar was already waiting between the gate and the patio beside the pool.

Stopping on the top step, Jet eyed Oscar. "Um, is he going to kill me?"

"Oscar," he turned his head to me, "he's okay." Pressing my hand down by my side with the palm parallel to the floor, I indicated he could relax. Stepping closer to Jet for a moment, Oscar caught his scent and then went to sit on his dog bed in the shade.

Coming forward, Jet removed a bouquet of flowers from behind his back. "I'm sorry, Rain. I jumped to conclusions."

Taking the flowers, I was unsure of what to do. No one ever brought flowers before. "Come in, I'll make you a drink." Stepping inside, Jet took in the open plan, the gas fireplace, and the large entertaining area while I found a vase for the flowers.

"Your dad owns this place?" Turning to admire the view, Jet's eyebrows lifted towards his hairline.

"Legally, I do. It was my mum's. She owned it before they met. My dad put all her estate in trust for me when she died, so it became mine when I turned twenty-one."

"She was a junior partner in her law firm, wasn't she?"

Unable to remember the last time I was able to talk about my mum without crying, I swallowed down my emotion. "She was. She knocked the old cottage that was here down to build this with the main intention of entertaining. We rent it out for holiday stays and come here for summer break each year." Setting the flowers aside in the vase, I licked my lips. Jet looked gorgeous as usual. "Coffee, tea, soda?"

Moving towards me, Jet took a seat at the kitchen counter. "Whatever you are drinking will be fine."

Needing to keep calm, I started making tea.

"I remember the story about what happened to your family. It made news overseas too. Your father mentored me when I did work experience in high school. I never picked up on the family connection."

The bonus, after all these years, was that I was very adept at disconnecting myself from what happened. "We decided it was best to move and for me to take my mother's maiden name going forward. At that time, my father intended to resume his appointment in court."

"The papers said the attackers were seeking retribution for their brother who was killed in prison. Your father sent him there, so they blamed him." Minding his phrasing, Jet observed me like I was a victim in one of his cases taking the stand to give my testimony. "He was a rapist, and your father gave him the maximum sentence."

"They all were. All four brothers' gang-raped and killed an eighteen-year-old girl. The youngest brother who went to school with her got the longest sentence because he was the one to kill her. The others encouraged him, but he did it. They justified it by saying she was the boy's girlfriend and she'd dumped him for some other guy. The older brothers got ten years, the younger got fifteen without parole."

Taking a big drink of the tea, I moved back out to the covered outdoor entertaining area and my canvas. Jet followed. "My paints will dry out if I leave it much longer." Picking up the brush, I returned to the landscape. Taking a seat, Jet watched me.

"Did the men serve their full time?"

"No, they were out in five. Rapists very rarely ever get heavy jail time, let alone serve the full amount. Only a week after the other three were released, the youngest was gang-raped by a group of prisoners and beaten to death. You see, the girl he raped, her godfather was a prison guard. Just happened that a few weeks earlier, he got transferred to the same prison."

"I read the mother was arrested as well?"

Black paint slashed my canvas. "She was parked in the car outside the entire time. She drove them there to do that to us, to do that to another family, and when the cops came, she phoned and warned them, and they shot my mother six times in the chest."

Blood filled the painting; I smeared in into the storm clouds of rage, covered the moon in it, let it bleed into the city beneath. "I'll never understand how a mother could encourage her children to decimate another family like that. It turned out she'd driven her sons to the first rape too."

"She obviously had a screw loose. How long did she get in jail?"

"Life." Lightning carved through the chaos of the painting. "Sentenced for three years for accessory, she was murdered inside of a week of arriving in jail." White smudged into the area surrounding the lightning, blending it, brightening up that one strip of the painting. "Other mothers didn't take kindly to what she encouraged her sons to do." Stepping back from the art, I considered it. The landscape was emotional, dark, and violent. It would sell for the best price, just like all my pieces like this in the past. Done with it, I started cleaning up.

Jet stood up to consider the painting. "What were you planning to paint today?"

"Rainbows and unicorns." Watching the side of Jet's mouth tease a smile with my joke, I checked the time. "Want to go out for dinner?"

"I don't really know this area or the places to eat."

"I do."

❖

Chapter Twenty-One
A WET DATE

OSCAR RAN BESIDE MY CAR AS I DROVE DOWN THE DRIVEWAY. I'D driven to dinner, and for the record, Jet was a terrible passenger. He kept looking for the break on his side of the car and gripped the seat the entire time like I was driving like a madwoman. I wasn't. He just couldn't handle not being the one in control of the car. Allowing us to both relax, I'd let him drive home.

Putting the car in park, Jet smiled. "Thank you for dinner. I've never had a woman insist on paying before. It's rather odd and goes against everything my parents raised me to do on a date."

"Was it a date? Or a meal between friends?"

"Oh, it was a date. I brought you flowers, remember?"

Getting out of the car, I shut the door and patted Oscar who was waiting patiently. "Well, my dad taught me whoever invites you to a meal should pay, unless it's negotiated in advance. He also taught to pay Dutch on dates, so that guys don't expect you to put out after it."

Raising a brow as we met at the internal garage door, Jet

smirked. "So, since you paid for dinner, am I expected to put out?"

Cheeks heating, I diverted my gaze and stepped inside. "No, I'm not like that."

"I know. Um, Rain?"

When I turned around, Oscar was blocking the door.

Chuckling, Jet lifted a brow. "I think I'm being told goodnight."

"Oscar, Jet's alright." Gesturing to his bed, I gave Oscar a pat as he came to me first then went to his bed. He curled up, eyes on Jet as he shut the door and followed me to the kitchen. It made me smile how protective Oscar was about me. Going to the cupboard, I grabbed out some ingredients and crystal jars I'd seen that I could use as serving dishes for desserts. After making Jet and I a tea each, I started mixing. In my Kitchen Aid, I tossed Philly cheese, sugar, and poured a healthy splash of Bailey's.

"I thought you were trying to avoid alcohol?" Jet raised a brow. When I'd just ordered juice at dinner, Jet followed suit and queried the lack of wine or cocktails.

Crushing some of the Maria biscuits, I chewed my lip as I focused, then smiled over my shoulder at him. "I have been, but I never drink if I'm getting behind the wheel. I'm not driving after this, and your place is stumbling distance, so it's all good." Moving back to the island bench and facing Jet, I sprinkled the crushed biscuit to cover the base of the jars.

Smiling, Jet drank his tea quietly while I scooped the thick mixture into the glass pots and sprinkled salted caramel bits over it. Placing the jars in the fridge, I whipped cream and cooked up some caramel sauce. Taking the jars back out, I topped them with cream, caramel sauce, and then some of those Belgium chocolate shavings. Setting one in front of Jet, I kept one out for me and put the rest back in the fridge. "Bon Appetit."

The delicious look on Jet's face when the Bailey's cheesecake was in his mouth was worth the effort. His eyebrows lifted, and his eyes widened as he sucked it from the spoon.

"After I straightened myself out with a lot of support from my dad, cooking became my outlet. Whenever I triggered, had nightmares, or just couldn't sleep, I'd get up and bake. My dad would wake up to a three-course breakfast, plus baked goods all over the kitchen surface. I'd send him off to work with a basket of goodies to share."

"Were you always this good, or did you improve over the years?"

"I was never bad. Cooking is chemistry. Measuring out substances and mixing them together at the right temperature to get the desired outcome. I can read instructions and follow them, so I started there and got experimental as I got the hang of it."

Scraping his dish clean, Jet stood up and took it to the sink, rinsing it off before turning to face me. I'd just popped a spoonful of cheesecake in my mouth when Jet's eyes made me pause. I sucked the deliciousness off the spoon as Jet approached. His eyes were intent on mine.

"I don't think you can finish that." Gently, Jet took the spoon from my mouth and put it back in the jar.

"I can't?"

Shaking his head, his mouth moved to mine. Our lips touched, there was no hesitant kiss, no gentle pinch. Kissing me, Jet tasted me with determination. Pulling back, eyes glazed, Jet smiled wickedly. "No, you can't." Grinning, Jet moved away quickly.

Blinking, I stood there confused before I realized he'd taken off with my cheesecake.

Taking a considerable spoonful, Jet moaned. "Damn, this is good."

"Hey!" I chased after him.

Jet moved, staying out of my reach as I tried to get my dish back. We were both laughing, Jet quickly devouring what was left of my dessert.

"Villain!"

Laughing, Jet threw the door open out to the yard. I chased. He was through the pool gate a moment after that. Grinning, I ran and tackled him just as he took the last mouthful and placed the jar on the sun chair. Swearing as he lost balance, Jet fell into the water. Turning at the last minute, Jet pulled me in after him. I screamed. Surfacing, we looked at each other, then burst out laughing. Tugging me to him, Jet started kissing me, but I shoved him away. "You just stole my dessert; don't think you are getting me as a chaser."

Smirking, Jet kissed me again. This time, I didn't resist. Wanting to feel his skin, I started unbuttoning his shirt.

All of a sudden, Jet shoved me away, his eyes dark and dangerous. "Don't!"

Jolting at the venom in his voice, I stood there blinking. Remembering his boundaries, the heat of the moment evaporated. My hands were shaking, my heart racing in my chest. My anxiety kicked into overdrive as I struggled to stay above water. Looking away from the menacing glare he was giving me, I swallowed. "I'm sorry."

Jet just stood there watching, chest heaving, fists clenched and angry. There was no touching him again, not even to soothe. Not while he was holding himself like this. It would only make it worse. Swimming to the side of the pool, I lifted myself out. "You can let yourself out the beach gate. Just make sure it locks after you." Slipping out of my dress, I squeezed it out as I walked to the pool gate. Jet didn't try and stop me, and I didn't look back.

Stepping inside, I closed and locked the door, walking straight for the laundry. Oscar was out of his bed, alert and watchful. Dumping my dress in the sink, I grabbed my towel from my earlier swim and dried myself off. Face in my towel, I cursed myself. Jet was clear in his boundaries, but I didn't think what I did would set him off like that. When I crossed the line, I thought he'd brush my hands away. Hell, I'd gotten three buttons undone before he snapped tonight. He didn't even try to redirect my hands at any time.

When I emerged into the lounge room, I could see Jet by the pool removing his shoes and socks. Swiping a frustrated hand through his hair, he sloshed out of the pool yard towards the beach gate.

Rushing to the door, I unlocked it. "Jet. Here, take the towel."

Appraising me, Jet blinked. His eyes cleared as he watched my trembling hand hang the towel over the pool fence and step back to the safety of the doorway. Moving to where the towel was, Jet dropped his shoes and undressed, remaining only in his boxer shorts. After drying himself with the towel, he wrapped it around his waist. Glancing towards me at the door, Jet approached slowly. "I won't hurt you."

Trembling, I stood my ground as he came closer. Meeting my eyes pointedly, Jet ducked his head and kissed me. It was tender, gentle, and slow. When he pulled back, he took a step back. "That was my fault."

Determined it was mine, I started to shake my head.

"Wait, Rain. I was so caught up in touching and kissing you, that I didn't even realize. I wanted my clothes off. I wanted to be with you. I wanted you to rip my shirt off me if that got me inside you faster."

Shivering, I was afraid to move an inch in case it set him off again.

"I have never been out of control with a woman. You do that to me, Rain. I get so caught up in being with you, I let everything go. It scares me."

"I'm sorry."

Jet's eyes observed me. "You shouldn't be sorry for making me want you, but for both our sakes, I'm going home now."

"You don't have to go. I promise I'll behave."

Closing the distance, Jet pinched my lips with his. My breath escaped me when that's all he did. "Is slow and gentle my only option?" My eyes watered. Jet didn't get angry or even look disappointed. "Then I need to go because I can't do that tonight."

Stepping back, Jet collected his clothes. "Stay anyway." I didn't know what my mouth was saying. My brain screamed at me.

Jet considered me. "Rain-"

"We won't have sex. We shouldn't anyway. If we are going to make this more, we should be able to spend time together without it needing to be physical. We'll watch a movie while your clothes dry."

Peering at his drenched clothes, a smile pulled at the side of his mouth. "Is there more cheesecake on offer?"

Narrowing my eyes, I tilted my head. "You'll get a sore stomach."

"I don't care. It will be worth it."

"Fine. But keep away from mine, or I'll sic Oscar on you next time."

Chuckling, Jet came closer with his clothes in his arms. "I'll behave, I promise." His lips brushed across mine, then pinched once. "Are you going to be able to do the same?"

My stomach somersaulted, and I had to press my thighs together hard. "Are we still talking about cheesecake?"

"Of course."

Dropping my shoulders back in defiance, I jutted out my chin. "Then, of course. I don't need to steal cheesecake because I can always make myself more."

Jet's deep, baritone laugh made my thighs ache I was clenching them so tightly. Letting him in, I closed and locked the door. After putting our clothes in the dryer, I grabbed another dress, then snuggled down beside him with two more cheesecakes to watch a movie. When that one finished, we watched another.

When the doorbell rang in the morning, I was still in Jet's arms on the lounge, and Jet was snoring.

Chapter Twenty-Two
STRETCHING BOUNDARIES

"Is he your model?" Sandra appraised Jet as he carried a few of the paintings out to Sandra's car for us.

"Shh, he hasn't seen those paintings."

"Really?" Sandra's eyebrows lifted. She looked disappointed. "So, he's not the stallion?"

"Not the one from the paintings, no."

"Damn!" Sandra studied Jet's ass as he bent over. "And I'm still jealous." Releasing a sigh, Sandra turned her focus to me. "Any exceptional ones I can highlight?"

Collecting the one I painted yesterday, I turned it to face her. "I only painted it yesterday. I've sealed it, but it may not be completely dry yet, so watch where you touch it."

Sandra whistled. "That one is going to fetch a good price for you. You should just paint the dark ones. You'd be raking it in."

"It's therapy that pays, not a career." I was always happy to unload the dark ones. Looking at them made me sick. Somewhere out there was a painting of a dark hallway with bloody drag marks down the floor. It was my highest selling painting so far.

"Can I look at the ones you are holding back?"

She knew I didn't give her all of them all the time. Some, I kept back for Christmas gifts or because I liked them, or because I hated them and wanted to burn them. With a sigh, I opened the door to the gym, and Sandra sorted through the ten canvases against the wall.

Appearing around the corner, Jet took in the room. "Can I use your gym today? They don't have one where I'm staying."

Raking my eyes over him, I lifted a brow. "If you do it naked, and I can watch?"

Jet smirked. "Half-naked; I'll lose the shirt, but you have to lose yours too."

"I'll go for my run while you use the gym. When I get back, I'll take everything off and watch you from the sauna."

Eyes filling with heat, Jet stepped closer, focus intent as he lowered his mouth to mine.

"Don't mind me." Jet and I turned to look at her. "Can I have this one?" She held a painting of the stars in the sky. I'd painted it one night while bored.

"It's shit."

Tilting his head to consider it, Jet dropped his jaw. "It's beautiful."

"He's right. This is really good, Rain. I've never seen a self-portrait of yours before, but this is spectacular. It took me a moment to see it."

"I saw it straight away. I'll buy it."

Blinking, I studied the painting. It was just random stars at first, but as I tilted my head, I realized there was a face looking back at me, but it wasn't mine. Hands clawing opposite elbows, I was struggling to breathe as my chest constricted, and my heart raced in my chest. "That's not a self-portrait."

Stepping forward, Jet took my hand in his and squeezed gently. "It's okay, I won't buy it. You should offer it to your father, though."

My tongue felt huge in my mouth, I couldn't even fathom a reply. I'd painted my mother's face into the stars of the sky. Wondering how many times I'd done that before and not realized it, I chewed my lip. I painted stars all the time when I was drunk and lacking any creativity.

"How about we leave that one for next time, Sandra. See if Judge May wants the memory first."

"Of course." Slipping the painting away, Sandra furrowed her brow. She wasn't aware of the details; she just knew I was a recluse because I'd been hurt. "I'll head off. I'll be in contact in a week or two. Enjoy your Christmas."

"You too."

Waiting for Sandra to let herself out the door, Jet went to the intercom and shut the gate while he considered me. "You okay?"

"Yes, I just hadn't realized I'd done that."

"How about I head back to the condo and get my stuff while you change for your run. That way, you can let me in before you head out."

"Stuff?"

"You don't expect me to work out in this?" Jet looked down at his slacks and button-down.

Shaking my head at myself for being silly, I was still thinking about that painting. "Oh, of course."

"I'd offer to come for the run with you, but I know you like to do that alone." Giving me a weak smile, Jet kissed my forehead. "I'll be back shortly."

After Jet left, I stood there for a few minutes considering that painting. Walking down the hall to my dad's bedroom, I opened the door. On the wall opposite the bed was the only other star constellation painting I'd kept. Dad convinced me he loved it and wouldn't let me paint over it years ago. My legs went out from under me as two faces emerged from the stars. Mum and Harry. I'd been painting them in the stars for years. No wonder dad hadn't let me destroy it. Taking several minutes to recover, I got my feet under me and went back to my room to change for my run.

By the time the front gate buzzer rang, I was dressed. Checking the screen to see it was Jet at the gate in his car, I didn't bother asking why he drove back, just pressed the open button. Calling Oscar, I collected his harness for the run.

"You okay?" Jet queried when he came in dressed in sweatpants and shirt.

"I thought we negotiated no shirt?"

Moving closer, Jet leaned one arm on the door jamb as he made direct eye contact. "After your run." His mouth captured mine in a toothpaste fresh kiss. As his arm pulled my body tight to his, I moaned and melted into him. Gently, Jet pulled away, much to my chagrin. "We can pick this up later. Right now, someone fed me too much cheesecake last night and I need to work that off."

"Um, you stole too much cheesecake cake last night. Don't go blaming me for your gluttony." Heading to the beach gate, I called Oscar to follow.

"See you when you get back. You can tell me what you are going to make me tonight."

Glancing over my shoulder, I smirked. "Exhausted."

A grin spreading across his face, Jet dropped his eyes to my derrière. Oscar and I set out on our morning run with enthusiasm. Pushing harder, I ran a little faster than usual because I kept thinking about watching Jet work out shirtless. Oscar was just enjoying my excitement for the run.

When we got home, I let Oscar off the lead to run around the yard and headed for the gym. Jet wasn't using the weight machines but was over at the chin-up bar when I stepped through the door. His shirt was already discarded beside my dad's kettle weights which were out, indicating he'd used those too. With his earphones in, he didn't hear me. Watching his back muscles bunch as he lifted himself up and down, I licked my lips. Moving to the sauna door, I pulled off my singlet and running shorts. Leaving just my crop top and knickers in place and slipped inside. Having turned the thermostat on before I left, it was the perfect temperature. Adding a few drops of eucalyptus to the steamer, I set myself up to lie across the top rack, legs up the wall, and head turned so I could watch Jet.

Finishing his chin-ups on the top stall bar, Jet turned around and started doing straight leg lifts to work his lower abs. Picking up my drink bottle, I sipped to prevent drooling. Dropping to the floor, Jet lay down and held the bottom stall bar while he rolled up onto his shoulders and then slowly lowered back down to lying, keeping his body stiff as a board while he did. By the time he stood, grabbed a lower and upper stall bar, and held his body out from the wall, I understood why he had a v pack without the rectus bulk. He proceeded to lift his body up and down, using his obliques and arms. The exercises he did utilize every muscle in his arms and core. He didn't need to do weights with what he was doing.

When Jet finished on the stall bars, he stood up and had a drink. That's when he spotted my clothes. Turning his head to the sauna, Jet winked as I lay there sweating. Jesus, it wasn't even that hot in here, but watching him was definitely getting my heart rate up. Setting his drink bottle down, Jet started doing some stretches. The man was flexible. He needed to be for how good he was at his martial arts, but I was impressed. When he finished, he drank the rest of his water and headed to join me in the sauna. He dropped his pants, boxers and all, letting me see he was ready for another workout.

Sitting up, I pulled my crop top over my head, my knickers came off next. By the time Jet pulled open the sauna door, I was ready for him. Stepping inside, Jet met my eyes as the door closed. "Do you want to have sex with me, Rain?"

"Yes." My body trembling as he approached.

Taking my hand, Jet gave it a gentle squeeze. My body calmed a little. "And you're okay to have unprotected sex with me?"

I bit my lip. "Have you-?"

"I haven't been with anyone else, Rain, and I don't have anything on me, so unless you do, it's either masturbation or sex without."

God! Was this even a question? "Without!" I squeaked enthusiastically. I was so damn randy I was ready to climax the moment he touched me. "Yes, to sex without."

Tugging my body against his, Jet's mouth captured mine. With our skin wet from the steam in the room, our hands slipped over each other. The thermostat wasn't that high since I preferred more steam room than sauna temperatures. Hands gliding down, Jet grabbed my ass. Jolting a little, I pulled back to meet his eyes.

"I'm going to pick you up." Grabbing me again, Jet rounded his hands to the juncture with my thighs, and as he firmed his grip, I used his shoulders to lift myself into his hold.

Meeting my eyes to check I was okay, Jet kissed me while he turned and took a seat on the bench. Kissing around his neck and across his shoulder, my fingers worked through his hair. To say I was a contradiction in nerves was an under-statement. I wanted this, wanted him more than I could explain. And still, I was trembling like an abused puppy terri-fied it would get kicked again. Keeping everything above his shoulders, I was afraid I'd trigger him, and terrified he'd trigger me.

Taking my face in his hands, Jet gently moved my head back, so I had to meet his eyes. Seeing his eyes were focused, I understood, that's how it worked for him. He pinpointed his absolute need and worked towards achieving it, even with sex. "Stay here with me. We're just putting two broken pieces back together. You don't force it; you just slot them together where they fit. We fit, Rain. There may be cracks or chips missing from the damage, but we still fit."

Blinking back tears, I gave him a genuine smile. He was such a romantic. Jet probably combined the idea of soul mates with us being broken souls.

Moving his hands to my waist, Jet guided me, positioning me over his need, all the while, keeping his eyes locked with mine. As he found my entrance, I bit my lip. Jet pushed gently down on my hips. My eyes rolled into my head as I released my thighs and slid down him. I was beyond wet for him. Kissing me heatedly, Jet didn't push, and I didn't pump, we both just let gravity do the work. Whenever my body fought his penetration, I inhaled, exhaled, and relaxed a little more, allowing him to sink deeper. The further down I went, the harder breathing became.

By the time I was impaled on him as far as my body was going to let him - and there was more ground to cover still if you get what I mean - I was panting. Kissing me, his own breath unsteady, Jet pressed a little on my hips to go that little bit deeper. I cursed to the ceiling. Taking the opportunity, Jet grabbed hold of my breast, moving the nipple into his mouth and sucking. My hips jolted forward, piercing me deeper. Swearing, I rocked my hips back. Using his free arm to encircle my waist, Jet quickly yanked my body back against him. I adored his strength, but the way he rammed into my depth made me cringe and whimper.

"Jet. Slow. Gentle."

Lifting his head, Jet caressed my face. "Have you tried it any other way?"

"Yes. Guys pounding me triggers me."

"What about you pounding me?" His hands were caressing me, keeping the fire stoked. "You'd never been on top before. What if you are the one controlling this? If it gets too much, just slow it down. I'll give you full control." Putting his hands in the air, Jet raised a brow. "Try it, Rain. Listen to what your body needs and take it." Placing his hands to the side, Jet used only his mouth to pleasure me.

Blinking, uncertain, I considered his suggestion. Jet was right, I'd never tried being the one in control or even having sex outside of a bed. He was giving me the chance to try, and if it hurt, I could stop. Bracing my hands on his chest and shoulder, I rocked back then forward. Still unsure, I started slow. Lifting his face, Jet gazed at me with lust glazed and needy eyes. In my head, I heard him telling me to stay here with him. When I lurched forward to kiss him, Jet caught my face millimeters from his, turned his head slightly, and then his lips were on me, devouring me. Matching my movements to our lips, as our need grew, so did the speed I moved over him.

Moaning as he kissed me, Jet caused spasms of delight to ascend from my core. My body tightening around him, I raced towards the edge. Jet's hands on my breasts urged me forward, causing me to pant his name across his lips whenever I drew breath. Jerking inside of me suddenly, I didn't even know Jet was close when he threw his head back and cried out as he came.

Grabbing my hips, Jet thrust me harder on him. My nails dragged down his chest as the feel of him coming took me to the edge and threw me over. Tumbling down the rabbit hole, I was unsure which way was up or down or if there was even solid ground. All I knew was absolute bliss, and Jet was breathing just as hard against my chest.

My arms wrapped around his head, holding him tight to me, I opened my eyes. Jet was hugging me just as tight. Safe in the strength of his arms, I was drunk on the endorphins pumping through my system.

Exhaling hard, Jet kissed my collarbone. "Where's the shower?"

"Next door. But my body is jelly."

Tucking me tight to him, Jet stood up. Wrapping my legs around him, he carried me next door to the shower. Turning on the water, Jet pressed me against the shower wall and kissed me tenderly before he pulled back to consider me. "You liked it?"

"Maybe. I'll have to try it a few more times to be sure." I wasn't saying it to be funny or cheeky. I seriously still wasn't sure if I liked it. It felt good, but it rode that edge for me, and I worried it would be too easy to go from heaven to hell. "It's different and could take getting used to."

Gaze falling, Jet huffed a little, and I realized he was hoping I'd enjoy it straight away.

"This is how you like it?"

Tucking a strand of my hair behind my ear, Jet met my eyes. "Not all the time. I like sex. I like everything from slamming to slow and deep. What I need is mood dependent."

My heart sank. "I don't know if I can give you what you need."

Caressing my waist, Jet rubbed his nose against mine. "You just did. We will work within your limits, Rain. But I need you to be open to exploring the perimeter occasionally, testing those limits. As we learn to trust one another more, I'm hoping our boundaries might be movable."

Tears filled my eyes at the sincerity in his. "Does that include yours? Because you frightened me last night."

Adam's apple bobbing, Jet nodded. "Mine too."

Taking my hand, Jet placed it to his mouth, kissing my palm, then he guided it to his chest and slid it down his body between us. When it reached his waist and kept going, he hesitated and visibly shivered.

"Jet, don't force this."

Swallowing hard, Jet gritted his teeth and kept going. "I want you to feel this."

Sliding my hand further, Jet continued until my fingertips

touched the base of him, still buried inside me, but enough of his trunk exposed that I could turn my wrist and wrap my hand around him. Receding just a moment ago, now he was growing hard again.

Sucking in a breath with my grip, Jet dropped his forehead to mine. "Feel how hard I am for you, Rain? I just shattered myself in you, and I want to do it again already. I've never desired or wanted a woman as badly as I need you."

Inhaling a deep breath, I released my hand from his growing length and touched his chin, lifting his face to mine. Dropping my head to the side, I kissed his jaw, tracing it back to his lips. Hesitating there, our eyes observed each other carefully.

"I'm ready."

Chapter Twenty-Three
WALKING ROUGH

JET REINVENTED THE TERM WALKING ROUGH. HE DIDN'T GO back to his condo for the rest of the week. Strangely, all his clothes were in his car. After a day of hanging out, and a night of multiple multiples, he went out to the car, collected his bag, and moved into my bedroom. At first, I didn't really think about it. Just like the day before, I went for my run with Oscar, but when I came back, his bag was on my bedroom floor. For a moment, I'd considered it, then I got distracted by Jet in the shower after his morning workout. After that, he just stayed, moving around me and my daily rituals. When I was busy, he sat reading for entertainment. When I was free, he made me his pleasure.

By the time Saturday morning came, after five days of riding bareback at every opportunity, I was feeling it. It didn't stop me wanting more, but I knew every place Jet had been this week, and by God, that man dug deep.

Noticing Jet walking just as gingerly coming into the kitchen, I chuckled.

"Morning." He slid into one of the bar stools. "I was thinking, we need to go to the shops and buy some good quality lubricant. That shit you use for your vibrator doesn't have long-lasting capabilities. We obviously need something a bit more robust."

"I think the problem is how robust you are."

Eyes glinting, Jet smiled. "My point being, we either invest in something with a little more staying power, or we abstain for a few days. I know what my preference is."

Chuckling, the heat in his voice made things pull tight downstairs, I grimaced and moaned all in one. That made Jet snicker. "Okay, we can go to the shops. We can walk Oscar down after our run. Can we discuss something else important?"

"If it's serious, I'm going to need coffee. Someone kept me up all night with her lustful ways."

Raising a brow over who was the one up all night, I didn't say it. Instead, I made him coffee while I discussed a more significant issue. "Christmas is only two days away. I'm guessing you are expected to join your family for the occasion?"

Jet's smile disintegrated. "Yes, I am."

"My family are arriving tomorrow night. Are we going to tell our families about this as something they can expect ongoing, or are you planning to leave tomorrow and call me when the need takes you?"

Eyebrows bunching, Jet inhaled hard. "I honestly hadn't thought that far ahead. It's not like I came away this week planning to have this affair with you. I actually came away to get over you."

My body froze, and I stopped breathing at the word affair.

Taking a mouthful of his coffee, Jet considered the kitchen

bench. "This wasn't a holiday romance, Rain. But Christmas Day may not be the day to tell my family I've started a relationship with my brother's ex-fiancé."

"So, I'm guessing we won't be seeing each other until the court is back in session." Taking a deep breath, I turned to start making breakfast.

Jet was quiet. Very quiet. My stomach dropped. He was always busy during the week. Our relationship would consist of weekends, probably spent between the sheets, and living separate lives during the week. What was I thinking getting involved with him?

After I cooked breakfast, we ate in silence, then I took Oscar for our morning run while Jet got his sweat on in the gym. When I got back, I didn't go in to watch him, just went into the shower. His work out changed day-to-day. Every second day Jet beat me to the shower. The other days, he was still on the stall bars when I got back.

The bathroom door opened as I stood beneath the fall of the water. "Can I join you?"

Turning around to watch him disrobe, I also didn't want my back to him. "Sure."

Stepping under the water with me, Jet wrapped me in his arms, his mouth finding mine immediately. We heavy petted, but before it could get out of control, Jet pulled away and started soaping up. Using the moment to escape, I sat on my bed, a towel wrapped around me while I tried to figure out where this was going. I wasn't the sort of woman who wanted a relationship where we lived in each other's pockets, but I wanted more than a weekend marriage. More than an affair.

With just a towel around his waist as he came into the room, Jet sighed and ran a hand through his hair. Sitting beside me, Jet took my hand in his. "Can I ask you something?"

"Of course."

"Would you have gone through with it if we hadn't have met, or if I hadn't have pursued you?"

Considering the question for several minutes, I eventually drew a breath. "I want to get married and have a family. Until I met you, Aubrey was the only person I could see that happening with."

"But you're not in love with him?"

"I love him as my best friend, but no, it's not lusting or love like most people have in a relationship."

Jet considered my hand in his. "Are you in love with me?"

"Jet-" I wasn't ready to answer this question. It was too soon.

"I can't go to my family and tell them I'm in love with you until I know this is going to be a real thing, Rain. Up until two months ago, they all thought you would marry Aub. He was picking out baby names for fuck's sake. Then I met you, and I had to have you, and I fucked it all up."

Taking my hand back, I stood up, refusing to look at him because I could see where this was heading. "You should go."

Standing up, Jet kept his distance. "Rain, I want you. I want you more than I've ever wanted anyone. But I'd rather keep this quiet from our families for now. Just until we know if we plan to pursue this long term or not."

Irritated by Jet's justification, I turned to face him. "You want an affair. That's why you used that word earlier. I want to date, to have a relationship, to let people know we are dating. Your parent's expectations of your brother were unrealistic. Aubrey's desire for me is fucked up, and your excuse for keeping me as a weekend fuck-toy is weak at best."

Mouth falling open, Jet stepped back his eyes wide.

I'd had enough of the Landy's dictating how I felt or what I wanted. "I'm spending Christmas with my family. That gives you two weeks to figure out if you can be in a proper relationship with me, or if we say goodbye for good."

Still wide-eyed, Jet forced his mouth closed as he observed me. "Rain...I don't see you as my fuck-toy or a dirty affair of which I'm ashamed. I'm just asking for us to wait for a month or so and let the dust settle about you and Aub before we turn up hand in hand and tell everyone we are dating."

Considering Jet, I pressed my lips together to hold back tears. "A month or so?"

Watching me, Jet nodded, his eyes wary. They were too closed off, too cautious.

Bowing my head, I inhaled and exhaled. "Fine." Jet's brow lifted as I raised my eyes to meet his. "You call me when the dust has settled, and you can openly be in a relationship. Until then, I think it's time for you to go."

Opening his mouth to argue, Jet closed it quickly and backed up a step. Chewing on his cheek for a second, Jet met my eyes and spoke to me as if I was one of his clients. "I'm sorry you feel that way. I've enjoyed our week together and am sorry to see it end."

Playing it just as cool as Jet, I nodded my head and kept my tone amicable. "Me too."

Moving to his bags, Jet dressed while I went into my walk-in robe to do the same. When I came out, Jet had his bags packed and turned to farewell me. His eyes were the coldest

I'd ever seen them. For a second, I hesitated to approach him, but I walked him to the door and out to his car.

Placing his bag in his boot, Jet came back to me. His eyes dropped to my trembling hands, but for the first time since we met, he didn't reach out to calm me.

The distance already growing between us was painful to endure. Sucking in a breath, I met Jet's eyes. "You make me the happiest I've ever been in my life. I don't want to pretend we're just friends anymore."

Gaze softening, Jet took my hand in his and squeezed it tenderly. His eyes connected with mine and then his lips were on mine, our body's melding as we kissed tortuously slow.

When we broke apart, Jet continued to hold me tight. "Don't make me leave yet. Let me stay one more night. I'm not ready to give you up."

The truth was, I wasn't ready to give him up either, plus I sucked at going cold turkey. "Okay."

Lifting me into his arms, Jet carried me back inside.

As he laid me beneath him on my bed, I met his eyes. "Stay with me."

Jet's pupils dilated as his breath left him in a rush. "Okay."

Waking to Jet getting out of the bed, I watched him dress and collect his phone before he left. Sitting up confused, I realized he'd been trying not to wake me. Getting up, I pulled a shirt and pair of knickers on before stepping out to head to the kitchen.

"Dad, I want to run something passed you," Jet's voice

echoed into the hall from the gym. "I'm going to be entering a relationship with Rain Noir."

Moving closer to the door, I held my breath.

"No, dad. With the view of marrying her and having a family with her. I'm in love with Rain. I've known she was the one the moment I laid eyes on her, just like you told me I would." Jet waited to listen to his father. "Can you suss mum out about it? I want to be able to tell Rain my intentions before I come home tomorrow." Jet lifted his face to the ceiling as he listened. "I've been with Rain this past week. Not intentionally, but it turned out the place I rented was literally a few doors from Rain's holiday home. I ran into her in my first hour here, and I've been with her since. I understand what you mean now when you talk about going away from mum. I don't want to leave Rain. Ever."

Chapter Twenty-Four
FAMILY ISSUES

❦

"RAIN!" JET'S PLEADING BARITONE ONLY MAKING ME GROW tighter. "Oh, God, Rain, I need to fuck you. If you don't stop, I'm going to pull you on top of me and slam that pussy so hard you won't be able to walk tomorrow.

"You're the one who asked me to do this."

As Jet pumped his hips forward, I pressed my fingers tighter into the knot I'd accidentally found. Gritting his teeth, Jet groaned as the muscle released.

Grumbling, I exhaled hard. "Stubborn little shit."

"Excuse me? Who are you calling little?"

To emphasize his point, Jet shoved forward again. Moaning, I sent up a prayer, my back arching as he kept going.

Jet groaned, his body shaking with restrained effort. "Jesus, I want to fuck you so hard."

"You'll hurt me."

Tensing, Jet thrust with a little more force. My body tightened, coiling harder. "Did that hurt?"

"Jet."

"Or this?" He thrust again. "Or this?" His hips found a

robust, steady rhythm. My fingers gripped his biceps hard. He was right, it was far from hurt, but I didn't know how long that could last. Rolling us, Jet put me on top. I automatically pulled my knees up, but when I tried to sit up, Jet kept my body pressed to his holding my hips in place. "Stay with me." Bending his legs up, Jet started slamming into me from beneath.

My eyes were wide, expecting any minute to be dragged down that hallway, but I clung to Jet's shoulders as my body opened itself to his persistent pound. He didn't go as deep as he could have if I'd sat up, but he made me feel him just the same. Biting his lip, Jet tightened his grip on me. "Come for me." I whimpered as his fingers became bruising. "Come on, Rain." He slammed his hips up harder, faster, his face contorting with his restraint.

"Not yet." I tried to hold him back by lifting up a little. That just drove him deeper. My eyes went wide when Jet lifted his head and caught my nipple between his lips, sucking hard as he pounded my snatch. Panting his name as my body coiled tight, Jet grunted, barely able to move inside of me. Shoving harder, Jet threw his head back and yelled as he unloaded with force. My eyes were wide at how amazing it felt. A moment later, I was crying out myself. Dropping my face, I bit his chest to try and stop from screaming, I was cumming so hard with him.

My bedroom door slammed. Jet and I both jumped and looked at the closed door, shocked. "Dad, Rain's having sex!" Storm's voice yelled down the house.

Cursing, Jet, and I quickly jumped out of bed to dress. Jet just got his pants on, and I was pulling on my dress when my dad knocked on the door. "Rain, are you okay?"

"Yes," I answered, absolutely embarrassed because I knew what my dad was really asking. "Sober and consenting. You're early."

"Oh!" Dad sounded surprised, and I guess he would be because he knew I was usually drunk to have sex. "Yes, Penelope dropped the boys off at breakfast, and we thought we'd surprise you for lunch."

"Well, definitely surprised."

I swear, I heard my dad laughing. "Okay, I'll take the boys down the beach with Oscar."

"It's fine. We just finished when Storm came in." Sure that I was redder than a tomato, I covered my face.

Jet burst out laughing. "Give us a minute to clean up, Judge." Moving me towards the shower, Jet waited until the water was running to put his mouth to my ear. "You need a shower, I was still cumming when you jumped off." Blinking at him, I finally felt the sticky mess running down the inside of my thighs. Closing my eyes, I shivered. Helping me undress again, Jet moved me under the water with him. "Shh, I know. I'll have you clean in a moment."

We'd covered this. I could handle unprotected sex as long as he came inside. The feel of it running down my legs if he shot shallow was too much for me. Kissing me gently, Jet cleaned me up, then he turned away to wash. By the time we entered the kitchen, I was more concerned with how to face my father. Still blushing like a sunset, I bit my lip when my dad raised a brow at me.

"I'll go down to Bunnings after lunch and get a door handle with a lock for you. Your brother is traumatized by seeing you getting boned, or so he tells me. Zephyr wanted to know if it was anything like the porn movie they found in

Penelope's wardrobe. I sent them down the beach, so I didn't have to hear any more of that conversation."

While Jet was covering his mouth to stop from laughing, I couldn't get any more embarrassed or horrified. "You should probably discuss that real sex isn't anything like the porn movies," Jet advised.

"Sure, right after I discuss safe sex with the grown adults," Dad gritted. His eyes came to me. "You know better. I made sure you knew better, especially considering your past sexual relationship."

"Dad, I do-"

"Rain, safe sex doesn't require showering after. It's nowhere near as messy." He hated being lied too.

"Judge," Jet cut in, seeing me retreat into myself. "If I may. We did start off with all precautions in place. But, ah, we had an incident. Since I was able to show Rain a recent test to prove I was clean, we agreed to be a little less cautious as long as we were monogamous. She's still on the pill."

My dad raised an eyebrow and looked to me. When I looked away, Dad didn't say anything. "I see." He took a deep breath. "And is this relationship going to be a permanent fixture in your lives, or is it more casual in its setup?"

"I'm hoping for permanent."

Lifting a brow at Jet's answer, my father looked unconvinced. "How are the rest of your family taking that?"

Jet's face dropped. "Rae is happy for us. I haven't spoken to Mum and Aubrey about it yet."

Picking up his coffee, Dad drained the cup then set it aside. "Well, that should be interesting." Dad's eyes flicked up to me before turning to Jet. "Will you be joining us for lunch?"

"If that would be okay with you?"

"Of course. Jet could you go and round the boys up from the beach, so we can head out?"

It was evident that dad was trying to get rid of Jet to speak to me. "Sure." Squeezing my hand, Jet kissed my temple before going out to the gate for the beach. Fidgeting, I waited.

"You told him you are on the pill?"

I cringed. "I was when I first told him that."

"But you haven't corrected his knowledge in the months since that last conversation?" Dad wasn't happy. I looked away. "Rain, you don't get to make decisions about these things alone. That's exactly the sort of thing Penelope did to me."

"I didn't do this on purpose. It's too late, so what does it matter?"

"It matters because he loves you, and you need to be honest with him. Jet is serious about having a relationship with you. You need to tell him the truth, and you need to do it before he goes home to speak to his mother and brother. This could change everything, for him, how he feels, and for how they are going to accept it." Dad looked up as the boys came running across the patio, chasing Oscar. "Tell him the truth, Rain. Don't lie to the man you love."

Walking back inside, smiling, Jet took me in, and his smile faded. "Everything okay?"

Dad stood up. "Boys, in the car. It's still a bit early for lunch, so I'm going to take the boys to Bunnings for that door handle. I'll pick you up in about an hour for lunch." Dad kissed my head. "Be brave, be honest, and know that I love you."

Waiting until they left, Jet sidled closer. "Your father doesn't approve, does he?"

"It's not you." Observing Jet's penetrating gaze, I sighed.

"Do you want some tea?"

Jet frowned. "I swear you were a big coffee drinker, but I think you only have one a day now. It's tea every other beverage. Is this connected to the no alcohol thing?"

Tasting my lip, I met his eyes. "Yeah, it is. I've been trying really hard to clean up my diet."

"I admire that. Your eyes are definitely clearer. When was the last time you had a few drinks?"

"The weekend we first slept together. The Sunday after I got home, I became violently ill. I always get an upset stomach when my emotions get too much for me." Putting a cup of tea in front of Jet, I took a sip of mine.

"So, your father made an excuse to leave," Jet cut to the chase. "I'm guessing that was so you could tell me goodbye, or something else?"

Taking a stabilizing breath, I pressed my hands to the cold stone of the island bench. "Yes." I waited for a few more breaths. "I should have told you this Tuesday, but we got caught up in things, and I knew it wouldn't make a difference now anyway." When Jet didn't interrupt, I sucked in another breath, then forced myself to control the exhale. "So, the week after all that shit went down with your family, I was pretty much in a bad way. Upset stomach most of the time, not really focusing on a routine or my health." Jet was sitting there frowning while I struggled to find the words. "I forgot to take my pills for a few days, and with everything how it was with your family and us, I wasn't too worried about it, you know, because it's not like I was about to go out and pick up some random guy."

"You got Oscar," Jet contested teasing.

"That was like a month later." Rolling my eyes, I resisted

matching the smirk on his face. Inhale with control, exhale twice as long. That is how you control an anxiety attack. "Anyway, I felt more stable emotionally, and I decided not to go back on the pill."

Jet's spine straightened severely.

Putting up a placating hand, I pleaded. "Please don't react yet; let me finish." Jet gave me a small nod. "I checked with my doctor, explained the reason for my decision, and asked about alternatives. She went through various options and ran some tests. Because of one of the test results, she advised I take a break from contraception for a year."

Jet was ready to yell; I could see it. The way his shoulders were set, his grip on the cup, the murderous look in his eyes.

"Jet, I assure you, if there were any chance you could have gotten me pregnant this week, I would have told you in advance and made sure you used protection. I would never purposefully take that sort of risk or get pregnant without my partner's consent."

Studying me, Jet didn't relax. "Why was there no chance you could get pregnant this week if you aren't on contraception?" Biting my lip, I looked away. Jet's eyes went to my tea. "We had unprotected sex the same day you got sick because of what my mother said. Vomiting and diarrhea can render the pill ineffective, even just one day of it."

My eyes filled with tears.

Standing up, Jet put space between us. "You quit your job and moved up here so my family wouldn't find out. So, I wouldn't find out. You weren't going to tell me?"

"I was trying to figure out how."

"How about, 'hey, you knocked me up. Do you want a say in it?'!"

If he thought I was going to sit there coyly while he ripped strips off me, he had the wrong girl. "So, you could talk me into getting rid of it like your brother did? What if I told you and miscarried a week later? It's not always about you Landy boys. It's my body, my life that gets changed by this. Your family doesn't know. If you don't want this, the door is over there. You can walk away from this, from me, and never have to see me again. I can't just walk away, Jet. Everything has to change in my life because of one decision we made. Nothing about your life has to be affected." Taking a deep breath, I softened my voice and met his eyes pleading. "Unless you want it too?"

Considering me for several breaths, Jet looked down at his shoes, then back up to me. "Your dad knows. He knew that night he took me out for a drink. He was asking me all sorts of questions about my plans and how I feel about you."

"And you wouldn't give him a straight answer. All you had to tell him was you cared for me and wanted to be with me, and he would have told you where I was going. Instead, you avoided the question and gave him noncommittal answers. He wasn't convinced I wasn't just another conquest, so he let me leave and supported my decision."

"But my being here today changed that?"

"Doesn't it?"

Meeting my eyes, Jet glared at me, then his eyes went to my tummy. There was nothing to see, the only change to my body so far was fuller breasts. Jet rubbed a frustrated hand through his hair. "Fuck!"

❖

Chapter Twenty-Five
FALLOUT

"Rain?" Dad called just over an hour later.

"Out here."

Coming out to the pergola, Dad looked me over. "Jet's car is gone?"

"He left. He swore, grabbed his stuff, and left."

Dad dropped his head. "I'm sorry."

"I don't think I'll be needing that lock on my door."

Dad took my hand in his. "He might just need time to absorb it. Remember what you were like when you found out?"

I'd been grateful I was with my doctor because when I started having a panic attack, she knew how to deal with it and reassure me. Then I got her to call my dad and tell him because I was terrified about how he'd react.

"Give him a few days. You'll know the moment he tells his family."

"If he tells his family."

"Veronica would murder him if she found out he had a child and hid it from her. She wouldn't care if it was illegitimate, and the mother was a prostitute he paid to screw. She wants a grandchild. Jet knows that. What he will be wary of is his mother's adoration of you. Veronica would have you married to one of her sons as soon as a marriage license could be arranged. If Jet refuses to stand by you, we both know Aubrey would step in immediately. Jet isn't stupid, he knows that too."

"Why does this keep happening to me? After everything, I was just learning to enjoy physical intimacy, to let someone in, and I go and fuck it up amazingly." Cheeks drenched in tears; I covered my face. "And let's not even talk about the fact that I have unprotected sex once and suddenly I'm up the duff. I mean, seriously? The Landy's must be packing super sperm for this to happen again. I'm surprised Veronica wasn't pregnant annually until she got Rae spaded."

Dad resisted laughing, but only just. Putting an arm around my shoulders, he hugged me to him. "Worst outcome? You're back where you were a week ago. No Jet, no Landy's, but a family who loves you, will support you, and a baby on the way."

"What if he wants to get married? We barely know each other."

"Do you think you two could be happy?"

"Yes. But I want to marry for the right reasons, not the wrong ones."

"As someone who deals with divorcing couples regularly, I'm sure Jet will feel the same." Dad stood back up. "Are you hungry?"

Rubbing my stomach, I groaned. "I could eat a horse." Jet knew how to work up an appetite.

"Aubrey," my dad spoke into the intercom as I came in from the pool. "Rain didn't mention you were coming to visit."

"Thought I would drive her present up and surprise her, Judge. Is she home?"

Glancing at me, Dad raised a brow. Swallowing nervously, I nodded my head. Dad's eyes dropped to my fidgeting hands before he pressed the button to open the gate. "I guess Jet told the family. That's something, at least."

"Is it? For it to be something to me, Jet should have been the one driving down the driveway."

"He's told the family, that means he intends to claim paternity."

"Well, with his work, the most I have to worry about is weekend custody arrangements." Sighing, I went back out to the pool.

It was late afternoon, three days after Christmas, and hot as hell. I'd had to wait until the sun was sinking before I could go out for a swim in the pool, which was warm enough to be a spa. In my book, having not heard from Jet since he left said everything I needed to hear. Slipping into the water, I swam out to the infinity edge. The colors of sunset painting the ocean pink and indigo.

"Hey, Merry Christmas!" Aubrey greeted.

Turning, I returned the greeting, making no effort to get out of the pool.

"I thought I'd surprise you. Surprise!" Aubrey looked down at the gift in his hands. "It's nothing spectacular, just some art supplies I thought were very cool."

"Thank you. Your gift is under the tree."

"Can I join you for a swim?"

"Sure." With a shrug, I turned my attention back to the ocean. Pressing my lips together, I tried to work out how to handle the conversation I knew was coming. If I could have got Jet to wait off on telling his family another month, then I'd be passed the first trimester and better able to handle this mess.

Gasping in the air as he surfaced, Aubrey stood to slick the water back off his face. "It was scorching today. A lot of cars overheated on the freeway. How did Oscar handle it?"

"He stayed inside with us for most of the day. He's having a swim with the twins down the beach now. That's why I'm staying by the edge, so I can keep an eye on them."

Spotting them, Aubrey laughed as Oscar shook himself, showering the boys with water. "He's good with the kids. That's a relief. How was your Christmas?"

"Good. I cooked, the boys ate, we played board games and just chilled. How about you?"

"It wasn't so bad. Jet was off kilter. Really withdrawn, which was unusual. He's been like that most of the week."

Understanding why he was in a mood, I swallowed. "I'm sorry to hear that. I hope he feels better soon and gets over whatever is bothering him."

"I heard he spent the week here last week. Rented a place a bit further up the beach."

"We ran into each other."

Aubrey frowned. "Seriously? That's all you're going to say. I thought we were friends who shared everything with each other."

"You're also his brother. There is such a thing as oversharing. Do you really want the sordid details of your brother and I at it like rabbits?"

Aubrey blew out a frustrated breath. "Do you love him?"

"I love being with him. I love the way he can talk to me without pussyfooting around me. I love the way he touches me, kisses me, works around my insecurities, and encourages me to explore new things. I love the way we can just be in each other's company and not have to say a thing."

"But do you love him enough to want to marry him?"

"Jesus, why does everyone make that the end goal? He's never been involved with anyone. Shouldn't we just be content with dating, with a relationship? Does it need to be a marriage straight out of the gate?"

"It does with Jet, yes. He's an old romantic, Rain. He believes in love at first sight, and he's told my parents he loves you, that he knew you were it the moment he first laid eyes on you. He's told them that no matter the circumstances that brought you into his life, you were always meant to be his."

My heart swelled, butterflies going crazy inside me. Jet still wanted me.

"Jet wants to marry you, Rain. But I want you to tell me what you want."

Taking a deep breath, I was ready to say so many things, but in the end, the answer that worked for me, which came from my heart, was the one I gave him. "I want Jet."

Aubrey considered me. "Are you sure? Trust me, you don't want to be signing a prenup with him unless you are sure it's for good."

I chuckled. "Again, I'm not jumping into marriage. We'll deal with the prenup when we are ready for that step."

"Why aren't we ready for it now?" A deep baritone that curled my toes spoke from the pool stairs. I turned to see Jet standing beside my father. "I know I'm going to marry you, Rain. I just got through asking your dad for your hand, so why does it have to wait?"

Turning to face him properly, I resisted smiling at what he was saying. "Because you haven't asked me. Even if you did, I don't want to rush into this for the wrong reason."

"What's wrong about loving me?" Jet challenged, stepping through the gate.

"Ego much? I never said I loved you," I debated moving towards him.

Jet smirked. "You didn't need to say it." He watched me step out of the pool. Picking up my towel, Jet wrapped it around me. "I knew the moment I laid eyes on you outside the police station, you were my soul mate."

"Police station?" I frowned.

"Three days before you stumbled drunk and half-naked into my arms, I was there picking up a file I needed for the court that day. You were on your morning run. You stopped to catch your breath out front, smiled at the sheriff, and continued on," Jet explained. "I was inside, but your smile captured me immediately, and I knew. I asked the sheriff for your name. He told me you were out of my league and to get lost."

I was in awe. I hadn't even known Jet had seen me before that night with Aubrey.

"Then three nights later, when I was dreaming about you, you stepped out of my dreams and into my house. I knew for certain you were it for me then. I just had to make you realize it." Taking my hand in his, Jet gave it his reassuring squeeze.

"If you're not ready, that's okay, but I think," his eyes went to my abdomen, no bigger than usual - well, if you discount Christmas Day gluttony. "I think the sooner, the better."

Blinking, I tilted my head appraising the gorgeous man before me. "You didn't tell them?"

Shaking his head slightly, Jet stepped closer and put his lips to my ear. "Let's elope. We'll tell them when we get back. I want to marry you and enjoy our honeymoon without the stigma attached."

The sound of water draining alerted me that Aubrey was getting out of the pool behind me. Stepping slightly to the side, so my back wasn't to him, I watched them both. They could have been twins if not for the age gap and the coloring. Aubrey was the day, and Jet was night.

Aubrey met Jet's eyes. "I get why you went after her. You should have told me why when I told you to back off. I would have understood."

Raising a brow at his brother, Jet wet his lips. "So, you'll give us your blessing?"

Aubrey took a deep breath. "If you make her happy, yes. The moment you hurt her; I'll be taking her back. Married or not."

The side of Jet's mouth twitched. "That's never going to happen." Taking my face in his hands, Jet made serious eye contact. "Say yes, eventually."

Butterflies swarmed through my insides as I smiled. "Yes, event-"

"Good!" Jet kissed me before I could finish. Melting into him, I moaned happily. "Did your dad put that lock on your bedroom door yet?"

Slapping his shoulder, I sobered. "I thought you left me. That you decided you didn't want me."

Jet exhaled dynamically. "I was blown away and needed time to get my head around what you told me. I picked up my phone to call you so many times over the next few days, but I wanted to see your face and tell you in person. I wanted to stand here and ask you to marry me with my family's blessing. So, I waited until Rae, and I convinced mum."

"You came here with Aubrey?"

"Ah, no. When I told him about us, and that I planned to marry you, Aub stormed out. I didn't realize he'd come here until I pulled into the driveway and saw his car. I decided to let you two talk while I asked the Judge for your hand."

"And he gave it to you?" I lifted a brow in question.

Jet laughed. "No. But he told me I better marry you and make you happy or you'd make a pretty widow. That and I needed to set a good example for the twins after they caught us. He said it's important those boys know real men take responsibility for their behavior. If they have sex, they need to be ready to commit long term."

"Was that speech for you or them?" I asked, humored.

"Definitely for me, but he made it about them." Jet pulled me tighter to him. "So, where are we eloping too?"

"I never agreed to elope."

"You really want the shotgun wedding with my mother involved?"

Already regretting my decision, I gave him a gentle smile. "She has no daughter, and your brother's bride won't look as fetching in a white dress if he meets the love of his life."

"You don't think Jim is his soul mate?"

"Jim?" I screwed my nose up. "No. I just can't see him calling that name passionately for the rest of his life."

"You're judging someone on their name?" Jet cocked a gorgeous brow over the hypocrisy.

"Yes. Your brother is going to end up with a Flynn, or Chase, or something pompous and rich," I declared, wrapping my arms around his neck.

"Well, it's good to know the name makes the man worthy."

"If you had been James or Mathew, I would never have said yes to that first drink."

"First time ever, I love the name my parents gave me." Jet moved closer. "Let's go to your room and lock the door."

"Your brother is here. I need to be polite to a guest. Plus, it would go a long way to rebuilding our friendship if us being together doesn't stop us from hanging out."

Jet huffed. "You're right. But he better not be expecting to share the bed with us tonight." My eyes went wide. Jet smirked wickedly. "Though, I made sure to bring the more robust lube with me this time."

"So, you're staying?" Dirty thoughts racing through my head.

"I've got another three weeks until I need to be back for work. I'm staying until I have to go, and then you're coming back with me."

"What if I want to stay here?"

When Jet smiled wickedly, I felt my knickers grow wet instantly. Putting his mouth to my ear, Jet sucked my ear lobe. "Do you truly think you can stay away?"

"You're evil! I've been seduced and bewitched by the devil."

"Wait until it's bedtime. I'll make you pray just as good as any other god."

And he did. And, though I tried to be quiet, I was glad my room was at the opposite end of the house from my brother's. Unfortunately, not the case for my father, but he slept pretty heavily. Well, I hoped he did.

❖

Chapter Twenty-Six
PRENUPTIALS

"MORNING," I YAWNED AS I STEPPED INTO THE KITCHEN TO make breakfast. My father and Jet were at the meals table, and Jet was scribbling on a notepad. "Sleep well?"

"Like a log," dad answered. "Thankfully, I still have the earplugs here from when I was married to the rhinoceros."

Understanding the insinuation, I felt my cheeks heat. Jet lifted a brow. "Which wife was that?"

"Number three. The mother of my boys. I don't regret them at all. She, however, was the worst decision I ever made."

"Will there be a number four?"

"If there is, you can write the prenup." Scowling at what Jet was writing, dad shook his head. "No, she won't agree to that, get rid of it."

Jet sat back. "This is standard of any prenup."

"You got her pregnant before the agreement was in place; therefore, no. You'll also guarantee her job in the family company remains secure and progression unhindered, or you'll pay alimony."

"I do not agree with that. I can't guarantee she keeps a job if her behavior affects her role."

Lifting a brow at the debate, I took a sip of tea. "Are you two writing our prenup?"

"Yes!" They answered in unison.

Striding over, I snatched the pen from Jet's hand and turned the pad so I could write on it. After scribbling furiously, I shoved it back in front of Jet. "They are my terms. Agree or don't marry me." I walked back into the kitchen.

Jet picked up the pad, annoyed. "If one or both parties decide to dissolve the marriage, the parties will agree to the following. The wife will move out of the Landy house on an agreed date within a month of the separation. Both parties will maintain anything they owned before the marriage and will split fifty-fifty anything purchased during the marriage. The mother will maintain custody of all children with the father having alternate weekends, school holidays, birthdays, and celebrations. The children will spend Mother's Day weekend with the mother and Father's Day weekend with the father each year, no matter if it falls on a weekend assigned to the other parent. Both parties agree to be amicable in the presence of the children at all times and not talk badly about each other, where the children could possibly overhear. If the husband has an affair or any sexual indiscretion with another person, the wife will be able to punch him in the face once without fear of prosecution."

"We might need to reword that a little," my dad chuckled. "But, I'm happy with it. I will insist on items like this house and bank accounts being listed."

"I agree," Jet concurred with my father before looking to me. "What happens if you cheat on me?"

"You can punch yourself because you obviously stopped servicing me for that to happen."

Jet lifted a brow. "Sex does tend to take a back seat in marriages."

"Jet, the only thing I would ever cheat on you with is my vibrator, and only if you stop wanting me first. I think you're safe."

"You could cheat on him with me," Aubrey yawned, coming into the kitchen.

"He has a point," Jet teased, but there was a serious undertone to the comment.

"Then add you can punch your brother in the face if he gets me drunk and takes advantage of me."

Jet smirked. "Deal."

"Hey! Though I do plan to get her drunk and get her knocked up so that it's my heavenly angels she births and not your evil spawn."

"The father is still in the room, people. Rain, go for your run. Aubrey, stop staring at her breasts, you're gay."

"They are still fascinating, and I'm staring because I swear, they are bigger. Did you get a boob job?"

"No!" Folding my arms across my chest, I cringed a little when they were tender.

"I don't believe you." Aubrey grabbed one. "See, they are at least a full cup size-"

Aubrey grunted as I knocked his arm away and punched him in the face. An entirely automatic reaction to being groped. Aubrey sat on the ground, holding his cheek, which was already bruising. "Shit, sorry!" Rushing to the freezer, I pulled out an ice pack.

"Don't apologize. He deserved that." Getting up, Jet came

and took the ice pack off me, tossed it to Aubrey, and then turned back to me. "You okay?"

"Yes, it's just automatic for me to react."

"So, it should be." Lifting my hand, Jet examined my knuckles. They weren't bleeding. "Tough hand, probably a bit of scar tissue there from your training."

"Training?" I feigned ignorance.

"I've seen you move to defend yourself a few times now, and I know Sensei Joseph does private training to a select few. I figured it out when your brothers could do the blue belt kata perfectly two weeks into lessons. I'm guessing they stand around mimicking you."

"Yeah, they do."

Jet smiled. "It just makes me love you more, Rain. That you not only overcame what happened to you, you went and did what you could to ensure it never happened again." He put his mouth to my ear and hand on my abdomen. "I expect our children will learn too." Kissing my cheek, Jet pulled back, smiling. He looked over his shoulder to see my dad writing on the notepad. "I need to get back to that before your father grants you half the estate."

"He wouldn't do that. I'm worth enough on my own."

Jet smirked. "I'm worth more." Kissing my lips, Jet went back to the table and the negotiations.

I looked at Aubrey. "Want to run?"

"Sure." Putting the ice pack back in the freezer, he walked out with me. Oscar was really protective of me with Aubrey and made sure he stayed between us. He'd been like that with every male who came to visit. Initially, he tried it with Jet, but accepted Jet was entitled to get closer than most. Dad was the only other person he let near me. Even the twins got a growl if they got too rough around me. It made me laugh.

"You've changed him," Aubrey conversed after spending half the run quiet.

"He seems the same to me."

"No, he's different around you. You don't see it because that's probably how he's always been around you. But, it's glaringly obvious to me."

"I'm sorry. I didn't mean too."

"No, it's good. I can see he really cares about you and see the connection he told us he felt. I can see the Jet I remember as a kid."

"What do you mean?"

Aubrey shrugged. "My first memory of Jet was him always being happy and looking after me. Then when he was eight, he changed. My dad says it all the time, how he just withdrew into himself. The smiles stopped, and the happiness disappeared. Dad was really concerned and wanted to get him a counselor. Mum apparently insisted that he go speak to our priest, that religious guidance would help. Dad said Jet only got worse."

"Did your dad ever figure out what caused it?"

Aubrey frowned. "I don't know. The weekend after I did my first service as an altar boy, dad came home with Jet, really angry. Like murderous with rage and wouldn't tell mum why. I thought Jet must have done something terrible after church. I heard dad telling Jet later that night that our priest had died. I realized Jet would have been there when he fell, and that dad was worried about how seeing that happen might have affected him. Jet just sat there, like he was in shock. Dad seemed more cut up about it than Jet did."

Taking that nugget in, I stopped running. Aubrey paused to face me. "What else did Rae say?"

"He told Jet he'd get him help. Someone good who would help him cope. He said something about Jet having taken the first step to help himself, Dad would help him with everything after."

"Do you think it helped?"

"The therapist? Yeah, Jet changed again. He never became that happy fun kid, but he started smiling again and talking to me. That's when he got interested in law, and he started studying hardcore." Aubrey tilted his head. "Are you okay?"

"Yeah." I shook my head to get the imagery out of my head, but Jet standing at the top of the steps looking down on his injured abuser kept playing in my head. "Sorry, I just didn't realize your brother hadn't always been like he is now," I lied. I'd bet good money that Rae suspected if he didn't know outright. "He's so focused and driven, it's hard to imagine him as a kid playing pranks on his brother." Starting to run again, I smiled as I remembered Jet stealing my dessert and me chasing him around the house. There were moments where the boy got out.

"My point being. The way he smiles when he looks at you. That's how I remember him being when we were kids. Always optimistic and happy. You bring that out in him." Aubrey took a quick look at me. "He brings it out in you too. You two should have met years ago. He's who you needed. Not me."

"Hey," I grabbed his arm, pulling him to a halt, frustrating Oscar by stopping again. "You have been there for me. You are my best friend. So, we messed up occasionally while trying to get our lives back on track. You don't derail a train at high speed and expect to put all the carriages back on the track all at once and that it will look the same."

"Your therapist tell you that?"

"Yes, but she was right. We got the locomotive back up, but it was smashed up. We fixed the aesthetics with time and healing, but it takes time, patience, understanding to get all the other carriages back online. Each one taking time to fix, and have it run right. We've been dragging ourselves through life, trying to ignore the parts that weren't working right. We did our best, Aubrey. Neither of us is to blame." I lifted my eyes to meet his. "Except for the drunken unprotected sex and what happened after. That was totally on your head."

"Thanks!"

"Own it. We all make mistakes." I looked down at my tummy but couldn't see past my boobs.

"Seriously, Rain," Aubrey noticed where my eyes went. "Did you get surgery?"

"Nope," I exhaled dramatically. "I got laid."

Chapter Twenty-Seven
ARRANGEMENTS

"JUDGE, CAN I ASK YOU SOMETHING ABOUT WOMEN?" AUBREY murmured out by the pool where he and my dad were playing chess. With the glass doors open to let the southerly breeze in, I could hear them inside.

"As long as it's not to do with my daughter and sex." Aubrey hesitated; Dad grumbled under his breath. "Go ahead."

"Is it normal for women's breasts to get bigger when they start having regular sex?"

Knocking over his pawn, Dad swore. "Define regular sex?" His voice lowered an octave in a warning.

"Oh, I meant regularly." Aubrey was sort of cute blushing. I didn't see him do it often, not like Jet, who blushed regularly for me.

Dad sat back. "Hormones do interesting things to our bodies. Good sex that a woman really enjoys can flood her body with hormones. I believe my daughter's body has seen a change in her hormone levels, which has affected her physical presentation."

"Oh! So, because Jet is making her come-"

"Checkmate!" Moving a piece, my dad got up, walking away. When he walked inside to see me sniggering on the couch, trying hard not to laugh openly, he pointed his finger at me once, menacingly. Pressing my lips together, I kept it in until he'd left the room.

Coming into the lounge area with his brow furrowed, Jet raised an eyebrow at me. "What's up with your dad?"

"Aubrey was just asking him for a Sex Ed lesson. He thinks my breasts have gotten bigger because you make me come so hard repeatedly. It was more than my dad could take."

"I'm going to get stuck talking the twins through the birds and the bees, aren't I?"

"Nah, he did it with Harry, he'll be fine. As long as they aren't referencing me." Thinking about Harry came with a flash of the lounge room. Harry's face. Blood. Pain. Jolting, I whimpered with the heartache.

"What was that?" Jet worried, sitting beside me quickly.

"Flashback." Shaking my head, I closed my eyes, listened to the beach outside, and let the sound of waves crashing secure me in this place. Taking Jet's hand, I squeezed it gently.

Touching my cheek, Jet turned my face to him. "Rain, I love you. Look at me. Stay with me." Opening my eyes, I smiled before diving into his embrace. Wrapping me in his arms, Jet kissed my head. He held me for several minutes until I pulled back, safe, in this place.

Clearing it away, I smiled at him. "How did they take it?"

"Rae already knew I was planning to marry you, but mum is having conniptions about not having a proper engagement." Sighing at his phone, Jet put it aside. "They are driving up tomorrow to stay the weekend and start the wedding planning."

"Really?" Aubrey asked. "That means the house will be empty."

Jet and I rolled our eyes, already knowing Aubrey was planning a weekend-long fuckfest with Jim. Leaning forward, Jet slipped his hand up my thigh beneath my sundress. "Damn, he stole my idea."

His good mood was contagious. "Your parents are coming here to see us."

"Even more reason to go somewhere else."

Huffing onto the lounge across from us, Aubrey scowled. "Oh my god! Get a room!"

Jet picked me up. "Okay." Waving over Jet's shoulder to a slightly annoyed Aubrey, I smirked when he smiled and shook his head then picked up the pregnancy book I'd been reading. His brows furrowed and head snapped back up to me.

"What the -?"

"No."

"What do you mean, no?" Frowning at Jet, Veronica's hand paused in her list-making.

"No to the church."

Veronica's mouth fell open. "No church? You can't be serious?"

"Deadly serious," Jet grumbled. "No church, and definitely no priest. I want a civil ceremony. Hell, I wanted to elope, but my bride insisted we give you a wedding."

Veronica looked horrified as she turned to me. "But Rain wants a church wedding."

"Actually-" I started.

"She wants to be married in the eyes of God. A civil cere-mony isn't even recognized by the church. No, it needs to be in the church, by a priest, doesn't it, Rain? I'll phone them and see what a good date is."

Jet raised a brow at me, the look clearly reminding me that this was my choice. He wanted to elope. Since I wanted to make his mother happy, I had to deal with her. "Actually, Veronica, I agree with Jet. You know my family isn't religious after what we've been through, and well, according to your church, I'm a murderer, so I would feel uncomfortable getting married there."

Taking my hand in his, Jet gave it a gentle squeeze. My hand drifted to my abdomen, checking. There was nothing wrong, but I remembered the feeling when they took Aubrey's baby out of me. The cramping was horrible.

Veronica looked like a guppy. "Is this not negotiable?"

"We are happy to oblige you in nearly every other way, mum. But on this one thing, I won't be moved."

I frowned. "Well, perhaps." Jet squeezed my hand almost painfully as Veronica's eyes lit up with hope. "Can we go for a drive? I want to show you both something."

The two of them looked confused, but Veronica was willing to humor me if it got her what she wanted. While she went to the bathroom, Jet pulled me aside. "We agreed on this, and you know why."

Placing a reassuring hand to his chest, I smiled up into his eyes. "You can still say no, and I will support you, but I need to show you this first. Will you just come along for the ride? Your mother may hate it anyway." Submitting, Jet went to get his car keys. "Dad, I'm taking Jet and Veronica up the bluff. Did you want to tag along?"

"Go ahead. I might take the boys for a surf," Rae smiled. Rae and Dad got along well, so they had been sitting out by the pool, letting Jet, and I deal with Veronica. While Rae was overjoyed with the news of us getting married, Veronica was still reluctant about it all. She adored me, but she always saw me with Aubrey, and she hadn't been able to shift him out and replace him with her other son yet. Which, I guess, was fair enough.

The four of us piled into Jet's car, and I directed him up to the bluff. We found a park in the car park and walked up the poplar lined driveway. "There are a lot of cars here," Veronica assessed. "Is it a park or something?"

Smiling, I kept walking. "Just wait."

My dad smiling too. He'd caught on already what I was about to suggest. We cleared the poplars, and the landscaped gardens before us opened out onto the ocean, high above where the waves beat against the cliff face below. As far as the eye could see, it was blue sky and the blue-grey sea stretching out to join as one on the horizon.

There was a permanent marquee set up filled with tables and chairs, all decorated for a wedding, and a small dance floor in the center. The gardens were lush and full of flowers this time of year. They had different themed pockets so that photos could be distinctive in a small space. The presentation like a mini-maze of various garden rooms. My favorite was the large tree with low hanging branches shading a lovely grassed area with a little pond to one side.

"It's beautiful," Jet smiled.

"It is, but there is more." Turning him to face back into the hidden corner of the gardens, I stepped back as he took in the church. It was old but fully renovated with restored stained-glass windows and a rebuilt bell tower. It was full of people currently, and the music was playing inside.

"Oh, it's lovely!" Clapping her hands in front of her chest, excited, Veronica walked off to have a better look. Giving me a wink, Dad followed Veronica.

Jet's smile fell away. Taking his hand, I gave it a gentle squeeze. "It's not a church. Well, not anymore. The church sold it about twenty years ago. The person who purchased it converted it into a wedding venue." I pointed out a chimney stack just visible over the top of the trees behind the church. "The old rectory is behind those trees and has been converted into a reception center. You can marry here in a civil ceremony and walk next door for the reception, or you can use the marquee and have the reception outdoors."

Jet looked confused for a moment. His eyes went to the joy on his mother's face, then to the smile on mine. Slowly, his lips lifted in a cheeky grin. "Here?"

I nodded.

Grinning broadly, Jet looked around. "It's probably going to be booked out a year in advance."

"On the weekend, yes. Weekdays are usually not so booked out."

Jet considered the idea. "I'm back to work in two weeks. We won't have the license ready for another three. Then there is the fact our guests will all work, but I guess that will keep the numbers down. God knows mum will invite every member of her family. That will fill one side of the church alone." Jet was doing calculations in his head. "It's doable." Pulling me in close, Jet met my eyes before he ducked his head and kissed me passionately.

"Excuse me," a polite woman interrupted. She waited until

we pulled apart. "I'm sorry, this is a private park and is for guests only."

"Yes, we know," Jet answered. "We were wondering who we speak to about its availability?"

An hour later, we were driving home with our wedding booked. "I don't understand why you are both in such a rush to do this. You should have an engagement party first and take time to plan the wedding properly," Veronica complained about the four-week deadline.

As fate would have it, another wedding canceled only that morning. So, not only did we get in quickly, we scored a Saturday late afternoon wedding. Reaching over the center console, I offered my hand palm up on Jet's thigh. Letting his eyes flick down, Jet put his hand over mine, entwining our fingers. Neither of us engaged in the discussion about dates.

Taking a deep breath, I looked out the window, a smile on my face and in my heart. It made me pull back a little, wondering over the strange feeling in my chest. When I looked at Jet, he grinned at me, his eyes polished obsidian. Warmth encompassed my chest, filling me with sunlight, chasing out the darkness in my soul. "I'm in love with you?" Recognizing this is what my mother meant when she told me you felt it not in your heart, but your stomach when the guy was right.

Jet's grin grew. "I know. I wouldn't be marrying you otherwise." He squeezed my hand gently. There was a lightness to him all of a sudden as if my acknowledgment calmed him.

Rubbing my chest, I concentrated on the feeling. "It hurts a little." Lifting my hand to his lips, Jet kissed each of my knuckles. "Is it like that for you?"

"Every breath I take where I'm not touching you is

strained. I started to think I was asthmatic when you went away."

"I'm not going to survive you breaking my heart."

Jet lifted his brow. "I take after my father. He's been entirely devoted to my mother since the day they met. I won't be any different, Rain. You're the heart breaker here, not me."

Looking away, I knew he was talking about Aubrey. Argh, that mess hadn't really been sorted. Aub was my best friend. I hoped we could keep that friendship firmly penned in going forward because even before I knew I loved Jet, I recognized that Jet was the one I wanted.

"Do you truly think I could break your heart?"

He turned his face to consider me. "No, Rain. You aren't that sort of woman. Aubrey dug his own hole and threw you into it."

"That's unfair on him. He was hurting too."

"It was more unfair on you and selfish of him." His hand brushed my cheek. "The fact you are willing to forgive him just tells me what a big heart you have."

His assurance made me smile. "All the better to love you with."

Jet smirked. "Say it again?"

"I'm in love with you."

Turning his face, Jet reached out to pull me into a kiss.

"Both hands on the wheel, and keep your eyes on the road," my dad grumbled from the back seat. "Take it to your room when you get home."

"Yes, Judge."

My cheeks heated, having forgotten we had company. "Sorry, Dad."

"You two remind me of Rae and myself when we met," Veronica cooed.

"Really?" I asked. "Then why don't you have ten children? I've heard you and Rae in the office."

"Well, we tried," Veronica mourned. "That's why there is such a big gap between Jet and Aub. I had three miscarriages, all girls. After Aubrey was born, Rae said he'd seen me hurt enough and had an operation to stop it from happening again."

Feeling guilty for bringing it up, I swallowed her heartbreak. "I'm sorry."

"I never knew that, Mum," Jet sympathized. "I'm sorry you went through that."

Veronica waved it away. "It's in the past. I'll be a grandmother soon enough, and with any luck, I'll get a granddaughter I can spoil." She leaned forward a little. "So, when are you going to tell me your due date?"

❖

Chapter Twenty-Eight
DESENSITIZATION

ARMS WRAPPED AROUND ME AS A HARD BODY PRESSED ME INTO the kitchen counter, a set of lips kissing the side of my neck. The hands didn't touch me, but my body seized, a sound of fear escaped my throat, and I went into the automatic response as a chair cluttered to the ground somewhere.

"Hmm, something smells good." One of Jet's hands grabbed a piece of carrot from the counter while the other blocked my elbow strike and pinned my arm out to the side to stop me using it. "Relax. I'm just pinching some carrot, sweet-"

"No!" My dad yelled, cutting Jet off. My heart was racing, but I wasn't trembling, I wasn't in flight at this moment, my body was tense and ready. As soon as he let me go, I was prepared to strike. "No pet names allowed. Her name is Rain. Use it, and only it."

Straightening a little, Jet started to ease back.

"No! Don't release her yet." Dad moved forward carefully. My eyes were locked on the kitchen bench, full, taking in everything around me. I was here in this room with family, and yet, I was there too. Typically, I was one or the other, not both.

Jet froze, his body tensing. The hand that stole the carrot found my free hand and interlaced his fingers with mine.

"Rain, its Dad. Can you look at me?"

Struggling to see clearly through the double vision, I swallowed.

Jet gave my hand a gentle squeeze. "I love you, Rain. Stay with me."

His words anchored me. Lifting my eyes to my dad slowly, this room coming into clarity, I met his gaze and slowly nodded my head.

"Okay, Jet," Dad exhaled. "Easy does it."

Keeping hold of my hand, Jet moved his body from mine initially, then released my wrist. Stepping away entirely, he gave me some breathing room. "Sorry, I just wanted to touch you."

"Never, ever do that," my father lectured. "Especially not in the kitchen."

"I can defend myself, Judge."

Dad shook his head. "Show him, Rain."

Jet frowned, looking to me. Glancing away, I lifted the arm he'd stopped attacking him to show him the chopping knife I'd automatically flipped along my forearm ready to drive it back into his side.

Breathing out a rush of air, the whites of his eyes showing, Jet realized what had happened. "He trained you in weaponry?"

"Just how to use a knife and how to disarm someone with a gun, and how to fire one." Placing the knife back on the bench, I stepped further away. Jet's eyes went to the scar on my torso, hidden by my dress, but I knew he was looking for where I was shot. He closed his eyes as my warning to never approach me from behind made sense.

"Had you not been fast enough to block and pin that arm, that would have been buried in you and my daughter would be devastated because she stabbed the man she loves, the father of her child, all over a piece of carrot," my dad worried.

Moving the vegetables into the dish, I added the drizzle of honey and shavings of cultured butter over the top and put in in the oven. "I'm going to go wash my face." Walking out, my hands were shaking from what I'd nearly done.

"Why no pet names?" Jet growled, but I knew his anger wasn't with me.

"They never called her by her real name. They used pet names, specifically the type a father would call his daughter."

Jet groaned in pain.

Closing my bedroom door behind me, I took deep, calming breaths. Moving into the bathroom, I washed my face. When Jet's arms reached either side of me to hold the basin, I jolted. He didn't touch me except where his arms brushed against me at my waist.

"I love you."

"Jet," I warned.

"I will not ask you to get over what happened to you, but I'm going to ask permission to help you get used to being hugged from behind for two reasons. Once your belly grows, this will be the only way I can hold you tightly, and because one day, our child may hug you from behind. What will be worse, Rain? Learning to deal with this now, or stabbing our child who just wanted to hug you?"

Choking on the idea, I sagged against the sink.

Taking the opportunity to move closer, Jet pressed his body against mine. I tensed. "Let's start slow. My hands aren't going to hold you. Just my body against yours."

I hated it. Meeting his eyes in the mirror, I gritted my teeth on a whimper. Jet could see I hated it, but he didn't look away.

"We could talk about names for the baby. Did you have a few ideas already?"

"New names. I don't like inherited names." My breathing was short and raspy, a shiver running through my body as I resisted the urge to fight him off.

"Did you want to continue your father's approach with the weather?"

"He's used all the good names."

"What about the seasons? Spring, Summer, Autumn, Winter, and Monsoon."

Gritting my teeth, I shook my head. "Definitely not."

"Astral elements?"

"Seriously?"

"Plants?"

"Jet!"

"Animals?" Raising his brows, Jet moved his hands to my hips as he put his mouth to my ear and started suggesting fauna. "We've got Raven, Possum, Koala, Kanga-"

"Be serious." I chuckled because it was apparent, he was just riling me up.

"Ooh, how about using law terminology. This one would have to be Actus Rea, and the next one would be Mens Rea."

"Because this one was the act without planning, and the next would be planned." Tilting my head, I lifted an eyebrow. "Way to tell our firstborn it was an accident."

Grinning, Jet moved one of his hands to rub my flat belly.

"Good point. Okay, seriously. I love the names, Edward and Bella."

"I was Team Jacob, so no." Closing my eyes, I enjoyed the way Jet's hand massaged. "Can we take this out to the bedroom?"

Jet chuckled. "I already locked the bedroom door." Nibbling his teeth down my neck, Jet slid his hand down my hip and thigh to pull up my dress.

"Stop!" Shoving away from him, I moved to the corner, my heart racing, barely able to draw breath.

Lifting his hands into the air, Jet backed away. "Slowly does it. I took it too far." Cursing to himself, Jet moved out to the bedroom.

Closing my eyes, I concentrated on controlling my breathing. How was the way he touched me any different from how he does from the front? It wasn't. It was just as gentle, just as passionate. I understood why I needed to move past this, but I didn't know if I could. Taking a few minutes to even out my breathing, I waited until I calmed down.

Jet was sitting on the bed when I walked out, his hands tapping beside his thighs as he contemplated things. "Sorry."

"You did nothing wrong. You're right, I need to get over this. I'm just not sure I can."

Jet stood up. "You can. Can I show you why you can?" Giving a hesitant bow of the head, I watched Jet move towards me. Turning me away from him, Jet stepped in to hug me from behind. "Stay with me."

Concentrating on breathing as he wrapped his arms around me, I stared at the wall across the room.

Taking my hands in his, Jet kissed just in front of my ear.

My pulse jumped when I realized he had me restrained. "Escape." His arms tightened.

Exhaling, I pushed my bum back, stepped a leg to the side, and behind him, and took him to the floor with me. Jet released me with a grunt. Rolling back into him, I threw my leg over, and Jet blocked the punch I threw. Reaching behind my neck, Jet grabbed me and pulled me down to his kiss. Freezing, I blinked at him for several seconds, then melted into him. A little confused, I pulled back.

Jet combed my hair back from my face. "You know how to defend yourself. Trust that you can get out of danger if it presents itself and allow yourself to be loved in the meantime."

My hand caressed down his torso as my eyes lowered to his shirt and fly. Touching the buckle of his belt, I slowly slid the leather through the buckle. Jet's hand grabbed my wrist. His brows furrowed. "I will if you will?"

Jet blinked in confusion. Waiting for him to replay his words to me and realize what I was asking, I didn't move my hands away. Slowly, Jet released his hold on me, and I continued undoing his belt. Fingers gripping into the lush carpet beneath us, Jet strained his arms so hard the veins were popping out.

"Breath, Jet. Just be here with me." Stopping with his belt open, I lifted my dress over my head. When Jet's eyes found my naked breasts, his grip relaxed. He was such a boob man.

Taking one of his hands placed his palm against my abdomen. "If you hurt me, you hurt our child." I needed to remind him because moments ago, he nearly lost control.

Jet's jaw tensed as I finished unzipping his fly and moved my hands up his chest. Lowering my face, I hovered my lips over his, but I didn't try and kiss him. "We'll start small. I get to undo your belt or shirt once a day. You get to hold me from behind once a day - not in the kitchen," I reinforced. "We will work up to me removing an item of clothing from you to you spooning me while we sleep, leading eventually to sex."

Hand caressing my cheek, Jet relaxed beneath me. "We don't have to go that far. I'm happy just to hold you, Rain. I enjoy being able to kiss you while I make love to you." His hands went to my breasts, kneading them, and flicking the nipples with his thumbs until I moaned. "And, frankly, while I love your ass, I love watching your breasts bounce, or having them in my mouth helping you to come."

To prove his point, Jet ducked his face and imprisoned one of my nipples with his teeth. Biting my lip on a moan, I firmed my grip on his shoulders. Grabbing my knickers, Jet pulled them off my bum. Tugging me forward, Jet positioned me, so I was sitting on his abdomen, and my breasts were directly over his face.

Lifting my hips, Jet finished the job I started by shifting his boxers and pulling his erection free, then I shuffled back until his head slipped between my folds. Hot, wet, and ready for him, I rubbed over him, loving the way he moaned. Releasing my breast, Jet directed my face to his, kissing me deeply as he slipped in an inch. As his hands pressed down on my hips, my nails dug into his chest through his shirt, and I took the lord's name in vain; Jet's too. The more sex we had, the tighter I seemed to get, and there had been plenty of sex.

Jet and I couldn't behave ourselves. As soon as we were alone, our hands and mouths were all over one another. Dad complained it was like having horny teenagers in the house a decade late. We didn't care. Dad resigned himself to taking walks along the beach several times a day, which was good for his health, so I was happy to encourage that.

We were enjoying the ability to be intimate with someone. For me, it was about enjoying sex and falling ever the more in love. For Jet, it was love and being intimate with someone he trusts. Then there was what I held within me. Jet's hands always moved to stroke my abdomen while we had sex. His eyes caressed my barely-there baby bump while I rocked over him.

Eyes rolling back in his head, Jet smiled as he let his head hang back. "Fuck! You pregnant makes me so horny. I can't get enough of being inside you."

"You were like that before you knew I was pregnant."

Jet grinned wickedly. "Trust me, I'm worse now."

"Do you think it will last?" Biting my lip as my body swept closer to release.

"Rain, I'm already planning the next kid."

His hips rocked up into me hard. My nails clawed over his chest as I hung back my head and bit my lip as I came. Jet grunted as my body seized around him. He thrust up, and with eyes wide open to our future together, filled me up.

Chapter Twenty-Nine
MOVING DAY

"ARE YOU SURE YOU DON'T WANT YOUR BED?" JET ASKED AS WE drove home.

"No, I want to leave it at dad's house, just in case I need to go babysit the twins." Truthfully, the idea of leaving my dad's house was hard for me, but it made sense I move in with Jet. "Your bed is fine."

"Actually, I was going to leave my bed in my old bedroom just in case you start snoring, or I need to work late."

"Why would I start snoring?"

Jet shrugged. "Dad said mum snored badly when she was pregnant with us boys, and she could only sleep on her back."

Narrowing my eyes at him, I lifted a brow.

Jet's eyes widened a little. "Which would be perfectly fine since you carry my child and all, but I don't want to disturb you when I'm up late, so let's just buy a new bed for our room." His eyes flicked to me, wary and then back to the road.

It made me turn my head and chuckle to myself. "You'll have to organize the bed yourself. Your mother is dragging me around to find a wedding dress as soon as we arrive. Then

I need to go home and pack what is going to be moved." Thinking of all that needed to be done, I sighed. "Perhaps we should wait until next week to move in together? We've got Barbara's wedding this weekend."

"We do?" Jet lifted his brows.

"Yes, we do. You're my plus one." I rubbed my hand over my tummy. "She's going to kill me if this bump shows in the dress."

Smirking, Jet put his hand over mine. "You can't see it unless you're naked. Plenty of women have a small tummy; yours won't even be a blip on the radar. Speaking of which. When do we get to lay eyes on our little reminder of why condoms are important?"

"Your mother has made an appointment with an obstetrician for next week. Apparently, she will order the scan to be done." I smiled at Jet's excitement. Tease as he might, he still smiled and had his hand on my tummy at every opportunity. "Did you like any of the names on the list?"

"What list?" When I glared at him through my brows, Jet frowned. "What? The list of names Aubrey gave me. I'm not even looking at it."

"Why not?"

"I'm not giving our child a name my brother picked out for his child with you." He took his hand away. "He's acting like he's still the potential father of your womb and he gets a right to be involved in everything to do with this baby."

"He's acting like an excited uncle. The twins are the same. They gave me a list of names too."

"Seriously?" Jet was bewildered. "What did they suggest?"

Taking out the list, I laughed. "Hurricane, Harry for short. Thor, Tempest, or Temperance if we are unfortunate enough to have a girl. Squall, Cloud, Arcus, Monsoon, Gale, Sirocco, Tornado, Atlantic, Dust, Whirl, Ice, and Blizzard."

"I'm sensing a theme."

"Well, Jet is actually on the list as being a weather event as well, to do with a Jet stream. So, they felt we should continue the weather theme."

Jet considered me, his mouth telling me he wasn't exactly happy with the idea. "Circle Temperance and Arcus. I like those two." I raised a brow. Jet raised one back. "Well, it's better than anything I've come up with yet."

"Not going to argue with that." He'd still been pushing Actus. "How about Atlas for a boy?"

"So, he can carry the weight of the world on his shoulders? I don't think so."

"Okay, well, where is the list Aubrey gave you?" I asked, putting my hand out for it.

Taking note of my hand, Jet fixed his eyes on the road ahead. "I threw it out."

"What?!"

"As I said. I don't want his input into the baby."

"Oh my god! He's your brother and my best friend. He's doing nothing out of the ordinary by giving us a list of names to help us think of something decent."

Gritting his teeth, Jet checked his blind spot, indicated, and pulled off the road onto the shoulder of the freeway.

"What are you doing?"

Stopping the car, Jet put it in park before he took a deep breath. "Harry and Vanessa."

I froze; everything about me stopped as those names fell like boulders into the ravine of silence.

"They were the names Aubrey suggested. I don't know if

he thinks I'm stupid or totally ignorant of what happened to you that I would even consider those names. Either way, he didn't intend to help, he was trying to cause a fight between us. I suggest those names, you flip out or worse, you regress, then I'm the asshole who wanted to name our kid after your dead mother or the brother that raped you."

I stopped breathing. "How do you know about that? Even Aubrey doesn't know. I only ever told my therapist."

Turning slightly to take me in, Jet exhaled, his shoulders dropping, his chin hitting his chest.

Clenching my jaw, I punched him in the arm once; he blocked the two punches I tried to follow it with. "Why? Why would you read the court files?"

"I was trying to understand more about what your triggers were. When you went away, and I thought you'd taken up with another guy, I wanted to know why you gave me up. I needed to know if I did something wrong that drove you away. You're too nice to tell me I scared you or hurt you, and I needed to know. You were meant to be mine, and you ran away from me. I needed to understand what I did wrong."

Breathing through the pain in my chest, I turned and faced forward in the car. "Take me home."

"Rain..."

"I can't deal with this or talk about this while I'm trapped in the middle of nowhere, Jet." Taking two deep breaths, I tried to calm my anger. "You read the police report, the fine details of the worst day of my life, but I've had that report read to me, Jet. It tells you the forensics. It doesn't tell you why I react to being grabbed from behind, why I hate being called pet names, why the stink of bourbon makes my stomach roll, and heave. It doesn't tell you everything they did. It just tells you the physical evidence, and that all healed years ago. Did it help you? Did reading that file tell you what you needed to know other than how much they hurt me? No, it didn't! Because the psychological damage wasn't in that file." We sat there quietly for a moment while I forced myself to swallow the hurt. "Take me home. Please."

"Rain, I'm sorry." Jet reached out to take my hand, but I snatched it away enraged.

"How would you feel if this was reversed, Jet? If your abuse had been discovered and documented. If I read those papers that noted the bruises from where he held you down, the tears in your anus-"

"Enough!" We sat there, breathing our joint anger into the car. "I get your point. You don't need to drive it home so horribly. I fucked up reading that file. I'm sorry. I probably wouldn't even have looked at it if it hadn't been reopened for more evidence."

Blinking at him, my mouth fell open, confusion smothering any words I'd been thinking.

Jet took a deep breath. "Your court-appointed therapist was finally able to complete the victim statement of events. She filed it, and I just happened to be there. It was too tempting to walk away from when the clerk went off to lunch instead of securing it first." When I sat there staring at Jet, his face softened. "That's all I read, Rain. Your victim's statement. You know anything you told your therapist was to be made available to the court and can be accessed by the public. They've waited twelve years to get that statement and close that file. If you want, I can help you apply to have the file sealed."

Tears falling, I stared at my hands fidgeting in my lap. "No.

My dad should know the truth. I won't ever be able to tell him, so he should be able to read that report and know Harry wasn't to blame in any way. I think he needs that confirmed."

Taking a breath, I looked out the window. "Aubrey doesn't know what Harry did. He wasn't malicious when suggesting those names. He was trying to allow them back into my life."

Scanning the list the twins gave me, I sighed. The very first suggestion of Hurricane they'd suggested Harry for short. I pointed it out to Jet. "The twins did the same. They both look so much like Harry. I'm terrified I won't be able to be around them when they hit puberty."

Reaching across the console, Jet took my hand, the comfort I felt immediately was almost a physical relief. "Before it happened, were you close with Harry?" I nodded my head. "Was Harry his full name?" I nodded my head. "We could call a boy Harrison or Hagrid, or anything along those lines, and he can be Harry for short. Not quite the same, but close enough."

Shaking my head, I turned back to Jet. "I like Hunter for a boy."

Jet considered it. "It's a good name." He took the paper out of my hand, flipped it over, grabbed my pen, and wrote Hunter. "We have our first name to consider."

Handing the paper back to me with the pen, he brushed his hand down my cheek then started the engine. Without any more words, Jet got us back on the road and drove us home. His home, our home, going forward. Once we got there, Veronica dragged me into the city shopping for a wedding dress. She'd made appointments at all the best boutiques and told them straight off we would be buying on the spot. It took until the third shop to find what I wanted. When I put it on, I knew it was the dress for me. Veronica didn't like the color, but she couldn't deny it looked good on me, and she accepted white just wasn't going to happen.

Afterward, I had Veronica drop me home. Dad was still up the coast with the twins. They were having his last weekend off together. Father and son bonding time. After calling Doctor Lind for an appointment, I took out a suitcase and started packing what I wanted to take from my bedroom. Dad suggested I only take the necessities, to begin with, just in case it didn't work out. Neither Jet, nor I, had ever lived with someone else before, and the added stress of living with Veronica might be more than I could endure. Truthfully, the hardest part would be being away from him and my brothers. Making sure everything was locked, I walked back to Jet's. I only had my suitcase, backpack, and handbag to carry.

Answering the door with a smile, Rae offered a welcoming hug. "I always knew you'd be our daughter too someday. Jet's up prepping for work next week. Pop your stuff down and come have a coffee with me." Following Rae to the kitchen, I took a seat at the table while he made us both a coffee. "Veronica is at her women's auxiliary meeting at the retired serviceman's club. She does a lot of volunteer work to keep her busy, but not so busy she isn't going to be around a lot during the day. For your own sanity, I would like you to consider coming back to work for me. Part-time, if that suits you better, but I think a few days of work with a reduced load would help you feel more grounded."

"I only left two months ago. Coming back, pregnant, and engaged to Jet. That's going to keep the water cooler gossiped up for months to come."

"You don't think your sudden resignation after going on a

few dates with Jet wasn't gossip fuel from the moment your leaving was announced?" Rae smiled as my cheeks heated. "Jet assures me there were no women in his life for a good six months leading up to you two meeting. If you come back, we will be honest. You were involved with Jet, you found out you were pregnant and weren't sure if a commitment with Jet would be an option. You left, but he followed you north when he realized how much he missed you and begged you to marry him." Rae considered my hesitation. "I'll tell you what, have the first week here to experience how things might be. I'm going to gush about becoming a grandfather at work, letting everyone know I'm so happy you and Jet have decided to try and make it work. I think, by next Friday, you'll be ready to come back to work, and the gossip will have already run its course."

Standing up, Rae kissed my head. "I'll carry your bag upstairs. You take your time to get comfortable thinking of this place as yours. You'll find Jet in his room when you are ready." Placing his empty coffee cup by the sink, Rae left me to consider his offer.

❖

Chapter Thirty
LOUDEST PRAYER

"COME IN," JET ANSWERED MY KNOCK. OPENING HIS BEDROOM door, I stuck my head in to see Jet sitting on his bed, laptop open, and a file open beside that. Glancing up, a smile lit up Jet's face. "Perfect timing. I'm just finishing up."

Stepping in, I closed the door. If I weren't already pregnant, I would have sworn I was ovulating. As soon as I caught sight of Jet, my urge was to jump his bones. Kneeling on the bed behind him, I gently placed my hands on his shoulders. "Can I hug you while you finish?"

Taking my arms, Jet wrapped them around him. "I wouldn't have it any other way." He lifted his face to mine as I cuddled down behind him so I could place a soft kiss on his lips. Grinning, Jet turned back to his laptop while I settled in, resting my face against his back. "Did you find a dress?"

"I did. Your mum doesn't like the color, but she teared up once I was wearing it."

"Did she convince you into anything else that I should know about?"

"Just a kitchen tea and a gift registry for both it and the wedding. I don't need that sort of carry-on, but it made your mum happy."

Tsk'ing under his breath, Jet shook his head. "You give in too easily. I'll have to be careful when the baby is born, or you will let her take over its upbringing."

Rolling my eyes, I jabbed him in the side. "I've basically raised my brothers. I think I can raise our child."

"Your brothers could use a little discipline."

"They get it with us. It's the downside to the fifty-fifty split that the courts favor these days. One parent always tends to be a good-time parent. Kids get no routine, it's hard to discipline them, and the parent who tries to pull their kids inline is seen as the ogre. The courts are to blame for most of the unruliness these days. Parents just get to a point where they give up because they can't fix it with the way custody is set up."

"That happened because dads weren't getting rights to their kids. Mothers were restricting access and cutting them out of their kid's lives." The growl in his voice told me those were terms he didn't like.

"I know why it happened. It doesn't stop it from being a stupid way to raise kids. I don't know. I'm definitely not against dad's having custody - you've seen where the responsibility falls with my brothers - but kids need routine and stability. Send both parents to a parenting class and then decide who should have weekday custody and give the other parent three weekends a month."

The sigh Jet let out leaned me heavier against him as if I were the weight of the world on his shoulders. "They would still fight over that arrangement. The courts just try to offer balance. Unless the parents are willing to put the welfare of their children above their hurt, jealousy, or selfishness, it will never be what is best for the kids."

Trying to ease back a little, I exhaled. "Agreed."

Finishing whatever he was working on, Jet closed his laptop. After closing the open folder, Jet stood up to go put them away. The way I pouted about having to let him go made Jet chuckle. "Let me use the bathroom, and I'll come back." Grinning as he went into the bathroom, Jet shut the door.

Pressing my lips together on an idea, I smiled as I decided to be naughty. Moving to the bedroom door, I locked it, undressed, laid down on Jet's bed, then picked up my phone to browse Pinterest for wedding ideas. "We still have to pick a cake. Your mother is insisting."

"Just let her choose; it will be faster," Jet called through the door. When he opened the door, Jet laughed. The deep baritone rumble made me squirm, only heightened when I looked up to find Jet naked. "Looks like we both had the same idea." Jumping on the bed beside me, Jet rolled me on top of him.

Squeaking in surprise at being lifted up suddenly, I then moaned when I felt him hard between my thighs. "I want you every time I'm near you."

"I feel the same, Rain." Tucking a strand of my hair back behind my ear, Jet met my eyes. "I love you."

Cheeks growing warm, I hovered over his lips. "I love you too."

Jet was slow and passionate in the way he made love to me. Exploring my body gently, awakening the nerve endings of every area he tasted, Jet made the experience almost magical. I loved the way he adored my body and the way he had to touch me.

"I purchased us a bed today," Jet panted as we lay recovering. "It will be delivered on Monday. Until then, are you happy to stay in this room?"

Smiling against his chest, I closed my eyes and cuddled into his warmth. "As long as I'm with you."

SUNDAY NIGHT, I was in the kitchen, making myself warm milk when I heard footsteps. A strange man walked into the kitchen in only a pair of jeans, stopping when he saw me. Eyeing him, I moved closer to the knife rack.

Tilting his head to appraise me, a smile bloomed across his handsome face. "You must be Rain? I'm Jim, Aubrey's boyfriend." He came forward, holding his hand out. "I've heard so much about you. Aubrey talks about you all the time and has photos of the two of you all over his room."

Moving around the bench to keep it between us when he tried to come close, I angled my body, ready to run for the door.

Jim's smile dimmed. "Are you okay?"

"Okay! Leftover cheesecake!" Striding into the kitchen, Aubrey saw me backing away from Jim, and his smile dropped. "Oh, crap!" Aubrey stepped between us, turning his back on Jim. "Rain, are you with me?"

Pausing, I blinked at Aubrey, took in the Landy kitchen, then exhaled a long and controlled breath. The Adrenalin pulsing through my body like a constant buzz, made my hands shake as I put one against my stomach. Fight or flight could make you nauseous. "Yes. Sorry, he just walked in, and I wasn't prepared for a stranger in the house." Stepping to the side of the meals table, I eyed where I'd left my drink, and forced a smile and fake confidence. "It's nice to meet you, Jim. I was just making warm milk to help me sleep." While Jim was still in the kitchen, I didn't move back behind the bench.

"Jim, why don't you take a seat at the kitchen table, and I'll fix us something to eat," Aubrey suggested, gesturing Jim should step out of the preparation area.

Taking the hint, Jim took a seat at the table watching curiously.

Smiling in thanks, I went back to making my warm milk while Aubrey pulled out the cheesecake that I'd made for dessert tonight. "I hate you."

Veronica informed me cheesecake was one of the foods pregnant women shouldn't be eating. So, I'd been stuck with a piece of fruit while everyone else got to eat my treat. Jet, god love him, declined, and asked for a bit to be packed in for work tomorrow, so he wasn't eating it in front of me. Rae thought it was sweet. Aubrey accused him of being a wimp and being scared of me.

Grinning like a Cheshire, Aubrey stuck out his tongue. "You're the one who got knocked up. Now, this cheesecake is all mine."

Shoving his shoulder playfully, I glared at him. "Enjoy it because it's the last I'm going to make until this baby is out and I can eat it again."

"That's just cruel. Denying your best friend baked goodies out of selfishness."

"I'm looking out for your health and your girth."

Aubrey grinned. "Don't you worry your pretty head. I'll work this yumminess off with Jim later." While Jim blushed, I rolled my eyes.

"Congratulations," Jim joined the conversation. "On the baby and the upcoming wedding."

"Thank you. Aubrey tells me you're a doctor. What sort?" Sipping my hot milk, I stayed standing at the bench, watching Aubrey make cappuccinos to serve with the cheesecake.

Turning red as a cherry, Jim showed his dimples on each side of his cheeks. "Ah, currently, trauma surgery. I've just started my residency. Hence, my odd hours for visiting."

It made me smile and relax how nervous Jim was around me. His eyes kept flicking between Aubrey and me. I'd seen that look before. Jim was smitten with Aubrey and hoping I would like him. "Aubrey tells me you've just moved in here with Jet?"

"Yes, this is my third night." Feeling a little more comfortable, I sat at the far end of the table from Jim.

Huffing, Aubrey peered in my direction as he poured their coffees. "Hopefully, you'll keep it down tonight. It's weird hearing your best friend praise your brother's sexual capabilities."

My entire face exploded in flames. "I'd apologize, but I'm not sorry, so it would be a 'sorry, not sorry' moment."

Aubrey came to join us, sitting closer to Jim and lifting his fork. "If you start tonight, Jim is going to help me compete to see who is the loudest."

"I've heard both. Rain will win." Making eye contact, Jet wrapped his arms around me from the side to kiss my cheek. "It's late, and I have work in the morning. Come to bed."

Smiling, I let Jet pull me out of the seat. "Give it a few

months, and you are going to need a crane to lift me up. Especially if this baby takes after you," I joked. Stopping on that thought, I assessed both the boys. "God! If it has your shoulders, I'm going to get ripped apart, getting it out."

"How is that any different to getting it in?" Snickering, Aubrey winked at Jim. "It's hereditary."

Jim eyed Jet up and down, and even I could translate that look. Pity for Jim, if anyone got to be the meat in the Landy boy sandwich, it would be me. My entire body heated with the thought.

Watching me, Aubrey smiled and shook his head. "Take your wife to bed before she suggests an orgy, Jet."

Slipping his arm around my waist and turning me towards the door, Jet cocked an eyebrow at his brother. "You'd say no?"

"While she's knocked up, yes. If I can't at least fantasize about getting her pregnant, it just won't work for me."

Jim frowned. "Am I missing something?"

Rolling my eyes, I snuggled my head against Jet's muscular pecs. "Aub is clucky and wants babies of his own. He decided when we were ten that I would be the incubator in which they grow."

"Oh!" Jim considered the three of us. "And you're okay with that?"

Voice growling in warning, Jet glared at his brother. "Not right now, I'm not. Maybe when he has a husband of his own, and he agrees to artificial insemination rather than doing it naturally."

"That shit costs a fortune, and there is nothing hot about cumming in a cup. We both know it would only take one sprog to get her up the duff. That's all it took for you."

When Jet stepped forward to argue, I put my hand on his

chest. "He's just riling you up. Let's go up to bed. I'll see how I go getting this Landy out before I agree to be impregnated with anymore. The only thing we can be sure of is that I won't be saying no to an epidural."

❖

Chapter Thirty-One
COLD FEET

"Rain?" Jet's worried voice answered the phone. "Aren't you home yet?"

Holding in another sob, I sucked in a breath and tried to sound calm. "Yes, hours ago. Are you back at the hotel?"

Today was the wedding, and I was staying at my beach house for the night. My dad, his girlfriend, Barbara, and my brothers were here with me. Jet and his family were at a resort up the road. Barbara's Husband and Jet's friends were also at the resort, and the boys had a mini bucks party last night.

Barbara and Veronica organized a surprise hens party for me, and we ran into the boys at one of the clubs in town. Jet and I latched onto each other immediately, only for Aubrey and Joseph to pry me free of Jet's hungry lips and octopus arms. The women quickly hurried me away to a different club.

Yawning, Jet waited for it to pass before trying to talk. "Yeah, they had me back by two. Is everything okay?"

"I had a nightmare."

The sound of Jet exhaling and shifting in the sheets came through the phone. "Do you want to talk about it?"

Biting my lip, I rubbed my tummy. "We were at your place, and I was out the front lawn playing with our child."

"Was it a boy or a girl?"

"I think it was a boy."

"Guess I'll need to keep working on that granddaughter for Veronica."

It made me smile. "You pulled up in your car after coming home from work, and I stood up to greet you as you walked towards me. Have I mentioned I love the way you smile at me when you see me the first time after you get home from work?"

"No, but the smile in your eyes as soon as you see me makes me even happier to see you."

Smiling to myself, I closed my eyes and rubbed the little bulge in my abdomen. Just hearing Jet breathe through the phone calmed me down.

"So, did I make love to you on the front porch with my entire family watching?"

"What?"

"The bad part of the dream?"

"Why would I dream that?"

"I dreamed that once. It was before we had sex. I was so eager for you. I dreamed I invited you to one of the family functions and couldn't resist you. We banged each other's brains out on the patio furniture with my family observing."

"That's disturbing. Were they booing?"

"Of course not," Jet scoffed. "This was before I knew your back history with my family. I knew my mum loved you, so in the dream, they all cheered us on, applauded, and insisted we get married upon completion."

Huffing, I rolled to the side. "I think you need to see a counselor about your over-inflated ego."

"My parents have always supported me in everything I've done, Rain. Even subconsciously, I expected they would support my choice of you."

"That must have been a shock when they didn't?"

"You and Aubrey were a shock. The contract was worrisome. Veronica's determination that my brother's sexual orientation was a temporary phase was insane. But Rae supported us immediately, and as soon as mum got on board with it, they more than supported us."

"True." Veronica shipped us harder than a Twilight fan shipped Bella and Edward.

"Are you avoiding telling me what happened in the dream?"

"No, you distracted me."

Jet remained quiet. Exhaling hard as I remembered the worst part about the dream, I wiped a stray tear away. "As you were walking towards us, this man came up behind you and put a gun to your head. He pulled the trigger as soon as you looked at him."

A tear fell down my cheek as I watched it happen behind my eyes. The image flashed and changed for a moment, over-laying with another memory, but I couldn't focus on anything but Jet falling dead at my feet on the lounge room floor. The ground moved, and we were back out the front of his house, his blood coating the front lawn.

Jet was quiet for a few breaths. "You watched me die?" When I sobbed in answer, Jet sighed. "Rain, that isn't going to happen. I mean, it may one day happen when we are old and grey, but it will be in a hospital from old age. We've survived the traumas of our youth. Now, it's about surviving parenthood because I'm sure our kids are going to be trying."

"Were you trying?"

"No, but I was thinking more about trying to raise sensible kids in a house with my mother present."

"I'm sure your mother may disagree with your assessment of the halo you think you wore as a child."

"She may, but she thinks I am much worse as an independent adult. We need to agree on one thing before our child is born. At no time will our child be participating in service in a church. In fact, it will take a lot for me to be convinced of a christening."

Pressing my lips together, I withheld mentioning that Veronica was already making plans for the baptism. The only way Jet was going to get out of it was for him to finally tell his mother what happened to him as an altar boy. Since Jet was determined he would never reveal it to another soul, it put Veronica and Jet in a stalemate situation with me playing mediator. "We could have a naming day."

"You know that won't appease my mother."

"No, but it is the middle ground. Rae can appease your mother. That's his job." Rae knew. I was sure of it. Aubrey told me that much, even if he hadn't realized it.

Sighing, Jet shifted in his bed again. "I'll speak to dad when we get home and get him to start the negotiation process."

Smiling at how my mind was totally distracted from the dream, I relaxed. "I miss you. I wish you were here beside me."

"I never noticed how empty my bed was until you weren't

in it with me. Come meet me on the beach. I can be down there in ten minutes."

"Jet, we are getting married in ten hours."

"And you need to sleep. I know the best way to get you to sleep well, and I promise you will have all the serotonin you need plus more if you come to meet me."

I chuckled. "Our parents would kill us."

"They don't need to know. Come on, I'll make you forget all about that nasty dream."

Smiling, I shook my head into the dim lighting of my room. "Not going to happen. The next time you get under my skirt will be to consummate our wedding, and your baby will no longer be a product of sin."

"Who said our baby is a product of sin?" Jet asked, sounding sufficiently scandalized.

"Your very religious mother. Though, to be fair, she said this while mourning the damnation of my soul, and admitting she always expected if you had a child, it would be by accident. The quick and effective volley of insults left me unable to react to any of them."

Jet groaned. "Jesus, that woman. I apologize in advance for all future cases of her oblivious insults. She truly doesn't mean them. That's exactly how she speaks to Aubrey and me, so it's actually a compliment in that she obviously cares about you like you were one of her own. She's just very passive-aggressive."

"I know, Jet. I've known both your parents for a very long time now."

"Are you sure I can't convince you to meet me down the beach? Even just for a quick kiss and cuddle?" When I giggled,

Jet chuckled too. We both knew where a quick kiss and cuddle would lead.

Truth be told, I probably would have gone, but the idea of walking down the aisle with friction burn to my bits was terrible enough to dissuade me. Add in the sand, getting in all the wrong places, and I was convinced staying in bed was better for my lady parts' ongoing health. "I think I'm good to sleep again now."

"Lucky you. All that talk of sin has me hard as a rock. You remembered to pack the lube, right?"

"Already in the bedside table."

"Good because I'm a traditionalist when it comes to how couples spend their wedding night."

My face was hurting from smiling so much. "Best, I get some sleep now, so I am not too tired tomorrow night. I'd hate to start our marriage by saying 'not tonight, honey. I've got a headache'."

"It won't be your head aching when I'm done with you, Rain," Jet growled playfully.

"I can't wait to say I do and kiss you again."

"Just kiss?"

"It's a starting point. Goodnight."

"Rain... Don't hang up. I want to hear you fall asleep, and when you wake up."

Smiling at the romantic he was, I sighed. "Okay."

Putting the phone on loudspeaker next to my pillow, I snuggled into the pillow. Jet must have done the same. The sound of his breathing quickly lulled me into happy dreams of Jet, and sex, and kisses that made my toes curl. He was still snoring when I woke up four hours later to Oscar drooling on my toes. Scrunching up my face in disgust, I chuckled to myself. Disconnecting the call, I dragged myself to the shower to start getting ready for my big day.

"I CAN'T BELIEVE you've pulled a wedding together in a matter of weeks," Barbara conversed as we walked out to the cars. "It took me years to get my wedding organized." There were tears in her eyes as she stopped in the driveway to smile at me. Those eyes fell down to my abdomen. The tiniest little bump was well hidden in my sleek silver dress. "Well, let's finish you up."

Smiling as she pulled the veil over my face for me, I tried not to bounce on my toes with excitement. The anticipation of seeing Jet and being his wife had me jumping out of my skin.

Tearing up, Joseph opened the car door for me. "You look beautiful, Rain."

"If you make me cry before I get to the church, you will all be in trouble."

Sliding into the backseat, I was grateful not to have netting or anything to deal with. Getting Barbara into a car with her wedding dress a few weeks back was a nightmare. That was with a limo with double opening doors.

Making sure my train was tucked in, Barbara dabbed at her eyes. "I'll see you at the bluff." She walked over to Rae's car and slid in next to my dad's current girlfriend.

Kissing his girlfriend on the cheek, Dad shut the door for that car and came to ride in the car with me. Waving, Rae hopped behind the wheel. Aubrey picked up the twins after lunch, so they could be with the groom's party, and Joseph was driving my dad and me to the wedding.

When Dad opened the door, Oscar tried to get in the car. "Oscar, no!" Dad scolded. Ignoring him, Oscar jumped in the car.

Laughing as he took up the seat beside me, I gave Oscar a pat. "You want to come too, don't you? But you can't come in the car."

"He can ride upfront with me," Joseph laughed, patting the front seat. He was driving my dad's car. There was no point in hiring cars when our family owned the equivalent of what you could rent anyway. When dad grumbled in objection, Joseph waved it away. "He'll behave. I'll keep him by me at the reception."

Oscar never let me out of his sight at home now, except when he took off to run the yard. He loved the Landy mansion and its expansive landscaped yards. Veronica hadn't quite warmed to the idea of a dog running over her parquetry floors yet, but he was well behaved, so she was slowly adapting to Oscar.

Once dad was in the car, we were moving.

"You nervous?" Dad asked.

"Excited." Taking a breath, I tried to dampen the butterflies in my stomach. "I really love him, Dad. Tell me it will last?"

Taking my hand in his, Dad gave it a gentle squeeze. "I can't see the future, Rain. I can tell you marriages take work and compromise. You and Jet are still getting to know each other, and soon, there will be a third person in your relationship who will demand the time and energy you currently give to Jet.

"Children are their own strain on a marriage. You two are

jumping in the deep end with only one swimming lesson under your belt. What you have going for you is that you are both quick learners, and you are both very much in love with each other.

"I've seen couples marry after years together and divorce within months. I've seen couples marry after dating for a few months, and their love only grows after each passing day. You and Jet have as good a chance as any of making this work. Believe it will; be willing to bend when needed, but also willing to stand your ground, and you'll see this through."

"Please tell me that's not your speech for the reception?"

"Oh, no, I would never be so romantic in public." His smile told me he was teasing me back. Smiling, I put my head on his shoulder to enjoy his comfort. He squeezed my hand. "I'm just down the road if you need me, Rain. Never forget that."

Over the last month, I'd missed seeing my dad each day after work. Part of me wished we'd moved in with him and my brothers instead of the Landy's, just so I could have him around regularly.

Several times now, Jet received messages out of the blue telling him we were having dinner with my dad. On the few occasions Jet worked late, he'd had to come to get me from Dad's place on his way home.

Jet never complained, and even called to suggest I visit them if he knew he was coming back late. The fact that Jet understood that some days, I just needed to be with my dad and brother's, made me love him even more.

At the bluff, Joseph opened the door and gave me his hand to help me out. Kissing my cheek through the veil, he stepped aside to shut the door. "I'll see you inside."

Oscar came to stand beside me, growling at the photographer when he approached. "Oscar, go inside and make sure Jet doesn't go anywhere." Oscar ran inside.

By the time we'd done the photos, only Barbara, dad, and I remained outside. "Let's do this," I declared and moved to the old church doors.

The music started up, Barbara smiled, gave me a kiss on the cheek, and stepped inside.

Taking his place beside me, Dad took my arm. "To be clear, I am not giving you away. I am holding your hand as I have through every major event in your life until now. Today, I'm giving permission for Jet to take over holding your hand from here on out." When he cleared his throat, I knew Dad was emotional. That was the only tell he had.

"I love you, Dad. I wish Mum and Harry were here." I said it without crying. Only just.

"They are, Rain. Always have been, that's why you paint them without even knowing. They've wanted you to know they were watching over you still." Wiping away the tear before it could fall, Dad kissed my temple. "Let's get you married."

We stepped inside to where Jet waited at the altar. Our eyes met, and my world narrowed to that one man. Jet's eyes were full of tears. All of a sudden, he looked down and started laughing. Aubrey and my brothers started laughing too. Glancing down, I found Oscar waiting proudly in front of Jet, sitting on Jet's foot so he couldn't move. He was such a good dog.

❖

Chapter Thirty-Two
A WELL-DESERVED HAPPINESS

THE 'I DO'S' WERE PERFECT.

The reception was wonderful.

The speeches were hilarious.

The dancing with my husband was magical.

And the wedding night?

Well, it was everything Jet promised it would be.

We enjoyed our first night as husband and wife at my beach house. Dad wisely elected to stay at the resort.

LYING IN BED, I stared up at the picture of Jet and I saluting our marriage with milkshakes. Since I couldn't drink alcohol at the wedding and I'd been craving milkshakes, Jet hired someone specifically to make swiss-style milkshakes at the reception. No ice cream; nothing dangerous to the baby, but the thickest frothiest malt milkshakes I'd ever had.

My hand rubbed over my swollen tummy. The last six months as Jet's wife were the happiest in my life. We were in our own wing of the Landy House, containing our bedroom plus two more sitting rooms and a study nook, which was now Jet's office at home. We'd finished decorating the nursery, but I'd asked Jet to build the cot in our bedroom, so the baby was close for the first twelve months. Smiling, and always obliging, Jet bought a bassinet for our room and left the cot in the nursery, so we could have options.

After the wedding, I'd gone back to work on a reduced load and only worked three days a week. Granted, they were the three days Veronica usually didn't have anything permanent to keep her occupied. Rae suggested those particular days and, having always found Rae to give me good direction, I agreed. Two weeks ago, when walking became waddling, and just going downstairs for something to eat seemed to take me half a day to get there, I'd taken maternity leave.

Turning my head in the early morning light, I watched Jet sleeping soundly beside me. Most mornings, I woke before him and enjoyed admiring how handsome he was, and that, even swollen and big-bellied as I was, he still couldn't keep his hands off me.

The baby gave another hard kick, probably complaining about the two rounds Jet gave me last night. This time, it kicked right in the ribs, making me grimace.

For two weeks now, its head had been engaged, and we were eagerly awaiting my due date, which was still a week away. Frankly, with how big this baby was, I was ready to push it out a month ago. During the last two visits to the obstetrician, she'd started gently preparing me for a c-section, but I really wanted to go naturally if I could.

Getting up from his bed by the bassinet, Oscar propped his head by my hand. Giving him a few pats, I rubbed at the growing ache in my pelvis. Rolling out of bed with a groan, my back ached like an elephant was sitting on it. Granted, the weight of my belly wasn't small, but this ache was buried in my bones.

Jumping up on the bed, Oscar went over to annoy Jet. "Oscar, don't, he's still got another hour until his alarm goes off," I scolded, but my heart wasn't in it. My womb felt like I was getting my period, except way worse than usual. "Oscar, cut it out," I moaned when he kept pawing at Jet.

Patting Oscar in his sleep, Jet moaned. As I somewhat stood up, I groaned and made my way slowly to the bathroom. Wondering how long I'd been aching for and if this is what woke me up, I used the toilet. While I was brushing my teeth, the cramping in my abdomen started again. Noting the time, I continued cleaning myself up.

"Why are you up so early?" Jet asked from the bathroom door.

Rinsing my mouth, I sighed. "I'm in labor."

"Really?" Jet was suddenly very awake.

"Really." Stepping into the shower, I turned on the water. "So, you can put some pants on because Mr. Woodmorning isn't getting his breakfast."

Glancing down at his morning glory, Jet walked over to join me in the shower. "Are you sure it's happening. You're rather calm."

As if to answer his question, while I stood waiting for the water to heat, warm fluid gushed out from between my legs. "Well, at least I was already in the shower."

Jet stared at the fluid covering his foot with slight disgust. "So, you didn't just wet yourself?" He stuck one foot then the other under the cold water to wash it off.

Chuckling, I kissed his chin. "No. My waters just broke. Let's shower, and then you can call the hospital and tell them we are on our way."

Smiling with sincerity, Jet wrapped his arms around me from behind. "Wow! Okay, it looks like today is the day." Helping me wash, Jet then quickly showered while I dried myself. Calling the hospital while I dressed, Jet told them my contractions were close to ten minutes apart, and they advised we head down as they'd only been sixteen minutes apart ten minutes before that.

As we drove to the private hospital I'd booked into, Jet called his paralegal and arranged someone from his firm to cover his day. It was lucky that he wasn't due in court today. "We still haven't chosen a girl's name," Jet reminded me as the midwife strapped the heartbeat monitor to my tummy. Contractions were now seven minutes apart.

"Nessa," I gritted, pushing down as another contraction hit. They were getting closer.

"After your mum?"

"She was only ever called Vanessa. She hated nicknames. I figure Nessa would be nice, and if she has Aubrey's personality, we can call her Loch Ness. Lovingly, of course."

Jet smiled. "Sounds good to me."

We hadn't bothered finding out the sex at the ultrasound because we didn't want to risk Veronica finding out by accident. We wanted it to be a surprise, so we kept it one for us as well.

The door opened as my obstetrician arrived. "Good morning. I hear your creation is in a hurry to be here for breakfast this morning?"

"Seems like." Gritting my teeth again, I panted a little with the severity of this contraction. Out of instinct, I bore down. "I might have slept through the first innings."

With raised brows, my doctor ducked her head between my legs and inspected the situation. "I know we discussed pain management, but I'm afraid we are not going to have time for an epidural, Rain."

"No, no, I don't want to do this without the good stuff." Jet gripped my hands as I tried to get up off the bed. "I can wait. I'll just cross my legs and... argh!" Another contraction.

"I'm sorry, Rain, but your baby has other ideas." My doctor sounded extremely sympathetic, but she still wasn't giving me the drugs, which wasn't endearing her to me.

On my first visit, the OB noted the scar tissue from my injuries and recommended an epidural, if not a c-section. Now, she turned to the midwife. "We're doing this now."

With those words, things started happening.

Peering up at Jet, tears filling my eyes, I was calm and relaxed when I thought it would all go exactly as I planned it. Now, it was all happening too fast. Pupils dilated; Jet wrapped me in his arms. "Stay with me. Just focus on me, and it will be okay."

Clinging to him as the next contraction gripped me, I pushed against the pain. Truthfully, I felt like I was severely constipated.

Jet's phone rang. Waiting until I was panting and able to let go of his hand, Jet took his phone out to look at the number. "It's Rae," he informed as he put it to his ear. "Morning, Granddad-to-be. Ah, no, we won't be down for breakfast. Rain and I are at the hospital. She went into labor at four this morning, and we've been here since six." Jet winked at me.

The next contraction was the worst yet. Gripping the bed

sheets hard, I gritted my teeth and tried to war with the pain, pushing down hard.

"Actually, it's happening as we speak. I have to go, Dad. Can you call the Judge for me and let him know? Thanks, Dad." Jet hung up as my doctor took up her place. She and the midwife were wearing gumboots.

"Are you expecting it to have puddles?" I snickered between gasps.

The midwife smiled as she joined us. "The floor can get quite wet."

Meeting my eyes between my legs, my obstetrician nodded her head. "Okay, Rain. Let's meet the next generation Landy."

TEN FINGERS, ten toes. Rose pink skin, a mop of black hair like his Dad, and big blue eyes. Hunter Samuel Landy took precisely fifteen minutes from the time the doctor said 'go' to slip into the world in a rush of amniotic fluid. He was smaller than I expected at only nine pounds but still larger than I would have liked. Definitely bigger than my lady bits would have liked too. He also had his father's enthusiasm for boob.

"Should he still be sucking this long?" I asked the midwife after twenty minutes.

"There's no milk yet. It's a comfort to babies. The more he sucks, the faster your milk should come in, and your womb will retract."

As if hearing the midwife, and only just realizing there was no food, Hunter gave up the nipple and snuggled against my chest.

"He's gorgeous," Jet murmured, stroking his mop of hair. "A job well done, Mum."

Chuckling at his praise, I offered him his first hold of his son. "Your mum will be disappointed."

"No, she won't." Taking his son in his arms, Jet held him perfectly. "Happy and healthy grandchildren. That's all she ever really wanted." Jet stroked my cheek. "Are you disappointed?"

I smiled up at the two men in my life. "No, I'm happy."

Coming back in with a wheelchair, the midwife put it beside the bed. She added patient bands to Hunter with the name Baby Landy on them, then held out her arms to take him. "Okay, Dad. You can take your beautiful wife to room twenty-four. Hunter is going to come with me for some testing, and then I'll bring him down to you."

Jet helped me up off the bed and into the chair. After grabbing our stuff, Jet wheeled me out of the labor ward and into the maternity ward. "Our family are out in the waiting room. Once you are settled and ready for visitors, I'll let them know where we are."

"Did no one go to work today?" I grumbled. I sort of wanted just a few hours with Jet and Hunter by ourselves.

"Your Dad did. He said he'll come down for the afternoon visiting time. Aubrey is at the office and will come down when I tell him you are ready. Mum and Dad are here, that's all. Rae would have gone to work, but he thought it best to be here to drive mum home afterward."

Exhaling, I placed my hand over his on my shoulder. Initially, Veronica wanted to be at the birth, but I'd ixnayed that straight out of the gate. While Veronica loved me like a daughter, she wasn't my mother, and I wasn't comfortable with the doctor being down there, I certainly didn't want an audience.

We entered a room that had a much larger bed than I expected. When I frowned up at Jet, he shrugged. "I paid extra to ensure you got the parents' room. I will have to go to work tomorrow, so I plan on staying the nights here until they let you come home in four days. You'll have classes to attend during the day and bonding to do, so nights will be my time to bond while you get some rest."

Tilting my head back to meet his eyes, I fell a little more in love with my husband. "How did I get so lucky to have you fall in love with me?"

Jet kissed my forehead. "Those are the exact words I murmur every night when you fall asleep next to me." Helping me up from the chair, Jet hugged me to him. "I knew the moment I saw you, that you were the one for me, Rain. I've never doubted it for a second."

"I think I knew it too. I'm just a little more stubborn than you."

Snickering, Jet directed me to the bed and then started unpacking my stuff.

Settling into the room, I had just got comfy on the bed when the midwife brought in Hunter. He had his own little crib and was wrapped up in a green blanket. "He's sound asleep," she informed, not whispering or even keeping a low volume. Placing the cot next to the bed, she sat down to go over a few things with me.

Once it was just the three of us, Jet was taking more photos of Hunter happily sleeping through his first hours. At one point, I drifted off to sleep. When I woke up, there was a lunch tray waiting for me, and Jet was holding Hunter in his arms. I smiled. It was one of those perfect moments. A moment where the world was a happy place, and nothing could hurt you. I expected to be panicked by all the dangers the world presented to my child, but, strangely, I wasn't as scared anymore.

Jet smiled at me, watching him. "Do you think you're up for company? Mum's waited patiently for hours now. It's good training for her, but it's also her first grandchild."

Sitting up, I made myself presentable. "Okay." I smiled, happiness filling me entirely.

Stepping forward, Jet kissed my lips tenderly. "I love you, Rain." Taking a deep breath, he sent a text on his phone, then jumped a brow at me. "It's about to begin."

Epilogue

JET

Pulling into the street, I woke my mobile in the handsfree cradle and tapped the Iron gate icon. The app linked through to the security system, and the gates opened as I pulled into the driveway. From the outside, the house looked still, but I knew that could be an illusion, a design to keep anyone watching unsure if anyone was even home.

Putting the car in park, I picked up my phone and the bag of flour from the passenger seat, along with the bouquet of lavender and rosemary. As I approached the front door, I opened up my voicemail and listened to my father's message again.

"Jet, it's Rae. Look, I just got home, and your mother is in hysterics. Apparently, she tried to convince Rain into you having Hunter baptized, and Rain flipped out. She's taken Hunter and left. I'm sure she hasn't gone far, but she did pack a bag for her and the baby and took Oscar. I've tried calling her, but she's not answering, so I've left a message with Thoren and you. I'm sure she's safe but knew you'd want to know sooner than later. Your mother said she did nothing to cause such a severe reaction, but Rain slapped her, and we both know Rain wouldn't do that unprovoked. Let me know she's okay."

Exhaling stiffly, I knocked at the door. The judge gave me access to the house some months back due to how often I'd be picking up Rain, but also in case something happened, and I needed to get in while he wasn't around, but I always knocked first. The door opened, and a sullen Judge May greeted me. "Jet. I heard you were stuck in court with a juvenile matter, I know how passionate you are about those, so I left work early and came home as soon as I got Rae's message."

Nodding as I stepped inside, I inhaled the scent of delicious food. "Were you nearly finished for the day?" Sliding my phone into my pocket, I handed the Judge the bag of flour, he took it without comment.

"I still had two cases on my docket for the day; an underage marriage and adoption. I've pushed them both to tomorrow. It's not like I ever have breathing room on my lists anyway. What's two more?"

"Is Rain okay?"

Inhaling fully, the Judge's pupils constricted. "Your mother is a piece of work sometimes." Shutting the door, the Judge led the way to the kitchen. "She's sleeping. Come have a drink before you go check on her. Let her rest a bit longer."

In the kitchen, the twins held a bowl of mush and took turns playing 'here comes the plane' to feed my giggling son. The scene put a smile on my face, despite the worry in my heart.

When Hunter saw me, he gifted me with a big smile and claps. "Hello, my Bambino. Are you happy?" Many gurgles and a few more laughs, then Hunter was focused back on his uncles and the food they held ready.

"Hey, Jet," Storm greeted as I kissed Hunter's head. "Rain said we could feed Hunter while she slept. There's a lot of yummies in the fridge if you're hungry, and freshly baked lasagna for dinner."

Before I could reply, Rain's dad handed me a plate of freshly heated lasagna before he grabbed two beers from the fridge. "Sit down, Jet. Your family are safe and not going anywhere."

Understanding that he was trying to put me at ease, I sat at the table. With a smile, I took a seat and ate while watching the twins take care of their nephew. "The boys seem a lot more settled of late," I noted when the Judge sat beside me.

"They have more stability now that they are living here full-time."

"Penelope didn't seem happy about the judge's ruling on the custody change."

"She has them every other weekend still, but only when it suits her. In essence, she was only worried the change in custody would affect her alimony. Once I told her I was happy to keep it as is, she couldn't care where the boys were."

"That was generous of you."

"Not really. Penelope's engaged to be married again, so once that's official, I'll be free of the alimony entirely anyway. She hasn't realized that yet, and I'm not going to be the person to tell her either."

Smirking, I finished my dinner, just as the twins finished feeding Hunter. "Here, give me my Bambino. You boys are good uncles."

"Rain needed to calm down. Knowing Dad was here, and

we could feed Hunter allowed her to go sleep. V really did a number on her today. Rain was talking about moving back home again," Zephyr informed. "Which would be great if you two decided to do that. Storm and I already agreed to move to the rooms in the lower level and let you and Rain have upstairs to yourself."

"Well, thank you. I'll speak to Rain about the living arrangements and see if we need to move before you go changing rooms."

Waving, the boys went upstairs to the media room to play games. "Keep it down," Judge called.

"It's nice they've given my mother a term of endearment."

"V?"

"Yeah. She can't be gran or anything like that, so V is nice."

"You might want to ask the meaning behind it before you agree."

Frowning, I observed the judge. "It doesn't stand for Veronica?"

"Not exactly." Lifting his beer, he took a long draught.

"You're not going to tell me, are you?"

"What was the Juvenile matter?"

"Sexual abuse by the father," I growled.

Judge May, having seen everything in his day, still lowered his head and shook it. "Evidence?"

"Indisputable."

"Sick bastard."

"Agreed."

"I saw some sick stuff in the criminal court, but at least that was all adults. Kids, and especially your own kids, that's a whole other level of sick."

"Growing up, I thought Family court was all divorces. It wasn't until I did my work experience with you that I realized child abuse and child protection cases all went to the family court."

"That's why you specialized there, to try and help kids?"

"It wasn't to deal with arguing couples and their greed and jealousy."

"Was it because of Aub?"

Taking a pull of beer, I considered how to answer that. "Kind of, yes. I've been protecting my little brother from anyone who might hurt him most of my life. At some point, I thought of all the kids out there who didn't have a big brother or weren't able to protect themselves, and I wanted to help them if I could. What I realized too late, is the one person I couldn't protect my brother from, was himself."

"You'll discover very quickly that as a parent, you can be rendered powerless, both by outside forces and your children. Rain was this effervescent soul of happiness and light before the attack. I lost my wife and both my children that night. Yes, Rain survived, but that girl up there is not the one I raised for fourteen years. Don't misunderstand, I love her just as much. But for a long time, it was like they'd left the corpse of my daughter here for me to helplessly watch her wither and rot. Everything I did to try and bring her back made it worse, so I stepped back and instead just created boundaries to prevent Rain from crossing entirely beyond saving. Your brother smashed the fence and let her through. I'll never forgive him for that, but I can't deny Rain dying is what saved her."

Tears splashed on the table as the judge stared at his bottle of beer on the table. Taking a breath, he straightened his back as if lifting the weight of his grief away. "But it was you, Jet, who brought her back to life. I saw it when she started dating you. Those first hints of my rainbow in a stormy sky could be glimpsed if you peered just right. She'll never be that little girl again, but you make the beauty of her soul shine through the murkiness. Don't destroy her, okay?"

"I won't. She's my rainbow now."

Considering me, the Judge almost hinted at a smile. "Your mother, on the other hand… here, let me take my grandson, you go tell your wife how much you love her."

"Do you know what Veronica said to her?"

"I don't need to know. My daughter came home with her bags packed, cursing her name, crying, and using the entire pantry to cope. Word to the wise, if she bakes sweets, she was triggered. If she makes meals and savory dishes, your mother reminded her she's bound for hell. Hope you enjoyed that Lasagna. There is a casserole with dumplings, a loaf of savory bread, and several other dishes my personal trainer would have a fit about me eating packed up in the fridge. I won't have to cook for a month."

Sighing, I looked to where Hunter giggled as I bounced him on my knee. "Your Nonna is very frustrating sometimes." Giving him a big kiss on the cheek, I passed him to his grandfather. "What happened to Rain's Grandparents? She never talks about them."

Eyes narrowing, the Judge chewed his cheek. "I was abandoned as a child and grew up in foster care. My parents weren't worth knowing. Vanessa's parents are still alive, but they didn't want to know Rain after the incident. So, she doesn't want to know about them. They reached out when she won an award a few years back for one of her building designs, but she pretended she had no idea who they were and told them never to call again."

Jaw tense, I was sure my anger was a mirror of the Judge's. "Why didn't they want to know her? Did she remind them of their daughter?"

"She was damaged goods and never going to amount to anything after the attack."

"The drugs?"

"This was before she disappeared into escapism. They said that while she was still fighting for her life in the hospital. I punched my father-in-law in the face and told him to get out. Rain didn't know, but she called her gran for her birthday some months later, and the bastards told her their daughter and granddaughter were dead and never to call again. I think that was the first time she drank enough to make herself vomit."

"They sound charming."

"He's the CEO of an endurance company. Tells you everything you need to know about him." Turning his attention to Hunter, Judge May smiled. "How about some tummy time?"

"Be careful, he scampers away quickly now. He's got the commando crawl down to a fine art."

Patting my shoulder, the judge got up and headed to the playmat Rain must have brought with her. The good one, the one for home. "Shit." Standing up, I went upstairs to Rain's old bedroom. It'd been a year since we moved in together, but she still hadn't packed it up entirely. You could be mistaken to think she still lived here.

Asleep on the bed, Rain looked angelic. A sad and tired

angel if the dark circles around her eyes and dried tears on her cheeks were any indication. Sighing, I closed the door and moved to the bed. Kicking off my shoes, I hung my jacket over the back of her desk chair.

Climbing onto the bed, I wrapped my arms around my wife, drawing her in against me. Eyes flashing open, Rain tensed. "It's just me. Can I hold you?"

Eyes filling with tears, Rain fell against me and sobbed into my chest. "Shh, I'm here. I've got you."

For several minutes, Rain cried it out. When she quietened, I just held her longer. "You need to tell her why."

There was no need to ask who or what, that was obvious. The problem was, I wouldn't. My mother put the church above all. It was the step between man and God for her, and they could never do any wrong. There would be no convincing her that her precious church was made of men and man's doctrines, not gods. The only words written by God were the Ten Commandments, which the church readily broke.

Thou shall not steal. The church had taken the innocence of many a child.

Thou shall not murder. Rape was not just the violation of the body, but also the murder of souls. Rain's father had said much the same. Those men tore the soul of his daughter to pieces, and she was lost to him, to herself. The woman I held in my arms now was because somewhere she found the strength to pull together the fragments until she had just enough to keep living.

"What did my mother say?"

"That if Hunter wasn't baptized, he'd end up a murderous hell-condemned soul like Aubrey and me."

"So, you hit her?"

"No, I reminded her that both Aubrey and I were baptized, and if Aubrey being gay condemned him to hell, then it was too good a place for child-raping priests that she seemed so sure I should trust with my son."

Closing my eyes, I gritted my jaw. How close had Rain come to revealing my secret?

"Your mother tried to slap me. I blocked her. She called me a baby killer. My hand just snapped out. I'm sorry, Jet. She's been harping about it for six months non-stop whenever she gets me alone, and I just couldn't take it anymore. You need to tell her."

Inhaling, I nosed her hair. "No. She'll get over it eventually."

"Then, I'm moving out."

"What?" Sitting up, I looked down at my angry wife. Was she leaving me because I wouldn't reveal my greatest shame?

The fire in her eyes softened, Rain brushed my cheek with trembling fingers. "I can't keep playing mediator between you too. If you don't tell her why baptism is never going to happen, I'm never going to hear the end of it. I'll eventually snap and drown her in a baptismal font. So, we need to move in here until your mother can get over it."

Exhaling in relief, I caressed Rain's tear-drenched cheek. "I thought you meant you were leaving me."

"What? No, never. I mean, if I do snap and kill Ronnie, there will be jail time, but I expect you to be totally sympathetic to my situation and to wait for me."

Soul lightening with her humor, I relaxed a little. "I wonder what the limit on conjugal visits per week is."

"Hey, this is not foreplay. Focus. How are you going to fix this?"

Blowing out a breath, I considered my beautiful wife. "For now, I'm going to go home, pack a bag and tell my mother that we will be staying here until she apologizes to you, and promises to let the baptism go. If she can't, then me and my hell-condemned family will move out permanently, and she won't be allowed to have anything to do with my spawn of evil."

Watching Rain take a deep breath, I tasted her delicious lips. "She believes Aub will never have kids, so she'll renege if it's the choice between having a baptism or never seeing her grandchildren."

"Stop using the plural. I haven't recovered from giving you the first yet."

Smirking, I adored my wife. "My point being, she'll give in very quickly. We'll still stay here for the week just to push the point." Plus, this was Rain's safe place.

Being here with her family always balanced Rain faster than my family's home. Probably because Rain's family knew how to move around her when those tears in the fabric of her soul showed up, and my mother just ripped them right open. Tasting her lips, I laid back on the bed, taking her with me.

"Jet, my brothers are just outside in the media room."

"And making enough noise to cover even your loudest climax." Pulling Rain on top, I decided that if my mother was right and my wife was destined for hell, I was going with her just to keep kissing her for eternity.

Later that night, I'd collected what I needed from home, given my parents my ultimatum, and returned to my wife's arms. Aubrey and Jim had turned up not long after, and they sat with Rain and me out on the back-deck drinking chamomile tea with Judge May.

"So, will the twins be moving downstairs?" Aubrey asked.

"Not yet. Right now, this is temporary," Rain's dad answered. "Though, I wouldn't be opposed to it becoming permanent. I've missed having my daughter here."

The Judge often invited Rain over for dinner and week-ends, which made it obvious he missed his daughter. "We'll see. That's all going to depend on Mum."

"As much as it upsets me when V has one of her moments, part of me wants her to be stubborn just for my benefit."

Aubrey snickered. "Are you calling her that too know?"

Rain's dad shrugged. "If the skin fits." Aubrey and Jim chuckled.

"Dad, don't encourage them," Rain scolded half-heartedly, though, I noted she was smirking herself.

"Okay, you need to tell me now. What does V stand for?"

"You know, the nasty lizard bitch from the mini-series V," Aubrey laughed. "Diana, her name was. The twins watched it and started calling Veronica, V."

Blinking at my laughing brother, I couldn't believe he was allowing the twins to basically call our mother a power-hungry lizard woman. "Isn't that an adult show?"

"They watched it at Penelope's," Rain sighed in resignation of the things the boys came home with from those visits. "Ronnie's not that bad. She's just very passionate about her religion."

Scoffing, Aubrey gave Rain a disbelieving look. "She's a zealot, like the lizard lady. The nickname works. Bonus that mum finds it endearing."

Shaking my head, I thought about it, and barely restrained

grinning at the comparison. Yeah, mum could be fanatical. "So, Judge, your name is Thoren. Did the weather names start with you?"

"I was found in a thunderstorm. Apparently, I wasn't even scared. So, that's the name the hospital gave me. Did you really never know my name?"

Giving him a shrug, I smiled. "You were always Judge. I guess it might be time to start calling you by your real name."

Considering me, Thoren shook his head. "No, Judge is good."

Blinking, I wasn't sure how to respond, but then Rain laughed. "Dad!"

Slowly, her dad's lips lifted in a smile. "Thoren is fine, Jet."

Gurgling came through the baby monitor. Checking her watch, Rain sighed as she stood up. "Ten o'clock feed. I might go to bed after I finish."

"I'll be up in a few."

Smiling, my wife radiated beauty as she kissed me then wished everyone a good night. As she walked away, I watched her counting my lucky stars to call that woman my wife. When I looked back, I found my brother and father smiling after Rain. Meeting each other's eyes, we shared mutual understanding. We all loved her, and we were happy just to see her happy.

It took two weeks for Veronica to give in on the baptism and settle for a naming day. By then, Rain had settled and really didn't want to move back. As much as I loved my wife's family, their house was significantly smaller, and Thoren and I were tending to get in each other's way, so Rain agreed to move back to the mansion.

Oscar was over the moon to have the grounds to run

around again, though, Rae believed Oscar's sudden vested interest in marking my mother's favorite rose bush until it started dying was his way of siding with his beloved owner.

As long as I had my wife and child and we were all smiling and healthy, I was happy.

Bonus Epilogue
OSCAR'S POV

"Oscar!" The twins cry as they get splashed by the water I'm shaking off. As soon as they arrived, we all raced down the beach to cool off. I missed the twins with their exuberance. They came by after school most days now, and we got to play after they did their homework. They were a lot more stable since coming to live with their sire full-time.

"Lunch!" my master yells from the gate. Racing the boys up the beach to reach the gate first, I try to dash inside. "Oscar, no." Rain commands me to sit by the door. Grudgingly, I do. "Good boy. You'll have to wait outside until you dry."

Pouting, I put my snout between my paws. Though, I know it won't take long to dry in this heat. Drying off with their towels, the twins give me a pat on the head and dash inside. The pup was all over his cousin's now, trying to get them to play with him.

"Let them eat, Hunter." Picking up her pup, Rain puts him in the chair next to his favorite cousin. He babbles at them while messing his food. The master rubs her rounded tummy as she walks back to the kitchen. "Settle down in there."

I roll over to dry faster. The pup in Rain's belly was restless, making the master's stomach revolt regularly. Rain was tired, and while still happy, the combination of work, a rambunctious pup to chase around, and her mate's needs were taking their toll on her energy level. Coming back to the door, Rain squatted down to pat my head before putting a plate of food down for me. It was her lunch, barely eaten. The pup caused that a lot.

"Good boy, Oscar." Stopping, Rain rubbed her tummy again. Nosing her belly, I lick her hand. Her scent was tired mixed with hope, and it was sharper too. Soon, we'd have a female pup in the house. I had a feeling she was going to be just like her mother.

Coming home from the shops, the mate worried about finding her squatting. "Rain, what's wrong?"

"Nothing," Rain assured as she let him help her back to standing. "Your lunch is ready." Smiling, her scent changed to happiness and desire. Making the gesture to tell me to eat, Rain let her mate lead her back inside. "Did you get everything on the list?"

"I did." Smirking, he pressed their lips together. These too mated at every opportunity, and the mate was very opportunistic. "Come on. You can help me wrap the presents, and then I think you need to rest."

"I'll grab Hunter and put him down for a nap first."

"Leave him with the twins. Zephyr, can you keep an eye on Hunter while we wrap the presents? Rain needs a rest."

"Sure, Jet," the responsible one agreed, deeply entrenched in showing the pup whatever he was watching on his tablet.

Finishing the master's lunch for her, I wandered inside, finding a spot by the window to enjoy the sun and have a nap. The noises from the master's bedroom told me they were mating again. He already had her with a pup, what was the point in this until that pup was born? It made no sense, but they had been the same when she carried the first pup too.

Lifting an eyelid when the boys cleaned up from lunch, I watched them move to the lounge to play their video games, taking the pup to his playpen and setting him up to play by himself. The pup wasn't having that. He waited until they were entrenched in their game, then scaled the wall of the playpen, and made his way to the open pantry door. This pup was a hungry little thing, always nagging his mother for more food.

"Woof!" *'Watch him.'*

"Hunter, out of there." Quickly running over, Zephyr removed the toddler from the pantry. "Storm, you didn't shut the door again. Rain's told you a hundred times." Carrying the little one back to the lounge, Zephyr hands him a tablet with a colorful game on it. That keeps the little one entertained.

"Where's Rain and Jet?" Storm looked around suddenly.

"Bedroom. Remember, Jet asked us to watch Hunter while they wrapped Christmas presents."

"Wasn't that an hour ago?"

"Yep!" Zephyr looked over his shoulder at the hallway. "Rain was going to rest too."

"Or they got distracted again," Storm huffed.

"More than likely."

"Aubrey says they're always doing it."

Zephyr cringed. "So, is he. Do you think he will get back with Jim?"

Storm shrugged. "I don't know. Jim was pretty angry about the whole Rain and Aubrey thing. I don't know why Aub told him. Dad said there are some things that you should just leave in your past and move on."

"Rain said Aubrey sabotages his own happiness. He used to do the same with her."

"What does that mean?"

Zephyr shrugged again. "Don't care. He's an awesome guy, and he's great with Hunter. He so wants to be a dad."

"Yeah, poor Aub. Hopefully, he'll find a wife soon."

"He's gay, Storm. He doesn't want a wife."

"But you can only have babies with a wife."

Zephyr frowned. "I know. I don't know how it works either."

Bowing my head to the ground, I watched the pup notice his cousin's distraction and sneak away. The pup was smart and kind but overly curious. Making his way to the door outside, the pup started to push through the doggy door. Getting up from my spot in the sun, I grabbed him by the back of his shirt.

"Osc, Osc!" the pup laughed as I used his shirt to carry him down the hall to my master's bedroom. Putting the pup down, I lifted up to push the handle down. The door opened a touch. The pup pushed it the rest of the way open and in we went.

The mate was in the shower, but my master was lying on the bed with a sheet covering her. Her breathing told me she was already sound asleep. Helping the pup up to be with his mum, I watched as he snuggled into her. The pup patted his mother's face a few times, then closed his eyes and joined her in a nap. Curling up beside the pup, I got comfortable.

When the mate came back into the room, I opened an eye.

He spied the full bed and laughed. Coming over, he kissed his mate lovingly on the head, then did the same to his pup. Admiring them both, a smile plastered on his face, he looked at me. "Keep them safe for me, Oscar. I'm going to take the twins for a surf. Call me when they wake up."

Putting my head down, I accepted the pat from the mate and enjoyed a nap with my family. When my master stirred, I trotted outside to the gate and called her mate. He waved from the waves to let me know he heard me. Happy, I checked the borders of my territory, freshening up a few of the faded markings as I went. When I was heading back to the house, I overheard the master telling her mate she was taking the pup for a swim.

Racing back in time for Rain to open the pool gate for her and the pup, I rushed through the gate and jumped into the beautiful cold water of the pool.

"Oscar!" my master scolded, but she laughed, as she always did.

Summer was the best!

Join the Beautiful and Deadly

Join Ebony's Mischief List

Sign up to Ebony's mailing list for the following perks:

- latest news on new releases
- heads up on upcoming promotions
- exclusive freebies like coupons to read Ebony's stories on Radish for free
- first chance at Giveaways
- get a free book

Go to https://ebonyolson.com for more information

Black Mark

THE COMPLETE SAGA

Mora has never had an easy life. Physically and mentally abused by her mother, she's never known what being wanted or loved felt like. Her only relief? Sex, bleeding, and playing the cello. And now, her new boss, Darius, has shown an interest in her character. Will Darius become another danger in Mora's life, or is he the absolution she's been internally wishing for?

Black Mark

ONE

Reaching the landing before the last flight of stairs, I paused to catch my breath. I preferred the stairs to the elevator, claiming it was for fitness, but in truth, I was extremely claustrophobic. Taking the deodorant out of my bag, I quickly gave myself a freshen up. My fine long black hair was pulled back in a tight ponytail, but I checked to make sure it was still presentable after seven flights of stairs.

The morning meeting with an upmarket clothing brand across town was still going. My boss, Stuart Shuman, had sent me back to entertain his next client until he could get back here. The client was the owner of Lynwood Corporation, the figurehead for bookings in the entertainment industry.

If you had the money, Lynwood offered the complete package for your event. They designed, developed and delivered everything from major public events, product launches, award shows, red carpet, the big fashion shows, gala dinners, concerts, corporate conferences, seminars and weddings for the rich and famous.

They would provide anything, from intimate acoustic acts

to comedians, magicians, costumed tributes and everything in between- and I do mean everything. Lynwood agents worked with the client and took care of booking top-name entertainment. They organized the decor, sound and lighting. If you could think of a popular event in England in the last four years with headlining acts, more than likely, Lynwood had been the driving force behind it.

After reapplying my lip gloss and straightening my sensible black work dress, I took the last flight of stairs and plastered my smile into place. Walking through the glass doors into the reception area, I found two men sitting in the waiting area, looking at their watches unhappily.

"Mr. Rafal." I smiled walking toward them.

The dark-haired man stood instantly turning toward me. His hazel eyes scanned me from toe to head, his mouth frowning, his pupils dilating.

Ignoring the mixed look of disappointment and interest I held my hand out. "I'm Mora Ellis, Mr. Shuman's executive assistant. He's asked me to apologize for running late. He's caught up with another client currently, but should arrive shortly."

He shook my hand then pointedly looked at his watch. "I have somewhere else to be by one," he said, a faded Scottish accent evident.

"Then I will have Mr. Schuman's partner and our director of operations start the meeting. Mr. Shuman can join when he can," I assured. Stepping past the potential new client, I moved to the reception desk. "Melissa, can you ask Mr. Hark to join us immediately, please?"

"Yes, Miss Ellis." Melissa's thick Scottish accent outshone Mr. Rafal's.

Stepping back, I eyed Darius Rafal. He was tall, easily six-foot-four, or an inch or two more. I'd met him once, five years ago when I'd first moved to England. He hadn't changed at all. He was clean-shaven, late twenties, his dark hair was slightly too long for business, but suited him well, accentuating his strong jawline.

Everything about Mr. Rafal was tailored and precise. His navy suit matched perfectly with his tie. A black onyx tie pin caught my eye before his hands fidgeted with the matching onyx cuff links, stealing my focus.

When I lifted my topaz blue eyes to meet his hazel eyes, one of his eyebrows rose at my gumption. His blond male colleague smirked and stepped forward holding out his hand.

"I'm Warren Mann, Mr. Rafal's executive assistant. It's lovely to meet you, Mora." The London accent was crisper than most of my colleagues. "I love your accent. South African?"

"Australian."

Warren's blue eyes shone with humor as he shook my hand. He scanned my face, his eyes literally taking in the arch of my dark brows, the small bridge of my nose which my glasses always slipped down, my barely existent cheekbones, and the perfect Cupid's bow of my lips. I felt like he was memorizing what I looked like.

He was older, easily in his mid-thirties, clean cut and almost military in his presentation. While the suit was tailored, he wore a short-collared button-down which prevented him from wearing a tie. It also meant the small collar didn't come high enough to cover the dark bruising of teeth marks on his neck.

"Your girlfriend has a bad crossbite." I met his eyes evenly.

He returned my gaze, surprised at my openness. "If she were my girlfriend, I'd pay for the braces. Luckily, that's not the case."

"Lucky for her not to be your girlfriend, or for you not to have to pay for the braces?" I queried evenly. No judgment, just discerning the facts.

Warren smiled brightly. "Probably both. Your teeth would leave a perfect bruise."

"That they do." Looking past Warren to his boss, I smiled politely. "If you'll follow me," I requested politely. I turned toward the conference room.

The tall, dark-haired and blue-eyed Alex Hark was walking into the room as I approached from the reception area. He shook hands and introduced himself before turning to me and murmuring, "Catch me up."

"Standard marketing proposal. Mr. Rafal runs Lynwood Corporation. We want a piece of the pie."

Melissa came in with a pot of sencha green tea and sat it in front of the clients along with a specific brand of lemon shortbread. Stuart liked me to research prospective clients and know what they wanted. He called it good business, I called it stalking.

"Where in Scotland are you from?" Mr. Rafal picked up the teacup as he spoke to Melissa.

"Aberdeen. You?" She tucked a fiery strand of her hair behind her ear and batted her lashes.

"Inverness." Putting the tea to his lips, Rafal turned his shoulder away from her. He hadn't been flirting. Now, his body language told me that her flirtations annoyed him. He was shutting her down before she got the wrong idea.

"Did you go to the University of Highlands and Islands?" Melissa pushed on enthusiastically.

Swallowing his tea, Darius placed it down carefully before turning hard eyes on Melissa. Melissa dropped her eyes and stepped back in almost a gesture of submission. "I studied economics and international relations at the University of Saint Andrews. I got my MBA at the Imperial College of London."

Placing my hand on Melissa's shoulder gently, I interrupted his haunting glare. "Thank you, Melissa." Never lifting her eyes from the ground, Melissa quickly left the room. "Unnecessary," I stated factually when she shut the door.

"I'm sorry?" Darius Rafal lifted those hard eyes to meet mine.

Resisting the temptation to flinch, I leaned my hip on the table next to him. "Melissa was just welcoming and friendly towards a fellow Scotsman."

"I don't need a new friend." Darius kept his challenging eyes locked on mine.

"Well, you could use some manners," I huffed, standing straight.

"Mora," Alex breathed my name in warning.

Without acknowledging the warning, I walked to the door. "I'll leave you in Alex's capable hands." I had no patience for anyone who mistreated a woman.

"I believe Mr. Shuman instructed you to entertain me till he arrived, Miss Ellis," Darius Rafal spoke evenly before taking another sip of tea.

Glancing back as I opened the door, I noted Darius sat with his back to me, his assistant restraining the grin that was already lighting up his blue eyes. "You have rather large strong hands, Mr. Rafal. I'm sure since you don't need any new friends, that you are quite capable of entertaining yourself."

Bowing his head, Alex cursed. Darius turned his angry eyes to mine. Giving myself points for not flinching under that look, I winked at him and walked out. The moment I did, his assistant burst out laughing.

"I apologize, Mr. Rafal. Mora has no patience for people who think they are better than anyone else," Alex apologized as I shut the door.

"Are you suggesting I'm a snob, Mr. Hark?"

"I'm not suggesting it, Mr. Rafal. Now, if you turn to page two of the proposal in front of you..."

"Jesus, Mora, you are going to get yourself fired." Alex grabbed my elbow, yelling over the deep beat of the music. We were inside Jasper's nightclub, called JJ's, in Camden Town.

"Hey, you're here." Gifting Alex a mile and ignoring the comment, I handed him a shot from the tray I was carrying. "We're over here."

Keeping the tray over my head, I navigated my way through the crowd to the lounges where my best friend and her colleagues had planted themselves. It was already ten and Sophie, and her orchestra friends, had spent the first few hours of Friday night at the pub near their rehearsal hall.

"I mean it, Mora. Rafal made a comment to Stuart about your attitude. He then pointedly mentioned he was meeting with a competitor of ours this afternoon. Stuart must think you lost us the contract."

"Pfft! That ass was never going to give Horizons the contract. He gave us thirty minutes. He spent two hours with Elliptical, and an hour and a half with Objective before they even came to us. We were just time fill. Stuart knew that. Why do you think he didn't bother racing back for the meeting? We got the Sanderson contract, by the way."

Grinning, I passed out the shots, throwing back one before I dropped down into the lounge beside Sophie, my best friend. Flicking her golden curls over her shoulder, Sophie batted her lashes at Alex. She leaned forward to grab her shot, ensuring her extraordinary cleavage nearly fell out of her top.

"Yeah, Alex, relax. You know Mora knows what's going on with all of your clients. She'd never piss off a big client if there were any chance you could get them." Sophie winked at him and crossed her legs, the skirt she wore riding up higher on her thighs. "Now, bring your sexy ass over here and let me lick the salt off you."

"It's vodka, not tequila," Alex argued, sitting on my other side.

"Do I care?" Sophie threw back the shot anyway.

Alex and Sophie were banging each other. I knew about it, though no one else did, especially not Alex's girlfriend. Sophie was already well past tipsy. That meant her social filter went out the window three rounds of shots ago. How Alex's girlfriend hadn't caught on yet was beyond me. I guess she was too focused on the potential I was hooking up with her boyfriend to even suspect or notice any other woman.

That's what happens when another woman finds out you aren't in a monogamous relationship. They instantly suspect you of screwing every man you talk to. Because, when the guy everyone thinks is your sweetheart starts getting it on with another woman in your presence, and you don't bat an eyelash that obviously means you are also screwing around.

"Leila will be here soon, so cool it, Sophie," Alex warned.

"Why do you invite her out with us? She hates me and spends the entire night giving me daggers or trying to psychoanalyze my relationship with Jasper."

Alex patted my leg and kissed my cheek, giving me a sympathetic smile. So of course, that's precisely when Leila arrived. Her face went bright red with anger, and I knew she was getting ready to start calling me several unsavory names again. Rolling my eyes, I grabbed Alex's chin and kissed him. It was closed mouth and awkward as hell, but I pressed my lips to his for several seconds before pulling away and standing. My eyes all for Leila. "Now call me all the names you want."

Alex was still sitting shocked by my kiss. He didn't even realize Leila was there till I'd walked away and Leila screeched like a cockatoo. "I knew it!"

Sophie was laughing so hard she tipped sideways on the lounge and nearly fell off. One of her friends caught her, and they laughed together. At the bar I signaled the barman for another round.

"Celebrating tonight, Mora?" Winston rolled up the white sleeves of his shirt, which only made the dark flesh underneath look darker.

"Hell, yes. I scored big today."

Winston grinned his pearly whites at me. "One more round, then I'm cutting you ladies off before Sophie gets herself in trouble. After this, single drinks only. Understood?"

"Fine! Punish me for the hot girl's shortcomings," I teased. Winston knew I could handle my alcohol better than Sophie. He didn't want to be cleaning up her puke in another hour.

"And what big score did you make today?" A deep voice whispered in my ear.

I turned to find Warren Mann grinning at me. The top two buttons of his shirt were undone, the jacket was gone and his eyes were bright and glassy. He'd had a few drinks already and was apparently there to relax. He reached out and tucked my hair behind my ear.

"I like your hair out. You look your age now."

Young is what he was saying, but then he was at least ten years my senior. I liked Warren. He was friendly, flirty, and just gave off those good vibes. He was looking over the little black dress that I was wearing, but his eyes paused for a moment longer than appropriate on the scoop neck, and how the material clung around my breasts.

"Not your boss, that's for sure." Smirking, I used my finger under his chin to lift his eyes back to mine. "You winding down after a long day?"

Warren held up a glass of scotch and ice. "Sure am. Want to help me?"

"Sure. Come join us."

Winston slid a second glass in front of Warren. "Thanks." Warren took the glass. "I'll just go grab my jacket."

Nodding acknowledgment, I watched the very buff Mr. Mann walk off into the crowd. "Last round, Mora," Winston reminded me as he slid another tray of shots in front of me.

Crossing my heart, I blew him a kiss. Giving me another one of his disarming smiles, Winston waved me off. Balancing the tray above my head like I still worked the bar to get through the crowd, I swerved my way over to the quiet corner we nabbed. When I put the tray down, the group all grabbed a shot. We saluted each other before throwing them back. I threw back my own shot while standing, then set it on the low table.

"There you are," Warren called behind me.

Standing straight, I turned around still filled with the success of my day. The smile disappeared when I saw my failure standing with Warren. Darius Rafal was gorgeous in daylight; darkness didn't detract from it. He now had a five o'clock shadow that made him look more rugged. It also made some primal sexual beast inside me start rolling around and purring. I was saved from actually purring out loud by Alex.

"What the hell is with you today, Mora? Are you PMSing or something?" Alex growled. He pushed past me to grab his jacket from the lounge. The way I was reacting to Darius Rafal made ovulating the more likely theory. Alex shook his head angrily. "You owe me big time. I have to go do damage control."

Sophie latched onto Alex's arm. "Leave the bitch. Stay. You deserve to relax. I can make it happen." Sophie licked her lips suggestively.

Alex hesitated, considering the option. He closed his eyes and shook his head. "Shit, you women are going to put me in an early grave." Pulling out of Sophie's drunken hold, Alex turned to leave. He saw Darius and Warren watching. He glanced back to me, annoyance clear on his face before he laughed and looked at Darius. "Be careful. This lot look like angels, but they are deadly."

"Love you too, Alex." I smiled.

Alex gave me a half smile over his shoulder, waved and disappeared into the crowd. Picking up my bottle of water, I took a long drink and plastered a smile on my face.

"Mora, you going to introduce us?" Sophie pointed to Warren and Darius.

"This is Warren Mann, he works at Lynwood, and that asshole is his boss."

Yeah, maybe Alex might have been right. I was definitely in a shit-stirring mood today. Though, it started with being in the room with Darius and his broad shoulders that would be great to sink my teeth and nails into. Maybe he'd thrown my hormones out of whack.

"Are you always so straight forward with all strangers?" Darius grumbled before giving his smirking assistant a dark look.

"With everyone."

"What are you doing with everyone?" A deep voice queried as strong hands wrapped around my waist and pulled me tight against a hard body.

Recognizing Jasper instantly, I grinned. Thank god I'd been drinking to handle this moment. "Being my usual charming self."

Darius's face shut down the moment Jasper touched me. Warren also seemed to sober up and stood straighter. Jasper turned my face to my shoulder and kissed my mouth tenderly. "I've missed you. Let's go back to my office." He nuzzled my neck before biting my shoulder hard enough to bruise.

Biting my lip, I let my head hang back as his hands moved lower to arrest my hips. Jasper lifted his mouth to my ear. "I want to eat that sweet cunt of yours while you wrap that beautiful mouth around my hard cock."

I groaned. To say I was randy after two weeks without was an understatement. Jasper turned me to face him, his green irises were barely visible by how large his pupils were. He wasn't model good-looking, but he had confidence and charisma that was far more appealing. He was a successful nightclub owner, so women weren't in short supply for him, and even in his early thirties, his body under those clothes was worth getting on your knees to worship.

Jasper kissed me hard, his fingers threading into my long black hair. When he pulled back, he licked over my lips. "My office, now."

He took my hand and pulled me after him through the crowd. Glancing back over my shoulder, I waved goodbye to Darius Rafal and Warren Mann, some of my joy dissipating. They'd surely be gone by the time I made my way back out to the club. Considering they didn't want our business, I'd probably never see them again.

Romance Suspense by Ebony Olson

Hotel Series

HOLLY CLAIRE TRILOGY

Henderson

Cassidy

Holmes

Holly's Trilogy: Books 1-3 Hotel Series (Compilation)

JESS BUTLER TRILOGY

Best Man

Black Mark Series

Black Mark's Resistance

Black Mark's Secret

Black Mark's Heart

Black Mark: The Complete Saga (Compilation)

Eleri Royals Series

Calypso

Standalones

Protective Instinct (December 2020)

Dark Fantasy / Paranormal Romance / Fantasy
by Ebony Olson

STANDALONES

Of Shadow and Light

Boundary

Silver Rogue

Halos (September 2020)

HIERARCH SERIES
(Radish Fiction Exclusive)

Succumb

Numinous

Masked

Exodus (Coming 2020/21)

RAVEN'S WING TRILOGY
(Radish Fiction Exclusive)

Phased

About the Author

Ebony lives in Sydney, Australia, with her husband, daughter, and six cats. She loves to read fantasy, thrillers, and paranormal romance, spending most of her free time with her nose in a book or writing.

Having always possessed an over-active imagination she spent her younger years regaling friends with fantastic stories, holding her audience captive with the passion and suspense of her characters plights.

Now in adulthood she has numerous published works and shows no signs of stopping her imagination from spreading across as many pages as it can find.

If you'd like to follow Ebony or simply say hi you can find her here:
Website: http://ebonyolson.com/
Ebony's Mischief & Mayhem Peeps

facebook.com/EbonyOlson.Author
twitter.com/Ebony_Olson
instagram.com/ebony_olson
amazon.com/author/ebonyolson
bookbub.com/authors/Ebony_Olson
goodreads.com/Ebony_Olson

www.ingramcontent.com/pod-product-compliance
Lightning Source LLC
Chambersburg PA
CBHW070055120726
47909CB00002B/395